THE CONTEST
You Can't Leave 'Til It's Over

A novel by
Timothy M. Braun

Sangre de Cristo Publishing, Inc.
Cripple Creek, Colorado

Copyright © 2010 Timothy M. Braun

ISBN: 0982815824
ISBN-13: 9780982815823

Printed in the United States of America

Cover design by Matthew Bowen, Indianapolis, IN.
Front Cover Model:
Crystal Trobaugh of Indianapolis, IN

Published by Sangre de Cristo Publishing, Inc., P.O. Box 1003, Cripple Creek, CO. 80813

Digital and paperback editions available at
www.sangredecristopublishing.com
www.amazon.com
www.smashwords.com

Dedication

This book is dedicated to my wife, Anita, for this book would not have been possible without her love, support, words of wisdom, and her belief in me throughout the long road to publishing.

Acknowledgements

A special thanks to the Writing Above the Clouds Writing Critique Group in Florissant, Colorado. Thanks to Diane Brunner and Sue Holmes for their help and to Matthew Bowen & Crystal Trobaugh for a great cover.

PROLOGUE

My name is Rico Sanducci. I'm a retired cop, a detective sergeant from a large department in New York. I used to work homicide, but now I'm a private dick. People hire me to solve murders and other crimes the police have given up on. Cold cases. I'm pretty good at it.

Two years ago, a strange, disturbed man, George Russo, contacted me through an acquaintance asking me to solve a mystery only he could describe. I traveled to see him because I'd never heard of anything like his yarn before. It was exceedingly bizarre.

That was the last time I've seen any income. It became a passion. I stopped taking any other work. I can't keep doing this, chasing an obsession that has overtaken my life. I have to get back to some normalcy, work another case I know I can solve, something to show I still have what it takes to unravel, to resolve, to bring to justice...and collect a paycheck.

At first, I didn't believe a word George said, partially, I suppose, because of where he was staying and where I had to meet him. But, I'm getting ahead of myself.

At first I just listened to him. Then I laughed at him. I insulted him, practically called him a liar. He didn't flinch, didn't bat an eye; but through the following weeks I couldn't get his tale out of my head.

After going back to visit with him several more times, going over and over the minutiae of his story, I felt in my gut the account might be true; he had too much detail, and he always stuck to the same set of facts. That's hard to do over a long period of time if you're lying or making up a story out of nowhere. But feeling it in my gut and proving it are two different issues.

To say this was a strange case would be like saying the sun rises in the east.

If his story is true, they were like rats in a cage, with the captors constantly poking them with sticks. The decisions they were made to make—the ethical choices alone would make anyone question their own moral compass. Was it some kind of social experiment, a sick joke that got out of hand? I know what I believe, but it's nothing I can prove.

I've been around the world tracking down leads and rumors...Singapore, London, Paris, Moscow, Dubai, and Beijing twice; each a false lead, a dead end. My funds are exhausted and my credit maxed out. I've used up everything I've ever worked for.

I have to admit; the perps were good, damn good... maybe better than me. They didn't leave a bit of evidence, not a single clue I could sink my teeth into. They slipped back into the underworld as fast as they initially appeared. What still bothers me, consumes my every waking minute—will they do it again, and who are they? I've stuck it out as long as I could, and I really believe they'll be back with another game, but where and when? And whom will they select for their next victims? They need to be caught and pay for their crimes. One day, they'll slip up, get careless, leave a clue and be found.

I've got a file cabinet full of interviews and documents, all leading to nowhere. Nothing. Nada. All the fake names I tracked down, the false contracts, the shell corporations; two years of investigation, of no income, of beating my head against the wall—I'm through, finished. I have to move on. Someone else will have to figure it out.

This is chiefly George's book. He wrote the majority of it. Much of the personal information you will encounter, the conversations, etc., have come from George's experiences or the manuscripts he copied. I've taken a little liberty with some parts of the story, to kind of fill in the gaps based on what I believe happened. I included details collected from my investigation and information that was supplied to me by informants and professional contacts I can't name here. There are particular key pieces of the puzzle that still elude me, but as you'll see, I did a best-guess estimate of what I believe actually transpired...but I can't be sure. No one can until these animals are captured and prosecuted.

As you can tell, I'm not a literary-type person. You won't find all kinds of big words or flowery details here, just a compelling story, one you won't see anywhere else. I'm just an old, retired gumshoe who tried to find the truth to a baffling puzzle; one that I hope is answered some-day...by anyone but me.

CHAPTER 1
The Offer

"Paul, I know it takes time, but it's been over three damn months. What the hell are you doing with my manuscript, lining your birdcage? Have you even started reading it yet?"

"George, there's absolutely nothing I can do for you right now. I'm backlogged and have other submissions I received before yours. I have to read those first. It's been very hectic around here." Paul paused. "Look, I know you have connections with other agents. Why don't you use them? The pressure here has been put on me to..."

I interrupted. "Find a great manuscript? A distinguished new writer? You've got one right in front of you. Can't you see that? Just read the damn thing and you'll see..."

"George," Paul stated, his voice cool and direct, "I suspect you have an incredibly good story, but I really don't think it's what we're looking for right now."

Fucking asshole, I thought. I'd heard all this before, many times over. It was their way of telling me to get lost. "Look, I know it's going to be successful if you just get off your..."

"No." Paul interrupted again. "It's not, George. *Trust me, I know.*"

Trust me, my ass, I thought. I knew I wasn't getting anywhere. I decided to try a different tack. "Look, Paul, I know you're busy and you have lots of manuscripts to read, but I really need this to sell. I'm about out of money. In fact, I'm dead broke."

There was a click on the other end of the phone— Paul hung up before I could continue my argument. I hit redial, which immediately sent my call to his voicemail. My first impulse was to tell him exactly what I thought of him and leave a spiteful message, but, I didn't want to burn any bridges, so, before I opened my mouth, I hung up.

"You dirty, rotten, son-of-a-bitch. I hope you choke on your next double-mocha latté," I yelled into the phone. I threw the portable handset across the small, cluttered room. It smashed into a double-tiered fifties-something white-oak lamp table. It woke my sleeping cat. The angora feline lifted his head, looked over at me, stretched his front legs, dug his claws into the worn faux leather couch, then lay back down and went to sleep.

I was steaming, to say the least. My novel, *Tragedy in the Schools*, which was based on a true story and had taken me a year and a half to write, had gone nowhere with several agents. I thought I could make a living writing novels and earn a ton of money, but finding a good agent to represent my manuscript had been more of a challenge than I'd ever dreamed. Right now I could give a rat's ass if it's even a good agent; any agent will do.

I really thought I had it all figured out, and for a long time believed many of those idiots would jump at the chance to represent my book. With my educational background and experience, who wouldn't want to read this work of genius? What I tragically failed to realize at the outset and only discovered in the past few months was most agents reject ninety-eight to nine-nine percent of all manuscript submissions. Not necessarily because they were bad novels, poorly written or of poor subject content, but usually because the author wasn't previously published; the proverbial Catch 22. Agents don't like to put in the time and effort to look for a publisher that will risk a new writer, and if the query letter doesn't meet their exact specifications, they'll toss it. More than likely, the fuckin' agents were just plain-ass lazy, or perhaps the author didn't say 'Pleeeze' enough times; didn't start the query with "Your Highness," or didn't sound like he or she would kiss ass to get represented. Quality doesn't seem to count anymore... it's whom you know or what genre is in fashion these days.

If I'd done my homework before deciding to become an author, I would have found there are very few that actually make a living writing great stories. I had heard, and then assumed, you wrote a good book, hired an agent, and sat back and watch the dinero roll in. What an error on my part that turned out to be! If I had known the truth, what I know now, I'd have taken a job washing floors at the local meat market. At least I'd have an income and wouldn't have blown my savings.

I was now going round and round with the fifty-third agent I'd queried. Six had requested the first three chapters of my manuscript, but I never heard a word back from them. Assholes. They sit on their thrones in skyscrapers in New York and look down upon their subjects. They say they're too busy to answer; they're probably too occupied making arrangements for their next liquid lunch.

Every other day for the past two weeks I'd called Paul. Each time, I hoped to hear some good news; hoped Paul would tell me he had finished reading my novel, how great the manuscript was and that a publisher was offering me thousands of dollars for the book rights, and maybe a little more for a movie deal. Delusional? Probably. Now he wouldn't even answer my calls, which pissed me off even more; no, depressed me even more.

I desperately need to sell this story. I'm even ready to negotiate a much lower amount than I figured it was worth. I need cash, that's the bottom line.

Of all the agents I'd spoken to, Paul had angered me the most. He constantly led me to believe he would be representing my book and sell it to a publisher. I was so sure he was the one; I hadn't queried any more agents as I awaited the contract. Now I realized Paul was no different from the rest, just another sleazy agent with his nose stuck so far up his ass that, if he sneezed, he'd blow his eardrums out.

I suddenly felt a twinge in my chest. My face felt hot, my hands shook. I was sure my blood pressure had spiked. I had to calm down. That fifth cup of coffee I'd just gulped down hadn't helped either. *Decaf, I have to buy some decaf. Where the hell are my blood pressure pills?*

I took several deep breaths and tried to slow my heart rate as I looked around the kitchen. Several days' accumulation of dirty dishes were still stacked in the sink and on the counter; the trash and garbage were overflowing. Old newspapers were piled six inches high on the table, next to reams of manuscript copies.

Sitting at my kitchen table, beads of sweat poured down my face and fell onto the blue Formica-topped, chrome-framed table. The damned steam heat was cooking my apartment again. It was either hot as spit on asphalt in a July desert, or colder than my freezer. There was no controlling it. The only times it was really bearable were during the transitions from hot to cold and vice versa.

I found my pills hiding behind the bag of cat chow on the counter next to the stove. I shook the bag, which my cat alerted to. There was almost nothing left.

"Well, if it comes down to you or me eating," I said to the cat as I poured the rest of the chow into his bowl, "you know who's going to starve."

My breakfast this morning consisted of two bowls of corn flakes with skim milk, which is all I can afford these days. I'm able to get a couple of boxes of donated food once a week from the local food pantry, but day after day of the same tasteless meals and no protein leaves me weak. You'd think I'd lose some weight, but I haven't; probably all the cookies I'm addicted to.

I haven't felt like doing any work lately, much less any writing. My savings are exhausted and I'm behind several months on most of my bills, including my rent. My landlord has been knocking on my door almost every other day. I wonder if it could really get much worse. My part-time job at the local hardware store barely allows me to feed myself, the cat, and pay my utilities; much less pay for any professional editing of my manuscript, which I know I should do.

I had to do something, go somewhere, anything to get my mind off my frustrations. As a distraction, I decided to take the trip downstairs and retrieve my mail in the lobby. I hadn't bothered to collect it in several days. Maybe an agent had answered one of my older queries. Shit, then I could forget about Paul and concentrate on a whole new possibility.

***

I cautiously stepped down the dark staircase, one step at a time. I had to place my feet at odd angles to avoid the trash strewn on the decades old, worn and creaky wooden stairs.

An old, out of shape and overweight guy like me should be living in a place with an elevator, a place I knew I couldn't afford. Traipsing up and down three flights of stairs in my condition just isn't conducive to my sought-after, comfortable retirement.

The gray enamel paint was gone from the center of each step, and the decades and decades of tenants pounding the stairs had grooved the center of each, with every lower level wearing deeper and broader grooves.

The days' old rubbish in the hallways reeked of rotting garbage; diapers filled with feces and urine, empty wine bottles, beer cans, cat piss, and stale, half-burnt cigarette butts assaulted my sense of smell. *How did I end up living in a dump like this, this hell? Am I doomed to spending the rest of my life like this?*

Here and there, large, well-fed rats scampered along the edges of the walls searching for any morsels of rotted food in the piles of garbage bags. Everywhere in the darkened halls the ancient wallpaper was peeling, showing long-forgotten coats of dull pink and green paint under several other layers of aged wallpaper. The paint on the railings had long worn down to bare wood a sort of hand-rubbed dirty sheen. The dim bulbs hanging in the hallways barely allowed me to see where I was stepping.

As I descended towards the lobby, I heard a woman's scream emanating from an apartment on the second floor, babies crying in another, but long ago I'd learned to mind my own business. Unless I found a dead body on the stairs, I was determined to keep to myself. But then again, I thought, if someone was already dead, why bother? Hear nothing, see nothing, and say nothing. Stay alive. Stay in one piece.

I reached the lobby of the main floor. At the bank of brown steel mailboxes built into the wall, I unlocked and opened the brass door and pulled out a small stack of letters and resident postal trash.

I looked at each item. *Bill. Bill, past due. Advertising junk. Bill, past due. What's this? A letter from a writer's agency? 'The New Writer's Agency,' another self-publishing outfit?*

I trudged back up the stairs staring at the envelope. My heart was pounding from the exertion and partially in anticipation of what kind of news the letter may contain. Was it a letter from an agent interested in my work, or just another come-on from a vanity publisher? I should have never looked into self-publishing. Now the solicitations never stop.

I hoped it wouldn't be another rejection, I couldn't take that right now—but then again, I didn't recall sending a query letter to this agency either.

I made it to my apartment door; it too was a wreck, marred with scars, cracks, and probably a dozen or so coats of worn-through shellac. I unlocked the three deadbolts and entered the sauna once again, throwing the mail on the kitchen table. Sitting down and wiping my forehead with the bottom of my shirt, I stared at the linen envelope for several minutes.

I always savored those small moments in time; the few occasions when the next precious instant could bring a turning point in my life; like watching the drawing of the sixth number in a state lottery when you discover you have the first five.

Slowly tearing it open, the accompanying letter was written on matching linen paper with an elaborate gold leaf emblazoned logo.

Dear Mr. George Russo:

   Congratulations! You are among an elite group of writers selected to attend a new writing contest. This first annual competition is for unpublished authors only. We have selected twenty participants, based on submissions we have read and whom we believe have the ability to write a winning manuscript.

The contest will be held at a vacation destination, the location to be determined by our Board of Directors. The all expense paid retreat will include all transportation, lodging, food and necessary items for the length of the competition. In return, the winner must agree to be represented by our organization with a standard agency-client contract.

We anticipate it may take a couple of months for everyone to complete a manuscript, so if you accept this offer and are chosen as a finalist, please make arrangements for an extended stay.

The winner will be awarded 'the prize of your life,' plus sixty thousand dollars. A twenty thousand dollar advance will be paid upon execution of the contract and you will be guaranteed publication by a major publishing house. An additional forty thousand dollars will be paid in monthly increments, once the book is published. We will elaborate on the details at a later date.

If you are interested, please complete the questionnaire, include a recent photo and respond to Mr. Henry Wright at the post office box below. Although we have sent out twenty invitations, we are limited to the first ten respondents.
Sincerely,
Henry J. Wright,
Agent, The New Writers Group
P.O. Box 12500
New York, New York 11111

Stunned, I sat and looked at the letter. It must have been fifteen minutes before I could shake the disbelief from my head. I'd never heard of a contest like this and I'd researched many of them. Most were open to just about anyone who was still breathing and could post the entry fees. This one had no entry fees and was only open to ten writers. Could someone have finally, really realized my potential, my God-given talent? Could I be this lucky? A twenty thousand dollar advance?

I wondered what kind of competition I would have. The other nine writers should also be unpublished, but must have some type of experience or they wouldn't have been invited. With my funds running out, here was an agent, or a group, who is willing to completely pay for all my expenses for two months while I write another manuscript.

Sitting there, I let myself imagine where the location of the competition would be. I hoped it would be somewhere warm—Hawaii, Mexico, the Fiji Islands maybe? Or how about Bermuda or the Florida Keys? Any location where the sun shined everyday would suit me just fine. I wanted desperately to escape the cold, snowy, icy winters of Buffalo.

I didn't need a second invitation or to think about it very long. I hurriedly filled out the application and the questionnaire.

I admit, there were some strange questions. *Who do you live with? Who are your nearest relatives and where do they live? How long has it been since you had contact with them?* At this point, I didn't care; I gave them all the details of my sorry life. They must have had a good reason to ask. Maybe it was part of a survey.

I searched for a recent photo of myself, and found one in the last yearbook from the school where I had taught. There were only two, probably part of my punishment; they weren't going to acknowledge me any more than they had to. The year prior, I probably had ten to fifteen different clips in there. Anyway, I cut one out. The pressure was on, I just had to be one of the first ten to accept the offer, and wasn't about to take any chances. After addressing and sealing the envelope, I rummaged around in the small drawers of the oak roll top desk looking for a postage stamp. Finding a stray one under a pile of papers, I affixed it to the envelope.

I donned my coat. The trip down the three flights of stairs this time no longer seemed like drudgery. My heart felt light, the heaviness I'd carried with me the last time down to the lobby had lifted. If I had been more agile, I would have taken two or three steps at a time, though I probably took them faster than I ever had.

I buttoned up my coat, shoved the door open and pranced out into the frosty, blowing wind. I made my way down the street to the corner where I dropped the reply into the post office drop box. As I headed back to my apartment, I wondered how long it would take until I heard back from them.

CHAPTER 2
Setup

The gusting wind blew cold and fierce as James held the black fedora on his head. His black, full-length, cashmere coat clung to the front of his body as he leaned into the gales, his head down to protect his eyes.

He watched in amusement as a tall, thin woman, wearing a mid-length fox fur coat which left her muscular legs exposed to the elements, struggled to balance in her stilettos as the wind pushed against her back. Shielding her eyes with a black clutch, she appeared to be wiping her eye as a dust devil swirled around her. She bumped into James as he stepped off the curb to cross the street. He glanced up at her, but ignored the jostle; he didn't want to draw any attention to himself. Especially right now. But he did turn and glance back at her; she was definitely a looker. With the crowded sidewalks and bumper-to-bumper traffic, that's the way it was in New York City. You kept to yourself, ignored the many intrusions and avoided looking anyone in the eye.

He walked to the next block, put on a pair of dark sunglasses, turned the corner and climbed several granite slab steps to the post office. Pulling open the massive glass door while reaching into his coat pocket for a set of keys, he went to box 12500, squatted down and opened the box closest to the floor. Keeping his head still, his eyes scanned either side of him, hoping he was blending in with the other patrons.

Smiling to himself and feeling like a spy in a low-budget suspense movie, he pulled a handful of business-sized envelopes from the box, and closed it. After relocking it and placing the keys back into his pocket, he pulled the fedora down further toward his sunglasses and placed the letters into an inside pocket of his coat. Making sure he didn't look directly into any of the many cameras located throughout the post office, he exited the building and retraced his steps back two blocks to his office.

His company, *The New Writers Group*, had rented a beautiful office complex on the twenty-fifth floor of the Lyman Building, a newly constructed thirty-story blend of new-age architectural glass and steel.

James rode up the glass-enclosed elevator, barely glancing at the city as he rose above it. He used to enjoy gazing out on the city from his high perch, but as with so many things in his life, it had lost its appeal long ago.

Stepping onto the travertine-tiled foyer of their office suite, he took a moment to enjoy the soothing sounds of water cascading down a copper-walled fountain. A work of art in itself, it was designed to greet visitors as they stepped off the elevator. He shrugged. Too bad there weren't any visitors to admire it.

He slowed down as he passed by his partner's office and overheard him interviewing someone on the phone for their next project. As he passed the glass outer wall, his partner cradled the phone with his shoulder and raised both arms with his hands pointed out, as if asking a question. James stopped and gave a thumbs-up. His partner waved him into the office, said something in Spanish to the party on the phone, and pushed the hold button.

"How many did we get?" Howard asked James as he took off his coat. He sat down in a soft, brown leather chair facing Howard's desk, sat back and crossed his legs.

"Looks like at least another ten responses, maybe more," he said, pulling the envelopes from the inner pocket of his coat and thumping them on his knee. "I'm going to give extra points this time for the earliest responses. I'm betting those will be the ones more willing to go anywhere we choose."

"Sounds good. I'm on the phone with that wetback, Juan, trying to round up another chaser. Looks like we may have a bite. I tried to get Guillermo again, but Juan says he's in jail."

"Will he have a problem this time with, uh—the details?"

"I'm not sure yet. Some coyotes don't have any qualms about doing what is necessary, some do. He may be just playing games with me, trying to get *mucho more dinero.*"

"Stay on it, Howard. I'll get busy on these right away. We've only got a few months to finalize this." James turned to leave, but swung back around to Howard. "By the way, how much does he want?"

"Not sure. He's talking about twenty-five big ones for the whole job, plus five for his finder's fee. Says that's what he's getting now for work like this. And, we have to supply everything this time."

Without speaking, James mouthed the words, "Too much."

Howard returned to the phone call as James left. In his own office, James dropped the envelopes onto his desk. He poured himself a cup of coffee and sat back in his chair looking at the pile of mail. *Ahh, who would be the lucky ones today?* He smirked. *Lucky?*

He opened the responses one at a time, slowly grading the answers of each questionnaire, eventually choosing the last four contestants. In a couple of months he would write letters to the fortunate ten he had selected.

CHAPTER 3
The Flight

My unemployment benefits had already run out and I was soon going to be hungry or applying for welfare. In several of the past months, I sold most of my food stamps to supplement my part time job just to help pay the utilities and keep them turned on. I had a hard time believing my own poverty.

It hadn't always been like this. Years before, I lived a comfortable, middle-class lifestyle. I enjoyed a career with the local school district teaching high school social studies. It never occurred to me that a career could go downhill so fast, all because of office politics, school jocks and coaches. One of the coaches came to me and privately insisted that I inflate a student athlete's grade. When I refused and told him I didn't run my classes that way, he said it was no big deal; it was done all the time. He was relentless and wouldn't let up.

I couldn't believe he was demanding such a thing. I'd heard rumors of other staff being bullied to change grades, but I'd never experienced it myself. School policy dictated the student be suspended from all athletics if his grades didn't meet a 'C' average, and this particular athlete was the school's superstar basketball player. But he was my worst student. Maybe the dumbest son-of-a-bitch I'd had in the past five years. I tried to be accommodating to a certain point, offering to help the student after hours or on weekends, and let him do extra work to bring his grades up. He refused. He just smiled at me whenever I made suggestions, but he never lifted a finger to help himself. It was as though he knew pressure was being placed on me and thought I would bend. I didn't, and the superintendent suspended him from the team.

After the school lost the divisional play-offs, the coaches blamed the loss on me. I became the scapegoat. No one said a word to the student; at least I never heard about it. Most of the teachers were quiet around me; they didn't even speak to me anymore. When I walked into the teachers lounge, everyone went silent. It made me nervous and angry that the other teachers relented and went along with the fraud, leaving me to hold the proverbial bag. I couldn't figure out whether they were upset at me for not going along, or ashamed of themselves for doing so. I assumed the latter and maintained an air of integrity and self-righteousness.

The rest of the year went incredibly slow. I was a pariah. At the end of the school year, I decided to quit teaching, and take some time off. A little later, when I needed something more to occupy my time, I used the experience I had gained in the ordeal as the basis of a novel and started writing. I had a small savings account and figured that would hold me until I finished a manuscript and sold it. That would be my source of income from now on. I didn't need to associate with anyone I didn't want to—no more being bullied or a scapegoat for me.

The offer of the contest revived my faith in my writing abilities; I spent the next couple of weeks editing my book and working my part-time job. Nothing else really mattered to me.

Each day I religiously checked the mail looking for that singular letter which would take me away from this rat-infested tenement shit-hole I called home, and give me a new life. I quit calling and writing all of the other literary agents. As far as I was concerned, I didn't need them anymore.

Two months after answering the offer, I'd almost given up looking for a reply when I received the letter I'd been waiting for.

Dear Mr. George Russo,

Congratulations on being one of the ten authors selected to compete in our first annual writing contest. You will be allowed up to two months to complete a manuscript.

You will be competing with nine other writers and all of your daily necessities will be supplied. If you are taking any medications, or have any other personal needs, please bring enough with you for an extended stay. We will provide for your room and board in an atmosphere where you can work uninterrupted day and night, if you wish.

Please bring this letter, along with the original invitation to the Westbank Airport on May 10th at 5 p.m. where a charter flight will convey you to your destination. You are limited to two suitcases plus a laptop computer carry-on.

Contact information will be provided upon arrival at your destination. Please do not divulge any of this information, as we do not want interference from external sources while writers are working. Any violations of this policy will be grounds for immediate disqualification and you will be sent home.

We hope you have a memorable experience and good luck in the contest!
Sincerely,
Henry J. Wright,
Agent, The New Writers Group
P.O. Box 12500
New York, New York 11111

"Yes! Yes!" I shouted. I was ecstatic and felt like a ten-year-old kid again. I didn't know what to do or who to tell, but I felt a heavy load lift off my back. I whooped and hollered, sang and danced until the residents in the apartment under me started knocking on their ceiling, yelling for me to quiet down.

***

I knew this was my ticket out of this dump and began preparing for the adventure. I advised my landlord that I would be leaving in three weeks, gave notice at the hardware store, forwarded my mail to my sister in California, and terminated my utilities and phone for May 9th.

I spent the remaining weeks packing all my personal belongings and gave my cat, Herman, to the local no-kill animal shelter. I knew half the people in this building would eat him if they had the chance.

I sold the better pieces of furniture and gave away the rest of it, moving the balance of my possessions into storage. I made just enough money from the sales of my furniture to pay the storage fees for the next several months. Calling my sister, I borrowed a few hundred bucks; enough money to purchase a bus ticket to Westbank and pay for a few personal items—including three months of blood pressure medicine. The rest of the money would have to sustain me until it was time to leave. I knew I was cutting everything close and hoped there wouldn't be any kinks in my plan. I kept thinking about what I would do if I didn't win the contest. I owed my sister; I wouldn't have a job or an apartment. I'd have nothing to start over again. That scared me, but maybe I would be forced to reexamine my life.

***

I arrived in Westbank in the afternoon the day before my scheduled flight and rented a cheap motel room while I waited to depart the next day. After settling in, I walked down the street to where I'd seen a public library. Something about the writing contest still bothered me, and now it was nagging at me. I'd always meant to check on the company promoting the contest, The New Writers Group, but it had slipped my mind with everything I had to do.

When I entered the library, I found a bank of computers with Internet access. A sign posted above them stated two dollars for one hour.

I paid the fee to the librarian and as I waited for her to activate my computer. There must be a society where all librarians learn their mannerisms and uniform protocols; she was neatly dressed with short-cropped gray hair and looked to be in her early fifties. There was a familiarity about her that couldn't abolish the stereotype.

I sat down to search for anything that would tell me more about the business. I couldn't find a thing. I even searched the Secretary of State's listing of registered business names and the Better Business Bureau's listings. Nothing. I should have found something that let me know this was a legitimate company, or terminated the trip. My gut was giving me a warning, but dollar signs danced in my head.

CHAPTER 4
Post Your Bets

Howard walked down the hall, his long legs making quick work of the distance to his partner's office.

"Hey, buddy, how about double or nothing this time?" He had a big smile on his face as he stared intently at James.

James slowly looked up from typing on his computer. His lopsided grin suggested he was intrigued. "Sounds interesting. I'll have to think about it. I've got what, a couple hundred-thousand of your money right now?"

"Yeah, but I've got a gut feeling on this one. Besides, this time I've got first pick. The odds are with me. You've won the last three, I'm due."

James glanced up at Howard again as he took a sip of coffee. "You don't even know who the contestants are yet. How can you be so sure?" After a short pause James continued. "Tell you what. Let's get a secretary to do all this typing and bookwork and I'll agree to your double or nothing right now."

"No way, partner. We agreed—no employees, no witnesses. Get it through your head; we either do this by ourselves or not at all. I don't want to be looking over my shoulder the rest of my life for a little fun now. All we need is some bimbo shooting her mouth off at the wrong time and we could be guests in the crowbar hotel for a long, long time."

James held his arms up in surrender. "All right, all right. I was just kidding anyway."

"Let me know when you've finished choosing the contestants so I can start my picks."

"They're ready now." He pushed a stack of folders across his desk. "We had a total of twenty-two applications. I picked the ten who I thought would be the best— three women and seven men—all single, all with remote families or no known family, and all live alone."

"Wow, we hit the jackpot," Howard replied taking the folders and sitting down in an overstuffed chair. "We've never had that kind of luck."

"How are the supplies coming?" James asked.

"We should be good, but you'll have to fly me out there next month to check on everything and take care of any last minute problems. I had work done on the generator yesterday. He said it's in good working order now. Should last at least a few months. You'll get the bill in a few days."

"Remind me to take the new cameras and recorders out this time," James said. "Did we get our chaser?"

"Yes, we got one, but we have to supply all his provisions this time, so put that on our list too."

"Tell them to bring their own provisions. We'll pay for them. What about weapons?"

"He's bringing his own, but I don't know if we should trust them to be clean."

"Talk to your arms-supplier buddy. We need absolute clean weapons here, no fuck-ups."

Howard spent the next half-hour diligently reading and studying each contestant's file. He called on his disposable cell phone and made an appointment to order the guns he needed. He would have to see his arms supplier face-to-face and pay cash.

"Okay, I have my first choice," Howard declared as he entered James' office with the stack of folders. "I want Harry. I think he's the winner. Sounds like a no-nonsense, macho type guy." Howard looked at the photo again and said, "He looks strong. I hope he is." He drew a large "H" on the folder with a thick, black marker indicating Harry was his pick.

"Good selection; he was my first choice also. I think I'll take Randy," James said. "He's young and probably pretty well-built. Besides, he's from a ranch. He'll know how to take care of himself out there." James inked a large "J" on Randy's folder.

"I thought you said they had no known families," Howard said. "Yet, this one is from a ranch?"

"Yeah, he's a working hand on a dude ranch, a wrangler, not family."

"Okay." It was Howard's turn again. "I'm going with Nicki. She's young and she's cute. They'll have fights over who is going to be her best friend and take care of her."

"I'm sure she'll be well looked after."

Howard smiled. "And look at that body. Hope it's not wasted. I'd screw her myself."

James chuckled. "You probably would. It's probably a glamour shot taken ten years ago."

A large "H" was put on her folder. They continued taking turns choosing their contestants until there were five "H's" and five "J's" on the ten folders.

"Still want double or nothing?" James asked.

"You bet," Howard said without hesitation.

"Okay, you got it. I'll get these profiles and pictures out to our clients today."

CHAPTER 5
Preparation

Four weeks later, James and Howard flew their private plane out to Denver International. They rented a Jeep, picked up the supplies from their plane and made the three-hour trip to the deserted town.

They made sure all the provisions for the contestants were stocked and everything was ready to go. All the food had been delivered and put away; towels, soaps, dishes, pots and pans, and everything they could think of that would be needed for a sixty-day stay for ten people, male and female.

By late afternoon they had replaced the old, bulky cameras and recorders with new ones. With the new technology, the components were so small you had to know where they had been placed in order to find them. Other pinhole cameras were secreted in the hotel lobby, in the kitchen where the group was sure to gather and discuss plans, and various places throughout the town. All were either wired to the several recorders hidden in the building next to the hotel or transmitted to them. In addition, all of the video images were relayed to a shack outside of town.

"This sure is a desolate fucking place," James remarked as he looked around the town and watched several tumbleweeds blow down the middle of the street. "Some *vacation destination*."

"Yeah, it's going to be sad to see it go. It's been in the family for over two hundred years," Howard replied. "We used to love vacationing here when I was a kid. We had horses brought in and spent the whole month riding the prairie. In the fall we helped with a roundup at a ranch about eighty miles from here. So, it used to be *our* vacation destination."

James laughed. "Well, it's going for a good cause. Look at all the dough you're getting for it. You'd never even get close to this much money if you ever put it up for sale."

"You mean *we* are getting for it. I ought to be getting a larger percent on this one."

"What, a couple of million or so isn't enough? You want more?

"I'm the one giving up my town for this contest."

"Well, yeah, but it's still a shit-load of money. Quit whining. You still get to keep the land," James said as he slapped Howard on the back. "Are the room keys tagged and out?"

"Check. On the counter."

James waved to Howard. "Let's go meet our chaser. He's supposed to be at the cabin by now. I want to make sure the video images are being relayed to him and give him the guns and his money."

"You go. I want to do a final inspection of all the rooms and test out the generator again. The spic's money is in my briefcase. I hope he can keep his mouth shut."

"This one better." James smiled. "If he knew what happened to the last one who shot his mouth off, I know he will."

"Make sure he *really* understands. I've been told he speaks good English. And take away any weapons he has with him when you give him ours. I don't want any loose ends coming back to haunt us."

The Jeep's tires flumed dust behind it as James made his way out to the campsite where the Mexican chaser had settled in. The site was hidden away deep in a canyon that couldn't be seen from the ghost town.

He came to a small, windowless, stone cabin with a cast iron well pump next to the front door. A barking dog, chained to the porch, pulled at the chain restraining him as James stepped from the Jeep and approached the cabin. He could hear the hum of a small motor from somewhere around the back of the cabin. Probably the generator, he thought. As he came within a few dozen feet of the wooden-planked front door, the dog started snarling and showing his teeth. James stopped and called out, "Anybody here?"

The door cracked open. James could see a scrawny, wiry looking man peering out at him.

"Whatta' ya want?" he asked.

"Are you Reynaldo?"

"Yeah. Who are you?"

"I'm the one with the money, that's all you need to know. We have some business to take care of. First of all, impress me."

"What? Wha-da-ya mean?"

"Tell me about yourself. Give me your record. I want to make sure you're the right man for the job."

Reynaldo stepped out onto the porch, which gave James the opportunity to size him up. He appeared to be about forty years old with a scraggly beard, greasy shoulder length hair, and rotted teeth. He looked as though he had worn the same clothes for more than a week. James tried to breathe through his mouth as much as possible not, trying not to smell the many odors emanating from this man. He wondered how long it had been since he had bathed since he was desperately in need of a shave and some clean clothes. His arms bore many multi-colored tattoos. Mostly from prison, James thought. His red and black flannel shirt was open in the front and the sleeves were cut off at the shoulder. His jeans hung off his bony hips, secured with a very worn piece of hemp rope, tied tight. James couldn't decide if there were more holes or denim to the jeans.

He was surprised he had no problem communicating with Reynaldo who spoke perfect English, unlike past chasers they had hired. He gave James his brief history, including telling him he was a member of the Mexican Mafia and had been most of his life, in and out of jail. Among the various scars and tattoos, James recognized the "MM" tattoo Reynaldo bore on his neck. He was convinced they had hired the right person for the job and gave Reynaldo his instructions, going over the details of changing the tapes in the recorders every night.

He went inside to check the monitors, making sure the new cameras were working and aimed correctly. A heavy odor of marijuana hung in the air. He discovered the cabin to be one room with a dirt-floor and a single light bulb hanging in the center of the ceiling. Against one wall, three small monitors with recorders lined several shelves. Each monitor projected a four-way split screen, showing the transmission of four different cameras. A sleeping bag lay in the middle of the room and a camping cook stove sat on a small table. A wooden chair placed next to the table was the only place to sit other than on the floor. Boxes of food and provisions sat against another wall.

Satisfied everything was in order, he went back outside.

"You know what I want. Do you understand how to change the tapes and operate the monitors?"

"Yes."

"Let me see your weapons," James demanded.

Reynaldo stood and stared at him for a few seconds, his muscular arms folded in front of him. "Hombre, I was told you would bring any hardware I needed."

"I did. I also know you wouldn't go anywhere without your own. So where is it?"

"I didn't bring..."

"Bye, asshole. You can leave now. Get your gear and get the fuck out of here."

James fingered the .25 caliber semi-auto in his pocket. He didn't know how Reynaldo would react. He had just kicked a pit bull in the balls and now waited to see if he was going to bite or back down.

"Man, what's wrong with you?"

"What are you, shit-for-brains? I'm saying get the fuck out of here. I don't need some jerk-off that can't follow directions. And that means you. Now get your shit and leave. I'll give the twenty-five thousand to someone else who'll do what I want and can follow orders," James yelled as he turned on his heel to leave.

"Wait a minute. You got the twenty-five?"

"Of course I do. I keep my end of the bargain. Twelve and a half now, the rest when the job is finished."

"I was told I would get the whole twenty-five up front."

James stared at the Mexican for a moment and laughed. "Do I have stupid written on my forehead?"

"Okay, okay. Wait here." Reynaldo disappeared into the one-room cabin.

James wandered over to a small corral next to the cabin where a brown and white paint gelding was drinking out of a trough. The horse looked up and walked over to the gate where James stood. He exhaled heavily through his nostrils and pawed at the ground while pushing on the gate. James reached over the rail and scratched him on the nose.

Reynaldo joined James a moment later with a revolver in his hand. He held it out and gave it to James by the barrel.

"How many times have you used it?"

"Just a couple, but it was in L.A. Not around here."

"Anyone shot?"

"No one killed. Just wounded a couple."

"Doesn't matter. It can be traced."

He inspected the piece of steel.

"Not bad. Smith and Wesson three-fifty-seven, custom hand grips." He opened the cylinder and pulled out a round. "Silver tip. Hunting vampires?" he asked with a smile.

"No, man. They'll knock you down hard."

James went to the Jeep, threw the revolver in the back seat and pulled out two gun cases, one for a handgun, the other, a rifle. He went back to Reynaldo who waited at the corral.

"What's the horse's name?"

"Dude."

"The dog?"

"Jasper."

"Can you follow instructions to the letter?"

"Yeah, man, just tell me what you want."

"First and last—no one leaves the town."

"You want me to...?"

"You do what you have to. I'm not asking any questions."

Reynaldo locked eyes with James. "I understand."

"One more thing."

"What's that?"

"You can never discuss or tell anyone what happens here. The last chaser we hired the opened his mouth—well, let's just say, he's not hirable any more. Comprehend?"

"Yeah. Got it."

James walked over to the porch with Reynaldo following.

"Here, you'll like these." James laid the two gun cases on the porch and handed Reynaldo several boxes of ammunition.

"The rifle's sighted in for two hundred yards." James said as he uncased a brand new Browning .270 Winchester, bolt-action rifle with a 4-12x-power scope. He then uncased a Smith & Wesson 9mm semi-auto.

"I want both of these back when this is over and you'll get your piece back."

Reynaldo nodded his approval as he admired the new pieces of hardware, running his hand over the new metal and walnut stock.

CHAPTER 6
The Flight

Around four in the afternoon, I took a taxi to Westbank airfield, a small private facility just outside the city. I hoisted myself out of the back seat of the taxi and paid the driver. I was tired, and so excited about the upcoming trip; I hadn't slept much the night before. But for now, sleep was the last thing on my mind. Adrenaline kept me in fast-forward.

Dragging my two bags out from the trunk of the cab, I looked around; I expected someone from the contest to be here to greet me. I'd pictured someone in a three-piece pin-stripe suit with a red tie, neatly combed hair and leather shoes. After all, I figured being chosen for the contest elevated me to a semi-celebrity status.

I waited several minutes, but there was no welcoming committee. Could this be the wrong place? I watched my taxi speed off into the distance. It had better not be, I was low on cash and I couldn't afford any more expenses.

The single runway airfield contained a small, gray wooden structure that served as a terminal. It had faded, whitewashed-framed windows and a steel roof that looked as though it was built in the 1940s, probably during the World War II era. Several small aircraft along the runway were tied down to stakes with wire cable and ropes. Next to the deteriorating, gray building was a flagpole. On top, a windsock fluttered up and down with the intermittent breeze. The place looked deserted.

A petite young woman walked out the door of the ancient building and approached me cautiously.

"Are you a writer, here for a flight, or are you a representative from the writing competition?" she asked.

"I'm a writer. I was told to be here by five for a flight. I take it you're also here for the contest."

"My name's Nicki," she said holding out her small hand. It contained a silver ring on every finger and thumb. "Yeah, I'm here for the same thing.

"Nice to meet you," I said, shaking her hand. "I'm George."

"There's no rep here yet—I suppose we'll just have to wait."

"I guess we will."

"Might as well join the rest of us inside."

"The rest? How many are here?"

"You make five."

"Lead the way."

I slung my laptop case over my shoulder, picked up my two pieces of green nylon luggage, and followed Nicki into the building.

The terminal had a waiting room consisting of about fifteen orange, vinyl-covered, chrome-framed chairs for visitors or passengers waiting for a flight. The room had several vintage coin-operated candy machines along with a coffee and hot chocolate machine. The wood floor was worn and scuffed from sixty-to-seventy some odd years of passengers, family and loved ones waiting for flights coming in and departing the airport. The large nail heads in the boards were worn to a silver sheen. There were three other individuals sitting in the waiting area and I assumed they were contestants, as they each had laptop cases along with two other pieces of luggage.

After scanning the room, my attention was drawn back to Nicki. She was a slender brunette with medium length hair, big blue eyes, and blue eye shadow outlined with black eyeliner. She wore tight, low-rise blue jeans, blue high heels and a white t-shirt under a black leather jacket. The outline of a belly-button ring protruded from her shirt. I figured she was in her late twenties, maybe early thirties. *Typical New Yorker or New Jersey broad, but, she is cute.*

"Well, what do we have here, another chump for the competition?"

"Ahh, shut up, Harry, you fuckin' redneck asshole," Nicki replied in a New-Jersey accent as she unwrapped a stick of gum.

"Another writer with a big head—probably already has a best seller he's been trying to peddle for the last six months," he continued.

I turned to Nicki. "What's with him?" I whispered out of the side of my mouth.

"Oh, that's Harry Finkle. He's a local asshole. Always has been, always will be. He's had a couple of short stories published by a horror magazine, now he thinks he's Stephen King."

"Sounds like you've known him awhile."

"For a few years. He used to be in a writer's critique group I was in. Tell you the truth, I think his writing sucks," she said in a low voice, but loud enough for him to hear. "He only got published 'cause he has a relative at a university who completely rewrites and edits his stories. That's the only way they would get edited, he'd never pay anyone to do it, the cheap prick."

"Yeah, and you're standing with the next Sandra Brown," Harry said. "She's supposedly written three international espionage thrillers, all still sitting in the bottom drawer of her desk. Maybe someday she'll get published-in some kiddie magazine."

Nicki gave him a dirty look and threw him the finger. Harry's eyes lit up along with a broad smile. I think he knew he'd gotten to her.

"Hey, Nicki. All those rings you got on, you got them anywhere else?" laughed Harry as he looked around at the other writers. "Open your jacket, let us take a look."

"If I do, asshole, you'll never know." She folded her arms, her jacket coming together tighter.

Harry was short compared to the other passengers, about five-foot six. He had black, neck-length hair with a two-day growth of facial hair. His square set jaw and dark eyes made his face look more like a prizefighter, but his protruding gut belied his lack of physical fitness.

"This ought to be fun," I said sarcastically as I took a seat across from one of the other contestants. "I'm glad everyone gets along so well. It's going to be a long two months."

The other two writers hadn't said a word. They seemed to enjoy the exchange between Nicki and Harry. The smirks on their faces gave them away. I'll admit—I kind of enjoyed it too.

"My name's Peter, Peter Maze," one of the men said as he rose to shake my hand. "Do you know where we're going?"

"I've no idea," I replied. "And I don't really care just as long as it's someplace warm. This whole contest seemed a little strange to me, but at the same time, I thought it might be a great opportunity."

"Does anyone mind if I smoke?" Peter asked pulling out a custom-made mahogany pipe along with a pouch of tobacco.

"I do," Harry said. "Go outside if you want to suck on that thing."

"I don't care what you think," shot back Peter, "I was talking to the others."

"Screw you," Harry said.

"Well, if you ever were to, Harry," Peter said slowly lighting his pipe, "you'd never go back to little boys."

Collective snickering broke out from all of the other passengers, myself included. This guy was a first class jerk, and probably going to be a real pain-in-the-ass. I instantly took a liking to Peter, though. He seemed like a laidback, classy type of guy with a sense of humor.

Harry got up from his chair, scowling at Peter and faced him, fists clenched. I really thought there was going to be a fight, but then he turned and walked out the door.

I smiled. "Nice sort of chap, isn't he? You know him too?"

"Unfortunately. Harry is known to a lot of writers around here. Seems no one wants to admit it though. I don't know how he was chosen for this contest. He can't write worth a shit. He must have submitted something someone else wrote."

"To tell you the truth, Pete, I don't know how any of us were selected. Seems they found our writing somewhere, but who gave it to them?"

"Maybe we'll find out when the rep gets here."

"If we're all going to be staying together for two months, I would suggest we all ought to try to get along," declared the last contestant.

"And just who are you?" Nicki asked, snapping her gum.

"I'm Jessie North," he said with a slight lisp, "I write poetry and short stories—usually romantic ones."

"Great," Nicki said with a groan. "Have you been published at all?"

"My dear," he started, "I've been published many times, but to my regret, not by any large publishers."

"Does that mean you're self-published?" she asked sitting on the edge of her seat looking directly at him.

"Unfortunately, yes."

"Is anyone here traditionally published?" I asked.

Everyone looked around at the others, but no one answered the question.

"Interesting," remarked Peter. "Seems we're all on a level playing field. The letter stated it was only for unpublished writers, but I had my doubts."

"Looks like it," I said.

"Let me ask one more question, if I may," Peter said. "Who here has a manuscript they believe would be a bestseller if they could only get a publisher or agent to read it?"

Slowly, we each acknowledged a great manuscript. Harry slid back into the building. Everyone quit talking.

"All of you trying to figure how to get rid of me already?" Harry asked. "Well, it ain't gonna' happen. You can all kiss my ass."

"Sit down and shut up, Harry. No one gives a shit about you," Nicki said.

"Please, please," pleaded Jessie. "Let's try and get along."

"Oh, shit," snapped Harry doing a double take, "Are you a faggot?"

"Why, are you?" Jessie asked, tilting his head.

"Yeah, Harry, interested?" Nicki asked with a huge grin. "You seem to have something for other guys. What's that called?" she asked snapping her fingers, looking towards the ceiling. "I think it has something to do with being...happy."

Everyone was smiling now. I was laughing. Nicki definitely knew how to get to Harry, and she had a way about her that just shut him down.

"Fuck all of you." Harry went over to the other side of the room and sat down by the window.

"One more question," Jessie asked, "how many of us have already started on a book for this contest—before we get to wherever we're going?"

Nobody admitted to starting a book, but all smiled at each other—except Harry, he was still looking out the window.

I admit it, I thought about starting a manuscript to get a head start, but I never did. I'm sure they all thought about it.

"I've got a question for everyone, if I may," I said. "How many here have had, shall I say, a bad experience with one or more agents?"

Slowly, everyone nodded affirmation, including Harry.

"Hey, look," Harry yelled as he stood up. "That must be our plane."

We all gathered at the old, dirt-streaked windows overlooking the airfield. Far off the end of the runway, a white twin-engine aircraft was descending, negotiating the crosswind and coming in for a landing.

The plane taxied up close to the building and cut its engines. All of us filed out the door to the now-quiet plane. A drop-down door opened revealing a middle-aged man wearing a white shirt and navy-blue pants. The door also contained the stairs to the tarmac. He stood in the doorway for a moment surveying the group of passengers, then walked down the stairs and over to us.

"Are you the rep from the contest?" Nicki ask as she stepped forward, obviously enchanted with the uniformed man.

"I'm Captain Rogers, the pilot," he stated. "I was told to pick up five passengers here. I take it you're the group, part of a competition?"

"Yes, Sir, we are," answered Peter.

"Well, grab your luggage. We're on a tight schedule. We have a weather front moving in and we need to take off as soon as possible. I need to take your invitations and acceptance letters. Those are your tickets."

"Where are we going?" Harry asked.

"I don't know the final destination. We have a stop in Chicago to pick up the remaining contestants and refuel; we'll find out when we get there."

"Chicago?" I questioned. "I was hoping we'd be going south, someplace warm."

"We may be," replied the captain, "We can go any-where after we pick up the others."

"Who's giving you the final destination?" Jessie asked.

"I don't know. I'll get radio instructions from my boss while we're in Chicago. They'll file the flight plans and we'll be off."

We went back into the terminal, retrieved our luggage and brought it out to the plane. The pilot stowed them in the cargo area.

"It's going to be kind of tight in there when we pick up the others and get everybody in, so make yourselves comfortable while you can," Captain Rogers said.

"Harry, why don't you take a seat with Jessie, I'm sure he could make you real comfortable," Nicki said as she winked at Jessie. Jessie gave her a candid smile.

"Fuck off, bitch," he responded. Nicki laughed and walked towards him.

"I'll show you my other rings," she taunted as she opened her jacket and rubbed up against him, thrusting her pelvis against his leg.

He pushed her away. "Get away from me, you whore."

As Nicki laughed, everyone else cracked half-hidden smiles—even the pilot.

Each of us gave the captain our letters, climbed the stairs, filed into the plane and took a seat. I sat next to Peter.

"We have one more small thing to get out of the way before we take off. My instructions are to have each of you sign one of these waivers," he said brandishing a large white envelope. "They wan to make sure everybody has their own health insurance and the like. I was told these are standard liability waivers. Read them, sign them and pass them forward," stated the pilot as he pulled a stack of papers out and handed out two-page contracts. "If anyone doesn't want to sign, let me know and I'll let you off the plane and return your luggage. If you have any questions, I'll try to answer them."

I briefly read through the paperwork. It was all legalese, enough that it should have been read and interpreted by someone more qualified than me—*a lawyer for example!* I glanced over at a couple of my new companions; some were signing the papers, others were looking around at the rest of us, probably wondering what the hell the papers actually said. It seemed every other sentence was wherefore or therefore.

Waivers were being passed forward. Shit! I didn't want to sign something I didn't understand. What to do? What to do?

A few minutes later, all the papers had been signed and passed forward to the pilot, except mine. He stood in the cabin doorway, looking at me—me looking at him. I swear he had a smirk on his face.

"As soon as the last waiver is signed, we can take off," he announced. Again, he looked at me.

"Would you like to disembark, Sir?"

I didn't know what to say. My future rested on winning this contest. I started to sign the waiver twice, but held back.

"We're all waiting, Sir."

By this time everyone was looking at me. Did they know what they signed? Did they understand it? Maybe they did. Maybe it's me. Maybe I'm the ignorant one. I signed the stupid thing and passed it forward.

The pilot secured the door and checked our seat belts. After reciting the standard safety mantras, he went through his preflight checklist, taxied to the runway and took off.

"I didn't quite like the way those waivers were worded," I said to Peter. "I didn't even get time to read the whole thing carefully. I wish they had included it with the application, then I could have had a lawyer look at it."

"Me neither, but what're you going to do now? From what I could read of it, it looked like it practically gave them the power to do anything, and we had no recourse. Did you see the part that said it was incorporated and interpreted under the laws of the country of Nauru?"

"What? Where the hell is that? Is it even a country?"

"It was in the fine print at the bottom of the second page. I've never heard of it either, and that part kind of scares the hell out of me."

"Tell me, if they had included the contract in with the acceptance letter and you didn't like it, would you have signed it anyway?"

Peter smirked. "Probably. I really want to win this thing. Right now I'd walk through fire if I had to. I need the money. I'm about four months behind on my child support and my ex is about to file papers on me again."

"I need the cash too. Promise me, if they kill me, sue the pants off them for me, okay?"

"Will do," Peter said. "Do I get to keep the money?"

"Only if you don't win the contest." We both had a chuckle.

After leveling out around twenty thousand feet, the pilot came on the intercom and told us the flight would take about three and a half hours. I looked around the cabin; everyone had settled in and was either reading a book or was trying to nap.

***

Several hours later the Captain Rogers announced he was preparing for a landing in Chicago and for all of us to put our seatbelts on. He also told us we would be on the ground for about an hour. We could disembark the aircraft, but if we did, we were to stay in the terminal. We would be taking off as soon as the plane was refueled.

As we descended, the plane circled several times over what appeared to be a residential neighborhood. At last the plane turned for a final approach and dropped the landing gear. I noticed we weren't landing at a large airport—it couldn't be O'Hare International.

"This is Chicago?" I asked. "Where're the hell are all the bright lights?"

"Must be another private airfield," Peter said.

The rough landing and taxi to the terminal indicated we had indeed landed on a dirt airstrip. We taxied for what seemed an interminable amount of time before we came to a complete stop and the engines were shut down.

When the pilot finally came out of the cockpit, Harry was first to question him.

"Where are we?"

"We're on the outskirts of Chicago. It's a small, private airfield where I can refuel and take off again fairly quickly."

"Why here? I thought we were going to O'Hare."

"No, it's too much of a hassle and too expensive to land at O'Hare International. We'd be tied up there for hours."

"Tell me, Captain, where in the hell is Nauru?" I asked.

"Where'd you come up with that name?" He looked slightly bewildered.

"It was in the contract."

"I don't know anything about the contract, you'd have to speak to whoever wrote it, but it's a small island in the southwestern Pacific."

"Thanks."

We all unbuckled as the pilot opened the cabin door and followed him down the steps out of the aircraft. We trailed behind him as he walked towards a small terminal, not unlike the one we were in three hours ago. The air smelled of diesel fuel, but the light breeze felt good compared to the plane's stuffy, dry cabin air.

I turned to Peter, "Does it seem weird to you that he knows where Nauru is, or is it just my imagination running wild?"

"Jeeze, George, ya think? We don't know where we're going, they give us a fucked up contract to sign and don't give us time to read it; it's from someplace in the world we've never heard of, and now we're at some hole-in-the-wall, shit-ass airport. Does it seem strange? Naw, George, not at all..." Peter cracked a smile. "But then again, you may just have a fucked-up imagination, too."

"Thanks," I said. It did seem a little odd, but he is a pilot. Probably knows a lot of places we don't. I was determined to look up this island nation on the Internet once we arrived at our destination. What in the world would make them use that country for the basis of their contracts? Did it have a great corporate structure and tax laws or was there something more sinister? It didn't compute.

Once inside, we found a small, faintly lit cafeteria-style restaurant that had already closed for the day. It had a low, yellowed, white-tile suspended ceiling which gave a cozy feeling. Although the restaurant was closed, the seating area was accessible. The large room held about twenty card table-sized dining tables covered with classic red and white checked vinyl tablecloths. Four nicked and scarred wood chairs were arranged at each table. A red shaded pendulum light hung directly over each table, it's dim light barely illuminated the space beneath it. Old autographed pictures of early aircraft and pilots decorated the pine-planked walls.

Five more potential passengers, two women and three men, sat at individual tables. They didn't seem to be communicating with each other and watched Captain Rogers and the five of us, seemingly waiting for directions. I'm sure they were scrutinizing each of us as we came through the door, checking out their competition, just as some of us were judging them.

"Are you the other writers?" questioned one young man dressed in western attire.

"Yep," Nicki piped up. She had been the first through the door behind the pilot. She checked out the cowboy from hat to boot.

"Howdy, Ma'am, I'm Randy," he said getting up from his seat and tipping his hat.

"Hi, Randy, I'm Nicki," she said extending her hand for him to either shake or kiss. Her shoulders went back, chest out, putting her breasts front and center. Her body language telegraphed to everyone she was looking for attention and was definitely interested in this young man.

Harry rolled his eyes. "You've got to be kidding."

I laughed. This one time I agreed with Harry.

Nicki shot Harry a sideways glance that I'm sure said, "fuck you," and then was all smiles as she directed her gaze to Randy.

"Where you from, Cowboy?" Nicki asked.

If I were to interpret the look she again gave Harry, it said, "Shut up, you dumb son-of-a-bitch, and don't screw this up."

"I work at a little ranch in Missouri," Randy said, "and you?"

"Oh, I'm from a little of everywhere, most recently from *New Joy-zee*," Nicki said in her finest accent.

I could see Randy was more attuned to her lower features than her face, but she certainly didn't seem to mind.

"Oh my God," Harry blurted. "This is sickening. She's from fucking Oklahoma! Her accent's fake, her rings are fake, and her tits are probably fake too."

"Shut the fuck up, Harry, you pencil-dick, red-neck asshole," Nicki shot back.

I knew it; I knew it! I knew that's what she was thinking!

"Do you know where we're head'n?" Randy asked, ignoring Harry's comments.

"They haven't told us yet," she replied. "The pilot said he would be told when we got here, so we're waiting to find out ourselves."

Randy sat back down, pulled a chair over next to him and took a flask out of his bag, unscrewed the cap and started to take a swig. "Want a nip?" he asked.

"Not now," Nicki replied with a quick wink. "Maybe a little later." She sat down next to him.

"Suit yourself." He took long drink and placed the flask back into the bag.

A 40's-ish, short, obese woman with shoulder-length hair dyed purple and green, sitting in the corner, cleared her throat loudly and stood up. "Does anybody know where we're going?" she yelled.

"Not yet," piped up a smiling Harry. He looked around at the others to ensure he had an audience for his insult to come. "You look like you just came from the circus. Were they here lately? You must weigh in at, what, around three-fifty? Were you their fat-lady?"

There was some muted laughter, a few snickers. The woman sat back down. "I can't believe you said that," she said as she started sobbing, loudly.

I couldn't tell if she was really crying, it did sound kind of fake to me, but I was still shocked Harry said what he did. That idiot just couldn't keep his mouth shut.

"Aw, I didn't mean nothing," Harry said, "I was just kiddin' ya."

"Boy, you make all kinds of friends wherever you go, don't you?" I asked.

"You betcha," Harry said as he sat down.

"You leave her alone," said the other woman as she walked over to the heavy lady. I couldn't help but notice how plain she was, especially in contrast to the circus lady.

She wore a floor length gray skirt topped with a white button down blouse and a Mandarin collar, her hair revealing the tight features of her face. The lines embossed around her eyes and in her forehead evoked a sense of harshness. "Don't pay any attention to them, Dorothy. Let's say a prayer together, maybe it'll save him from eternal damnation."

"Ada, get the hell away from me," Dorothy bellowed as she waved her arm, obviously not crying anymore.

I later learned Ada was a Christian short-story writer. I wasn't surprised.

Stunned at the rebuke, Ada returned to her table and sat down, her hands folded on the table and her eyes downcast. I assumed she was praying.

I looked over at Peter and smiled. "She reminds me of my second grade teacher, Mrs. Bellawood. Meanest bitch I ever had the displeasure to meet."

"Which one?" Peter asked with a chortle.

"The multi-colored one."

"Yeah, and the other one reminds me of my Dean of Students in high school."

A middle-aged black male came over to Peter and me and introduced himself as Ralph Jones. He told us he was a journalist who'd turned mystery novelist. I guessed his age around thirty-eight. He was the only black writer invited. He seemed like a nice enough guy, but kind of quiet.

***

Small talk among my fellow writers continued for about forty-five minutes, until the pilot came through the door. "We're re-fueled. Everyone who was on the plane from New York, please re-board now. The rest of you grab your luggage; have your invitations and letters ready. Meet me out at the steps of the plane."

"Where're we going?" Ralph asked.

"I don't know yet. As soon as I know, you'll all know. I'll call in and ask once we are all boarded and then make the announcement to everyone," stated the pilot.

"I need help," Dorothy stated looking around for someone to volunteer.

"What for?" Randy asked.

"To get her out of her seat," Harry murmured.

"I heard that," declared Dorothy. "My bags."

"Stow it," demanded the pilot, glaring at Harry. "I'll get your bags. Just get out to the plane."

The five of us from New York went out the door first, followed by the Chicago five. While we were boarding, I noticed Captain Rogers bring Dorothy's bags out. He then obtained the paperwork from all of the new passenger's, loaded their luggage, and passed out waivers to each, instructing them to read, sign and give them to him on the plane. After we were all onboard the pilot closed the cabin door. He made sure everyone had their seatbelts securely fastened and started collecting the papers.

"What are these for?" Randy asked.

"They're just standard waivers in case of accidents and says you agree to the lengthy stay at the location chosen by the contest. It also says you have your own health insurance in case you get sick, plus a bunch of other clauses. Read it carefully. If you don't agree to it, I'll let you off now," replied the pilot.

"I don't like to sign a waiver that says we agree to go somewhere where we don't even know where it is we're going," remarked Dorothy.

"Please come forward, Ma'am. I'll help you off the plane," the pilot said.

"No, no. That's not what I meant." After a moment she said, "I'll sign it. It's just..."

She signed the waiver.

The other four also signed the waivers and passed them forward.

"Have you heard what our destination is yet?" Peter asked.

"We'll all know in a few minutes," the pilot said. "I can't take off without my office filing a flight plan."

The pilot returned to the cockpit with the waivers and started the twin engines one at a time while again giving the required safety speeches.

A loud voice yelled out, "Where are we going?" to which the rest of the passengers started echoing the same question.

The captain came back on the intercom and stated, "I was just notified we are headed for Aspen, Colorado. Our flight time will be about four hours. Anyone not wanting to continue, please let me know now, and I'll let you disembark from the plane."

Everyone looked around. No one stood up. All were silent. Then a round of applause filled the cabin.

"It isn't Fiji, but I guess it'll do," I said to Peter. "I was really hoping for someplace a little warmer, but I've heard Aspen is nice in the summer, maybe a little cool at night, but it'll do."

"Fiji would be too hot, but I'm glad it's not New York or Los Angeles," Peter replied. "Too crowded for my tastes. I know I'd have a hard time writing."

"Please prepare for take-off," announced the pilot.

The plane taxied out to the runway, and was cleared for take off. The pilot applied full power. The plane used every inch of the runway before gently climbing into the clouds and heading for Aspen.

After we leveled out, the pilot told us we could move about the cabin, but to stay buckled in if we were seated. A gentleman stood up and introduced himself as Stewart. He asked us all to introduce ourselves. We all stood up, one at a time, and gave our name, where we were from and a brief synopsis of our writing career.

After hearing each of their histories, I was sure the contest was in my pocket.

CHAPTER 7
The Stopover

Day One

The pilot turned off the cabin lights for the long flight and most of the passengers took advantage of the darkness by getting some sleep. A few turned on their personal light and read. It was a smooth flight, no air turbulence at all. The only noise in the cabin was the relentless drone of the engines.

At one point or another, each person retrieved a small boxed lunch and bottle of water from under their seat. Mine was tuna salad and a bag of chips. You'd think they could've supplied something a little tastier. I was so tired from my restless sleep the night before, after the small meal I passed out for a couple of hours.

When I woke up, Peter was looking at me with a broad smile.

"What?" I asked.

"Are you going to let anyone else sleep?"

"Wha..., wha-da-ya-mean?" I wiped my eyes and smoothed back my hair. Things gradually came into focus.

"You were snoring so loud, the pilot came back here to see if something was wrong with the plane. He said he felt a strange vibration."

I laughed. "Yeah, right." Pete seemed to have a good sense of humor; I figured we might end up pretty good friends.

Around three hours into the flight, I noticed we seemed to be losing altitude. It was gradual, and no one else appeared to notice it, but the lights on the ground looked closer. I wondered if we had made better time than expected.

While I reflected on the altitude we were possibly at, the captain came on the intercom. His voice sounded anxious. "May I please have your attention. I'm experiencing a problem with one of the engines. I've lost some oil pressure and it's starting to overheat. I'm going to have to put the plane down fairly soon until I can figure out what's wrong. I've spoken with the home office and they've found a private airfield nearby that is willing to let us land and stay over for the night until another plane can be brought in. There's no real emergency and nothing to worry about; this is just a precaution. Please buckle up and prepare to land."

Stewart had been silently, studying the other contestants until now. "Just my luck," he said plainly, "nothing ever goes smoothly."

He was in his mid-40's, distinguished looking, a politician by trade. I found out later he allegedly had been caught taking bribes, and was given a break by the prosecutor as long as he resigned his office and stayed out of politics for a number of years, which he reluctantly did.

He began writing political thrillers after his forced retirement. All of his novels reportedly had a crooked District Attorney as the main character, which was his way of getting back at a system that, in his own mind, had unjustly ended his career. He wrote all his novels under a pseudonym. I thought if he had any balls he would have used his real name, but it didn't matter, he never published any of them. I wondered if they were good books and he just never submitted any of them to an agent, or so bad, none of them were ever published.

"I'd rather land and wait for another plane," stated Jessie who was sitting next to Stewart, "than stay on this one to the site of the crash."

"Sounds reasonable to me," Peter said.

***

We lost altitude quickly, one of the engines sputtering as the pilot put the flaps down. A noise from the undercarriage made everyone apprehensive, as they sat up and looked out the windows. Ada was sitting in the rear, praying fervently.

The captain must have sensed our nervousness. He came over the intercom and announced, "Don't worry about that noise, folks, it's just the landing gear going down."

"Where the hell are we?" Peter asked. "I don't see a light anywhere."

The engine continued to sputter as if it was going to cough one more time and die.

"Look, over there, I see lights," Nicki said.

"Landing lights," Stewart said, sounding relieved.

"Just in time," Dorothy whispered loudly.

The rough landing signaled we had touched down on another dirt runway. The plane taxied up next to what appeared to be an old school bus that had been painted white, with no other markings. The few landing lights outlining the runway shut off after the plane landed. The airstrip had no facilities, no hangers or terminals. It was completely dark outside except for the lights of the plane.

"This ain't an airport," Peter commented. "It's a landing strip in the middle of nowhere."

"Ladies and gentlemen," announced the pilot, "the hotel where you will be staying tonight has provided a bus for the ride to the hotel. Please claim all your baggage and belongings, as we will not be re-boarding this plane. The bus ride will be about a half-hour long, so please use the plane's restroom if you need to before we depart."

The pilot shut down the engines and opened the door. Cool night air rushed into the plane. It smelled good and clean, nothing like the big city. He went over to the bus, started the engine and turned on the headlights to provide lighting for the passengers. He came back to the plane, opened the cargo hatch and removed the entire load of luggage, which he helped carry over to the bus.

"Where are we?" Ada asked.

"Somewhere between Chicago and Aspen," retorted Harry. "Does it matter?"

Peter looked at his cell phone. "I don't have a signal out here. Does anyone?"

One by one, everybody took their phone out and looked. No one had a signal.

"We must really be out in the boonies," Randy declared.

It was a cool, clear, and crisp night. Somewhere in the distance coyotes were singing their nightly songs. Millions of stars shone brightly in the sky but the moon was missing.

"It sure is dark out here," stated Dorothy.

"Yeah, but look at all the stars," Nicki said. "Isn't it romantic? I've never seen so many."

"You never see all the stars in a city," I said, "too much light and air pollution."

"Yeah. This place looks to be right up your alley, Nicki," declared Harry, "black of night, seven men, and all the time in the world."

"You're just jealous, asshole," snapped Nicki. Her frown turned into a smile as she looked around. She walked over to Jessie and whispered in his ear. He shook his head and smiled. Nicki strutted over to Harry and ran her hand down his chest. "You want to get laid, *big boy*? I can fix you up."

"Get away from me you slut." He slapped her hand away.

"But, Harry, you seem so *horny*." She grabbed him in the crotch.

Everyone, including the pilot, burst out laughing at this scene...except Harry. He was steaming and speechless.

"Everyone on the bus," yelled Captain Rogers. We all meandered over and stepped up onto the bus one by one with the exception of Dorothy. She tried to step up but there wasn't anything to grab onto.

"Someone help me up," she demanded.

"Is there anything you can do for yourself?" Randy asked.

"Yeah, I can play with myself," she retorted.

"Oh, my god," Randy said shivering, "*that* image scares the hell out of me."

The pilot stepped over and helped pull Dorothy up onto the step. He got into the driver's seat, ground the bus into gear and pulled away from the airfield.

How the hell does he know where to go, I thought? I walked up the aisle to the pilot. "How do you know where this hotel is?"

He pulled a sheet of paper from a pocket next to the driver's seat. "Directions."

I sat back down.

We stayed on dirt roads the entire way to the hotel, only traveling about twenty-five miles per hour. The old bus had a manual transmission on the floor, which the pilot didn't seem too comfortable with. He ground the gears, double and triple clutched it, finally resting into a drivable gear. The seats were almost as hard as sitting on the steel floor would be. The padding offered minimal comfort it was so compressed from years past. Every pothole and bump in the road sprung everyone up and down in their seat like jack-in-the-boxes; we were bounced around like rag dolls.

"Where are we?" Peter shouted to the pilot.

He looked up into the rearview mirror. "We're on the prairie in Wyoming, somewhere close to Colorado. Other than that, I don't know. I could give you coordinates, if that would help."

"No, don't bother," he replied.

As we bounced along the dirt road, the narrow headlight beams only illuminated a small area on the sides of the road; brush, prairie grass, a few rabbits and a scrub tree here and there were all that could be seen. Once in a while I would see a steer or two with yellow or blue ear tags. They would raise their heads from grazing as the bus rumbled by, kicking up a cloud of dust that hung like a curtain in the still air.

About twenty minutes later the bus passed through the gate of a fenced-in area. He pulled up in front of a large wooden, wind-worn building brushed with faded blue paint. From the headlights I could see it was trimmed in a whitewash. Although a light was on inside, the windows were so dirty you could hardly see through them. A sun-bleached sign hung over the front door that read *Hotel*. Weeds and tall brush outlined the perimeter of the building.

"This looks like a *minus* four-star hotel," Peter stated.

"Where's McDonalds, Burger King, Denny's?" Ada asked, "I'm starving."

"This is it?" Dorothy asked, her voice high-pitched. "This is it?" Her arms were outstretched, trying to encompass the incredulity of it all. "We're supposed to stay *here* tonight?"

"We're here," announced the pilot. "Make the best of it until tomorrow. I was told there are supposed to be ten rooms and ten keys on the counter. Everyone take one and get settled in a room. There'll be instructions for everyone in the morning."

"Instructions?" I asked. "What instructions? Aren't you returning with another plane in the morning?"

"I don't know if it will be me or not. I haven't been told. It'll be tomorrow sometime, but I don't know if it will be in the morning. Someone will let you know as soon as they can."

"Where are you going?" I asked. "I don't like being left out in the middle of nowhere with no communications."

"I have to take the plane in for repairs."

"I thought it was broken, that's why we had to land. This doesn't make any sense. We had to land and stay here because the plane needs repairs, but you have to leave in the plane so it can get repaired."

"The engine was badly overheating. I'll have to wait awhile until it cools down, check for adequate oil pressure, then head for the nearest airport that has maintenance. Without all the extra weight on board, I should be able to make it, even if it's on one engine."

"He's talking about you, Dorothy," Harry said.

"I'm talking about everyone," the pilot snapped.

Peter was the first to get off the bus, claim his luggage and head for the hotel. I followed. I could hear a faint hum—a motor running somewhere—it seemed to be coming from behind the hotel.

"What's that humming noise?" I asked to no one in particular.

"I'm betting it's a generator," Ralph said straining to hear where it was coming from.

"Great," Stewart said. "We're camping out for the night. Who's making breakfast in the morning?"

"Don't look at me," retorted Ada who was following us.

"Maybe they're bringing it in when they pick us up in the morning," I said.

"I wouldn't put any money on it," Peter stated.

We stepped up onto the porch and into the hotel.

The lobby was sparsely furnished. There were several wicker chairs arranged around a small card table. A threadbare, red and gold oriental carpet adorned the wooden floor under the card table, its fringes frayed and half-gone. An old leather couch looked forlorn against the far side of the room. Decorations were scarce as well. The only items of note were some old, rusty tobacco, whiskey and beer signs that hung on the walls.

Dingy, white-lace curtains, tinged with yellow, covering the lower windows drooped from a rope strung between large nails sticking out from the trim.   The lighting we had glimpsed through the dirty windows glowed from a wagon wheel chandelier hung above the table. The filthy glass sconces probably blocked more light than it let out. Several of the bulbs were burnt out.   Matching wall sconces protruded from two of the walls.

The worn, wide-planked, bare wooden floors creaked as Peter and I walked across to the solid oak hotel desk. On the desk were ten keys, with the tags turned face down. Peter picked up a key and looked at the tag. *Room 10, 3rd floor.* He put it back and looked at another. *Room 2, 2nd floor.* That must have been better. He kept it. He picked up his bags and started up the stairs. "See you all in the morning."

"What kind of place is this?" questioned Nicki.

"I suspect it's an old ghost town, partially restored," Ralph said. "Kind of quaint, if you ask me."

"This is horrid," cried Dorothy. "Could someone bring my bags in?"

"Did I hear a *please*?" Jessie asked as he walked past her and picked up a key.

"Would someone *pleassse* bring my bags in?"

"Do it yourself," Stewart said. "We're not your bellboys."

I picked up a key that said Room 8, 3rd floor. Shit! I turned over two other keys—both third floor. Lucky me. I didn't see any elevators around and I didn't want to walk up all those stairs either, but I figured it was just for one night, what could it hurt? I stuck around for a few minutes more. Dorothy was going to end up with a room on the third floor, and I knew there'd be a debacle. I guess my warped side wanted to see it.

She was the last one to get her key. Room 10, 3rd floor.

"I can't be on the third floor," she wailed, "it's... it's too much."

She went over to Nicki, who had managed to get a room next to Randy on the second floor. I figured she was just where she wanted to be.

"Will you trade me rooms?" she asked, almost begging.

"Piss off," Nicki said grabbing her bags and pulling them up the stairs. "It'll help you work some of that—that bad attitude off."

Randy had brought his bags up to the second-floor landing, returning to help Nicki with hers. I smiled. If I were he, and about fifteen years younger, I'd have done the same.

Dorothy looked around the room at the other contestants, her Bassett Hound eyes pleading for a sympathetic soul to help her. No one would look directly at her; the rest of us grabbed our bags and headed up the stairs. She went over to the leather couch and plopped down, sobbing. She couldn't force or coerce anyone to help her this time. I decided I would come back down and give her a hand if no one else had after I had seen my room.

***

I finally made my way up the stairs to my room on the third floor. It was as strenuous as climbing up the stairs to my apartment in New York City. My chest was heaving as though I'd just forged a new trail over the Catskills.

Jessie was just ahead of me. He went to room nine and unlocked the door with the skeleton key attached to his tag. I had the room next to him.

"Quite a hike up those stairs," I said as I unlocked my door. "I hope it's just for the night."

"I wanted the top floor," he replied.

"You did?"

Jessie was a healthy young man and looked in moderately good physical shape, but who would want to walk up two flights of stairs if they didn't have to?

"Yeah. There's no one above me to wake me up," he said pointing to the yellowed ceiling. "After eight years of listening to the 'thud, thud, thud' of feet across a floor, toilets flushing, and people screaming at each other when you're trying to sleep, I'll take it every time."

Thinking back to my own apartment, he had a point.

Opening my door and turning on the light, I found myself in a room that smelled a little musty, but was clean. The décor was late 1800's, a little gaudy for my tastes. The old pink wallpaper was peeling in several corners of the room; a large brass bed with a huge head frame was shoved up against the wall. The floor was the same as in the lobby downstairs with wide pine boards. A couple of cheap, dust-covered paintings of half-naked women decorated two of the walls, and a brass chandelier hung from the twelve-foot high ceilings, throwing a circle of dim light onto the center of a faded and ragged oriental blue rug.

Jessie came running into my room.

"This must be an old house of ill repute; a real whorehouse," he said. "This is great!"

I laughed. "It must have been." He ran back out.

A dark oak bureau with a white washbasin on top sat below one of the pictures, and an aged wardrobe closet was positioned on the opposite side of the room. A lunch bag was sitting on the bureau. I opened it and found a peanut butter and grape jelly sandwich inside along with a bag of potato chips and another bottle of water. *Don't they have anything but water?* It hit me then and seemed a little strange that this was very similar to the meal we had on the plane. Probably cost them even less than the tuna fish.

I sat on the bed and wolfed down the sandwich. I was hungrier than I thought. There being no box springs on the bed, the mattress sagged heavily. Any support the bed might have had was worn out years, maybe decades before. I finished the sandwich and pulled the mattress off the bed along with the sheets and pillow and placed them on the floor next to the bed frame. That would be my bed for the night. I wondered how old the mattress was; did it have bed bugs or other critters that would infest me later? I laughed to myself wondering how much screwing had been done on this mattress in an old whorehouse.

I went out into the hallway and peeked into some of the other rooms as the occupants went in or came out. Each looked the same as mine with a few minor nuances. The pictures were different—the rug and wallpapers had slightly different colors—the wardrobes were a little larger or smaller.

I then went to find the restroom facilities. At the end of the hall was a door standing partially open. I pushed it wide open and saw that everything was white! The white enamel-painted room had a white porcelain claw-foot tub with matching knobs and a light brown rubber hose coming off the faucet with a spray nozzle at the end. A white rubber plug with a chain held the water in the tub. The white toilet was antique, like the rest of the building, with a white pull-chain water closet mounted on the wall. A small amount of rusty water sat in the bottom of the toilet. A little white sink stood alone on the opposite wall, held up with two chrome legs, its porcelain handles matching those of the tub. The dingy white linoleum floor had worn out and faded long ago and was completely worn through in places, displaying the wood floor under it.

Jessie probably considered staying the night at the hotel a real experience—one that would take him back to the early 20th century.

Some of the others didn't share the same optimism or attitude as he did. I thought the place was a dump, historic or not, but I could put up with it for one night. I just kept telling myself Aspen will be great, and we'll be there tomorrow. I went to see what everyone else thought of the place.

Ralph told me he considered the place a disaster and was insulted that he, a great journalist, would have to put up with less than comfortable lodging. There had to be a conspiracy here, someone was setting him up.

Ada's door was ajar. I knocked. She was more than just a little upset. I wish I hadn't asked her how she liked the place.

"I can't share a bathroom with men! I've never even shared a *house* with a man! Men pee all over the toilet seat and leave a mess. Besides, they don't even know how to put the seat down. And look at these pictures—they're sinful! I can't even look at them." She grabbed one off its nail, turned it to face the wall, and placed it on the floor. I handed her the other one.

"Sounds to me like you know men pretty well," I chided.

She looked at me, took a couple deep breaths and calmed down.

"I had brothers. I guess I'll have to get up early and be the first in."

I bid her goodnight and went down to the second floor. Nicki and Randy didn't seem to mind anything. I'm sure they had other things on their minds and nothing short of a fire would distract them from having a *great* night. I think the biggest decision they had to make was which room they were going to "sleep" in.

***

After everyone had disappeared upstairs to his or her room, I guess Dorothy must have realized no one was coming to help her. She went outside where her bags still sat in the dirt and brought them in, one at a time. She rested on the couch between each trip to catch her breath. About that time, I went downstairs to check on her.

"I'll help you upstairs this time, Dorothy, but you're going to have to start helping yourself."

"Thanks, George. I am grateful."

"I'll take your two bags up to your room. Number ten, right?"

"Yes."

"You'll have to take your computer bag. I'll leave these in the hall next to your door."

I picked up the two bags and trudged up the stairs. They were quite a bit heavier than mine and I had to stop on the second level to rest. After making it to the third floor, I placed them in front of her door.

Dorothy trudged up the two flights of stairs, one step at a time, resting halfway up each level. She finally made it to her room. I watched her as she unlocked her door and went in. I waited for what I knew was coming next. When she saw the furnishings and the spring bed with the thin mattress, she let out a howl that brought everyone from the third floor to her room.

"*Nooo*, I can't live like this," she shrieked. "Look at this place."

We all looked into the room and shrugged collectively. It was exactly like our own rooms.

"Damn-it, Dorothy, it's just like everyone else's room. It's just for the night. If you don't like it, haul all your shit downstairs and sleep in the lobby or out in the street," Stewart said. "I'm going to bed, it's been a long day."

"Wait till she sees the bathroom," chuckled Jessie as everyone walked back to their rooms. "If you hear another howl, you'll know why!"

CHAPTER 8
Captive Audience

Day Two

The next morning when I went downstairs, a couple of the others had already been up with the early sun, which I suspect had risen around six. A thick fog had begun setting in and surrounded the hotel—nothing could be seen past a stone's throw.

Peter walked out the front door with me and onto the small porch, stretching his arms.

"How about running down to the local convenience store and picking up a couple of coffees?" Peter asked.

"Tell you what," I said smiling, "you fly and I'll buy. It'll only take you a couple days."

"I wonder when they're coming for us."

"The way the pilot was talking, it may be this after-noon."

"I'm hungry and I'd love a cup of coffee. Those shitty-ass sandwiches they supplied just didn't cut it."

"I know. You'd think they could have afforded something just a little better."

As he turned around to go back inside, Peter spotted a brown leather pouch on the wood deck, sitting against the wall, next to the front door.

"George, someone must have left their case out here. Know whose it is?" He picked it up and examined it for a nametag.

"No, I don't remember seeing that with anyone. Maybe it's Dorothy's; her shit was the only things left outside last night. Open it and check it out."

He unlatched the buckle and looked inside to see if he could find something to identify its owner. Pulling out a manila envelope with a label addressed to *The Contestants*, he showed it to me. "I don't think it's Dorothy's," he said.

"Uh-oh," I said. "That fucking pilot. I knew there was something wrong. Everything seemed a little too organized for a last minute emergency."

Opening the envelope, he found a letter addressed to the group. "Oh, shit. This doesn't look good," Peter said.

I read the letter over his shoulder.

GOOD MORNING, CONTESTANTS:

There is a full kitchen through the door to the rear of the hotel lobby. I'm sure by now most of you will want some coffee or tea. In the kitchen you will find a coffee pot, coffee, and plenty of food.

There has been a change in plans. It has been decided you will be staying here until your manuscripts are finished, so make yourselves as comfortable as you can. Some information you will need to endure and some rules you MUST abide by:

1. Do not try to leave. The fence around the town is electrified. Stay away from it.

2. If you decide to try your luck and leave, you are between one hundred and two hundred miles away from any other civilization—depending on which way you decide to travel.

3. You should choose a leader and decide on chores and jobs to sustain yourselves.

5. You have enough food for at least two months, if you conserve.

6. You have enough fuel to run your generator for two months, if you are frugal. Don't waste it, as it also supplies your water from the well, your hot water, your cooking, and your lights. Turn it off when it is not needed.

7. I'm sure most of you have already started a book for the contest. Put it away. For this contest, you will all collaborate on one book, but keep separate manuscripts. The premise of the book shall be your experiences getting to, staying at, and living in this hotel and town; the writing of this book under the conditions prescribed above, and the interactions of the different personalities of the contestants.

8. Do not wander around in the other buildings. It is dangerous. The wood is rotted and there are rattlesnakes, scorpions and other nasty creatures you may not want to come into contact with.

9. I am sure someone will want to try his or her luck and succumb to the possibility of leaving. If they don't make it, when we find their body or bodies, you will find them buried in the southwest corner of the town. If anyone else expires, please bury him or her in the same location. There is a shovel on the side of the hotel.

In closing, let me be blunt. You were all chosen for this contest because you believe you have best-selling author abilities. You now have the opportunity to prove your aptitude, so write as if your life depends on it. No one gets to leave until everyone is done with their manuscript, or sixty days, whichever comes first.

P.S.—As a bonus, you will find a supply of liquor in the basement. Enjoy it and make it last. Good luck to all!

"This must be a joke," muttered Peter.

"Doesn't sound like a joke to me," I said.

He reread the letter, took it inside and showed it to Stewart and Ralph, who were engrossed in their own conversation.

"Here, read this," he said. "I found it outside on the porch."

Both read the letter.

"This can't be real," Stewart said, looking in amazement at Ralph and Peter. "We were supposed to go to Aspen. He said we were going to Aspen!"

"Ah, but if you remember the waiver we signed, it didn't say 'Aspen', it just said *in the locality chosen*," Peter said. "This must be the *locality chosen*. The pilot lied to us."

"I wonder if he knew he was lying to us?" questioned Stewart. "As a matter of fact, I wonder if he really had engine problems."

"He knew," I said, "and I doubt he had engine problems. Everything went too smoothly, just like it was all planned. He just happened to have engine problems. He just happened to find a hotel in the middle of nowhere to put us up and there just happened to be a bus at the landing strip to take us here. Bullshit, he knew. He's probably part of this competition."

"Yeah, how many of us would have gotten off the plane if he told us 'You're going to be staying at an old ghost town out in the middle of nowhere, with no contact with anyone, and no modern facilities?'" Peter asked.

Minutes later, Ada and Harry came down the stairs to the lobby.

"Has anyone come for us yet?" Ada asked.

"Someone's been here, but not *for* us," Peter blurted. "Here, read this. It was on the porch this morning."

He gave the letter to Ada and Harry.

After reading the letter, Ada gave it back and said, "What is this, some kind of a sick joke? They can't do this!"

"They can't keep us here," Harry said.

"That's the ninety-two dollar question," Stewart said. "Who are *they*?"

"And the other question is, where is here?" I asked.

"We don't know yet, but I suppose we'll find out pretty soon. Let's go to the kitchen and see if we can make some coffee. Whoever wrote this was right on that point, I need a couple of mugs," Peter stated.

We followed Peter through a door to the rear of the lobby, which opened to a large, semi-modern kitchen. An oversized, rectangular white-painted wood table with dark green legs sat in the middle of the room, surrounded by ten tan-painted wooden chairs. Avocado colored appliances offset a pink and light green room. Several white-trimmed, dirty windows, thick with dust from years of neglect barely let in adequate sunlight. An ornamental tin ceiling, with a coat of dingy white paint obscured its intricate detail. Fluorescent lights hung from the high ceiling, and the floor was covered with the same linoleum as in the bathrooms. It, too, was marred with years of wear. The many white-coated cabinets were slatted giving an appearance of wainscoting. A large room off the side of the kitchen proved to be the pantry and held hundreds of cans and boxes of food. Another small room off the other end of the kitchen contained a 1970's era gold-colored washer and dryer pair. The cabinets above them held pails of generic detergent and bleach.

On the counter next to the stove was a coffee pot, but it was going to take some time to make the much-wanted coffee—it was a 30-cup percolator type.

"Does anyone know how to operate this monstrosity?" Harry asked. "Where the hell is the coffee?"

He opened the cabinet above the coffee pot and found a plain white can of generic coffee.

"Isn't there any Starbucks, Folgers or Maxwell House?" Stewart asked. "Anything brand named?"

"This appears to be it," Harry said.

"I've made percolated coffee before," Ada said, "but it's been a long time. I'll have to experiment with the amounts."

"There's directions on the can," Harry said, handing the can to Ada. "See what you can do. If you have to experiment on the first pot, error on the side of strength. I like my coffee *strong*."

Ada looked around to the others, as if looking for any objections. No one said anything. Maybe they didn't want to start a fight with Harry so early in the morning, but this time I agreed with him.

We went through the cabinets, finding the dishware, silverware, cups, saucers, and baking and cooking utensils.

"Seems everything is here we might need," stated Ralph.

"Yeah, for anyone who is staying," Harry said. "I don't know about any of you, but I'm not."

"Me neither," Ralph said.

"Well, let's get the rest of the group down here and have a powwow. If this is a joke, it's a good one, but if it isn't, we need to decide what we're going to do," Peter suggested.

Ada stayed in the kitchen to make the coffee and the rest of us filed back into the hotel lobby.

"The fog is lifting," Harry said, "I'm going to take a look around. The letter said there was an electrified fence surrounding us. I'll check it out."

"I'll come with you," Stewart said.

"We'll get the rest of the group up," Peter said. "Ralph, if you take the second floor, I'll take the third."

"Okay, meet you back here."

***

About a half hour later, Harry and Stewart returned from their foray around the town. When they entered the lobby, everyone was present and had completed reading the letter. Several were arguing and shouting at each other. They stopped as Harry and Stewart entered the room, awaiting their findings.

"I'm going to sue the pants off these assholes," Dorothy yelled. "We have to get out of here!"

"Are you through, Dorothy?" Stewart asked. "We're all in this together. We have to discuss what we're going to do."

After everyone quieted down he gave his report. "It appears we are in an old western ghost town that is only about two blocks long. The good news is the building we're in is in the best shape of them all. Everything else is dilapidated, falling down and unusable. It seems the prairie surrounds us as far as the eye can see." He paused, as if waiting for questions.

Dorothy obliged him. "Where are we?"

"I don't know where the hell we are, but I think we're somewhere in Wyoming or eastern Colorado, as the pilot said. Of course, it could also be southern Nebraska or western Kansas—or someplace like that."

Harry continued. "The bad news is that about a hundred yards beyond the town encircling us on all four sides is a chain-link fence about eight feet high. The gate we came through last night now has a stainless steel chain around it with a huge padlock securing it. There're signs about every twenty feet warning of high voltage, and they weren't kidding. I threw an old piece of wire I found on the ground at the fence. It lit up like the Fourth of July, so it is electrified with a very high voltage, like the letter stated."

"So what are you telling us?" Dorothy asked. "We're captives?"

"He's saying we're prisoners," Jessie said. He was grinning like a dumb ass and his eyes were all lit up—similar to a kid at Disneyland. "This is exciting!"

"It appears so." Stewart rolled his eyes. "Some vacation destination this turned out to be."

"There's a road, if you want to call it that, leading out of here that appears to head east. It looks more like a wagon trail than a road," Stewart said.

"We can't be held here, that's illegal," cried Dorothy. "What are we going to do?"

"We? Whadda' ya mean *we*?" Harry asked. "Just what in the hell do you think you're going do? All you can do is sit there on your fat ass and cry."

"Leave her alone," Jessie said.

"Shut up, you fairy," shot Harry, "unless you want to back up your words."

"Ah, shut up yourself, Harry, and quit acting like a tough guy. I know you're all talk, and soon everyone else will too," Nicki said.

"Ignore him, Nicki. We ought to be thinking about getting some breakfast," Randy said. "I'm starving and I think better with a full stomach."

"With all the exercise you two got last night, I'd be hungry, too," Harry said. "If you guys are going to fuck all night, at least do it on the floor and have a little respect for the rest of us who want to sleep. Those beds make a lot of noise."

Nicki was blushing, looking toward the floor with her hand on her forehead shielding her eyes. Everyone else, including Randy, was smiling. I knew what Harry had said was true, but no one was going to say anything else. It seemed every person was awakened at least once last night by the noise of the old bedsprings and the frame pounding against the wall.

"The coffee should be ready by now," Ada said. "Who wants some?" We all raised our hands in unison. I guess it was too many for her to handle by herself.

"You'll have to help yourselves. It's on the counter. I hope it tastes all right."

"What's out there we can have for breakfast?" Jessie asked.

"You'll have to go look, but I saw a bunch of different types of cereal and pancake and waffle mixes," Ada said.

"Cereal?" Nicki asked. "Yuck."

"I didn't see any milk or juices," Ralph said.

"No, there doesn't seem to be any fresh milk," Ada said, "but I saw cases of powered milk."

"Powdered milk?" Dorothy asked scrunching her face. "I haven't had that since I was a kid, and I hated it then."

"I know, you want the whole milk, the stuff with all the cream and fat," Harry said sarcastically.

Everyone headed out to the kitchen, except Ralph and Peter.

"Coming?" Stewart asked.

"All of a sudden, I'm not that hungry," Peter said.

"Me neither," Ralph said.

"Suit yourself," Stewart said.

In the kitchen, the other eight of us searched the cabinets for something to eat. It was a nightmare, everyone for themselves. Ada mixed a couple gallons of powdered milk and most had various types of cereal with the whitish, watery solution. I found a box of generic cornflakes that I added the whitish water to. It looked gross, and tasted even worse, but I was hungry and quickly downed the bowl hoping to bypass my taste buds.

Randy and Nicki decided to make pancakes. She found some syrup for herself. Randy wanted grape jelly on his, which she found in the pantry. Nicki found a skillet, mixed the batter, and cooked a couple of plates of pancakes on the electric stove.

After filling our stomachs, some of us stacked dishes in the sink; the rest left them on the table. Nothing was cleaned up; no dishes were washed or rinsed. We all wandered back to the hotel lobby.

"What do we do now?" Jessie asked. He obviously was not interested in being the leader. He was waiting to see what everyone else decided to do.

"I told you I'm not staying here," Ralph said. "It can't be a hundred miles to anywhere. I'm going to take some water and food and get out past the fence. I hope no one objects."

"Why would anyone object?" Harry asked.   "Who gives a shit what you do or what happens to you."

"I do," said Ada. "I care about all of us."

"Fine. You go with him," Harry replied.

"What about getting caught?" Jessie wondered.

"By who? I'll take my chances. I think it's a bunch of bluff and bluster to tell you the truth. I didn't see anyone anywhere outside the fence guarding us with a machine gun. We're probably our own captives. Besides, if there is someone watching us, what are they going to do, shoot me? March me back here?"

"When are you planning on going?" Stewart wanted to know.

"Now, as soon as I can get ready."

"Don't you think you ought to have something to eat first?" he asked.

"No. I don't eat breakfast. I'll have to leave my stuff here. Hopefully, I'll pick it up when I get back. If you'll watch it for me, I'd appreciate it."

"Of course I'll watch it, but can't I talk you out of this? Maybe we should wait and see how this plays out a little. We ought to stay together just in case someone does come and get us," Stewart implored.

"Why? Don't you get it? This is a bunch of bullshit. You still believe this is a contest? You still think there's a sixty thousand dollar prize? Look at this place. Can't you see what's going on? Do you really think that a company that can afford to pay us sixty thousand dollars would have to put us up in this dump? Do you think they'd be feeding us peanut butter and jelly sandwiches and bottles of water? This is someone's cruel joke; we're being led around like a bunch of sheep. They aren't going to do anything except leave you here to rot. I've got to figure out which way to go after I get out, that's all. If I get to anywhere, or find anyone, I'll send the authorities."

CHAPTER 9
The Rescue Attempt

Ralph left the group and went upstairs to his room to wash up, change and prepare for the trek. He put on a pair of jeans, a long-sleeved shirt and jogging sneakers. He took a light jacket, as it had been foggy and chilly the night before. He came back down stairs and gave Stewart the key to his room.

"Does anyone have a flashlight or a knife?" Ralph asked.

No one answered.

"I've got a little pen light in my luggage," I told him. "You can use it if you want."

"That would be great, George, thanks. I need to find a container for water and figure out what food to take."

He went to the kitchen. In the pantry he found cans of beans and packages of dried beef. He took five of each and two cans of peaches. He couldn't find anything to store water in, but found a paring knife to open the cans with.

Back in the lobby, he asked if anyone had a backpack he could use.

"You can use mine," Jessie said, "I'll get it."

"Does anyone know where the basement is?" Harry asked. "The letter said there was booze stored down there."

"Alcohol? You want alcohol this time of day? That's the devil's drink," Ada said.

"Aw, get off your high-horse, woman. I need to find a water container for Ralph. If there's a basement, there may be something down there. He can't go anywhere without water."

"It's the door over there," Randy said pointing. "We, uh, kind of found it last night. There's a bunch of old plastic gallon milk containers down there. Does anyone have any aspirin?"

"I have some," Ada said, "But I'll not waste any on the results of liquor. You'll have to suffer your sins."

"Thanks, Ada, you're a real gem," Randy replied, holding his head.

"I have some, Randy. I'll get a couple for you when I go upstairs," I said. I'd brought a whole bottle, so I figured I could spare a couple.

Ralph went down into the basement. He came back with two plastic gallon-sized jugs, and a bottle of vodka. "For medicinal purposes," he said holding up a bottle of vodka.

We went into the kitchen, rinsed the jugs out with water and a little bleach, and then filled them with water. Tying them together with a length of rope, he left about three feet between them.

When we got back to the lobby, Jessie had retrieved his backpack and Ralph placed the food and the medicinal liquor in it. I went to my room and got my penlight, a couple aspirin, and a couple extra batteries. Returning, I gave Randy the aspirin. He took them and went immediately to the kitchen, I suspected to get some water. I gave the light and batteries to Ralph.

"How are you getting over the fence?" Nicki asked.

"I'm not," Ralph replied, "I'm going under it. The letter said there's a shovel lying on the side of the hotel. I checked and it's there. I'm going to dig a small trench."

"Well, good luck. I hope you find someone and get us out of this hellhole," Dorothy said. "And soon."

"I'll help you dig the trench," Harry said. "You're going to need to save your energy."

"Me, too," added Stewart. "I'll help."

"I'll give ya a hand, too" I said.

Ralph grabbed his backpack, and Stewart the two gallons of water. After a few goodbyes and well wishes, we filed out the front door. I picked up the shovel lying along the side the building. Harry wandered off for a few minutes, but soon caught up with us carrying an old board, about his height and six inches wide.

What's the board for?" Stewart asked.

"I figured we could use it to wedge up the lower part of the fence. Make it easier for him to get under. We won't have to dig as much."

Ralph smiled. "Good idea."

We found a place about twenty feet from the gate where the ground was already a couple inches below the bottom of the electrified fence and Harry started digging. The loose sand and rock made for easy excavation.

"Don't hit the fence," I warned. No sooner had I said it, Harry's shovel touched the fence. Sparks flew. It scared the shit out of me. I expected Harry to fall or get knocked out. He just stood there laughing.

"You moron, the handle is wood. It doesn't conduct electricity."

In about a half hour they had a trench deep enough for Ralph to crawl under and Stewart used the board to wedge the fence up next to the trench. Ralph slid under easily, pulling his two gallons of water and backpack through after him.

"Well, if I make it, I'll hopefully see ya's in four to five days. If I don't, it's been nice meeting all of you," he said from the other side of the fence.

"You'll make it," I said, giving him a thumbs-up.

"I've decided to follow the wagon trail road and head east, I'll make better time on a path rather than fighting the prairie. So, I was thinking, if I don't make it or if you don't hear from me and one of you want to try again, go west. Maybe you'll be luckier."

Ralph put the backpack on, slung the two gallons of water over his shoulder and headed out across the prairie. Stewart, Harry and I stayed and watched him as he disappeared from sight.

"Think he'll make it?" Stewart asked.

"I guess we'll find out in a few days," I said as we turned and walked back to the hotel.

***

As we entered the hotel lobby, we found Dorothy in the middle of a rant.

"You can't smoke that thing in this hotel, it stinks."

"And I don't give a shit what you think," Peter said, "What I do in my room is my business. If you don't like it, tough shit."

"Does every other word have to be a cuss word?" Ada asked.

"But it comes up through the cracks in the floor. My room is right above yours," Dorothy complained.

"Ada, get some earplugs," Peter said. "I'll tell you what, Dorothy, if you lose a hundred pounds and start doing everything for yourself, I'll quit smoking my pipe in my room—otherwise, we're not in Chicago and the smoking police aren't coming through the door to your rescue."

"All right," Stewart intervened. "We've got better things to do than sit around and argue all day. It's almost noon and we had better start making a few decisions."

"Like what?" Nicki asked as she rubbed her shoulder against Randy.

"We have to figure out what we are going to do with the generator and the fuel. Is it going to be every man for himself, or do we organize and each person take turns fixing meals for everyone? What about shower and bath schedules, cleaning, washing dishes and clothes? If we are going to be here for a while, even say, a week, we need to stop the fighting and figure out what we are going to do. And we really need to cooperate if we're to make it through two months," Steward lectured. "On top of all that, the letter said we have to collaborate on a book."

"You people need to clean up after yourselves, especially in the bathroom. It's disgusting," Ada complained. "Shaving cream all over in the sink, water on the floor...and we've only been here one night. I fixed the coffee and mixed the milk this morning, but now there's a sink full of dishes, and cereal all over the place. It's like a bunch of pigs ran through the kitchen. No one bothered to clean up after themselves, and I'm not doing any more until the jobs around here are shared."

"I agree," Dorothy stated. "Why can't you guys put the toilet seat down when you're finished?"

"I suppose I could ask you why you can't put the seat up when *you're* finished?" Harry retorted. "There's a lot more of us here than you."

"Because..."

"Could we get serious here for a few minutes and quit the squabbling?" Stewart interjected. "I can't believe we're already arguing about which way the toilet seats should be. Next, it'll be which way the toilet paper should hang."

There were several moments of silence.

"If Ralph gets through, I figure we ought to hear from someone in about three to four days," I said. "If by day five we haven't heard anything, we have to count on being here for quite a while longer. The letter said we had enough fuel for two months, *if we conserve.* Whether you realize it or not, the generator is our lifeblood. It pumps the water from the well to a pressure tank. No electricity, no water."

"Guess we all have to just drink the booze then, eh?" Randy joked, smiling towards Ada.

"Won't touch *my* lips," she retorted.

"That's fine, dear, more for me."

"Listen to George, damn-it, he's making sense," Stewart demanded. "We run out of fuel, we die. It's as simple as that. Don't you get it?"

"They wouldn't let us all die here, would they?" inquired Dorothy. She looked as if she had just had an epiphany.

"The question is, would they even know it?" I asked. "Whoever *they* are."

Everyone was quiet.

"What do you suggest?" Peter asked, breaking the silence.

"To begin with, we have to figure out how much fuel we have, then how much the generator consumes in an hour. If we know that, then we can reasonably figure out how much we can use per day. I'd suggest we give ourselves a few weeks beyond the two months, just in case."

"So divide it by seventy five days instead of the sixty?" Jessie asked.

"Right."

"I'll fend for myself," Harry said, "I ain't doing nobody's dirty dishes, cooking, laundry or bathroom cleaning.

"Me either," Nicki said, holding onto Randy's hand, "we'll take care ourselves."

"You got that, darling," Randy said giving her hand a squeeze.

"Anybody else?" I asked. "That leaves me, Peter, Jessie, Dorothy, Ada and Stewart. Who wants to see what's available for lunch while I go and find out how much fuel we have?"

"I'll see what I can drum up; I think we ought to bake some bread today too. I know everything is here for it," Dorothy said. "We're definitely going to need some."

"I'll give you a hand for now," Ada said.

Peter and I followed the sound of the generator out to a shack in back of the hotel. As we entered it, we found an older, electric start generator, which appeared to be about a fifteen to twenty thousand watt, enough to power most appliances in the hotel. Behind the shed was a five hundred gallon gas tank on a stand that sat up higher than the generator. By now, we knew the generator had been running for at least 14 hours.

"I need to look in the tank and see how much fuel we have," Peter said. "Give me a hand up."

I cupped my hands and Peter stepped up. He unscrewed the cap and peered in. "The level's down about twelve inches from the top. I'd say that gives us approximately four hundred and fifty gallons left."

I did some quick math in my head. "Shit. That doesn't sound good. I think that's only going to let us run it a few hours a day. Let's go back inside and decide what we're going to do," I said. "There's going to be a mutiny."

"How would you suggest I present it? I can't think of any good way."

"Straight out is probably the best. They aren't going to like it, but neither do I."

Back in the hotel, while Ada and Dorothy were baking bread, the rest gathered in the lobby.

"How's it look?" Stewart asked.

I shook my head. "We're going to figure it out and let everyone know in a few." I think Stewart knew we were in trouble.

I sat down in the kitchen with Peter and figured out on paper what we had and how long it would last, down to the last gallon. We wanted to be sure of our figures.

***

About a half-hour later we gathered everyone, except Ada and Dorothy, together in the lobby to give them the news.

"It's a fairly large generator," Peter said. "I had one that was a bit smaller, so I'm going to estimate this one uses about two gallons an hour under full load, in other words, when we turn it on. It will probably always have a full load on it since everything we have is electric. I think it'll always be heating water."

"We have many appliances that are using the juice it puts out—the electric stove, the water heater, the well pump, lights, refrigerator, and the washer and dryer, and we need them all. We believe we have about four hundred and fifty gallons of gas left. That gives us about six gallons a day for seventy-five days. In other words, about three hours of usage a day," I said.

"Three hours a day?" questioned Harry. "Ten people are supposed to shower, cook three meals, wash clothes, dishes and clean in three hours a day? And what about lights?"

"Nine," I said. "Ralph's gone."

"I know it's going to be tight, but we have to do it if we are to stay two months and survive. We'll have to go without lights at night, but it stays pretty light out until about eight thirty now anyway," Stewart said.

"So now we have to decide when we are going to turn the generator on and off," I said. "I don't know if we can all take showers everyday. I don't think the hot water heater will generate that much heated water in the time frame we have."

"It can't do that in *three hours?*" Nicki ask.

"We can't use all three hours in the morning. We need water and electricity in the afternoon and at night, also," Peter said. "I know you and Randy and Harry want to fend for yourselves, but this affects all of us. We all need to decide together and agree on when we turn the generator on and off, and for how long."

"Hey, why don't we all shower together and save electricity?" slurred Randy. He was obviously either drunk or heading there.

"Shut up," Jessie said, "this is serious."

"Screw you, you little faggot," Randy said as he lunged toward Jessie, "I'll fix you."

Stewart and Peter grabbed Randy by the arms and forced him back down onto the couch.

"Leave him alone," Nicki said, sliding in next to Randy.

"You should ease up on the booze, Randy, it may be a long two months," Peter said.

"Kiss my ass."

"Suit yourself, but if you keep this up, I'll dump all the booze that's in the cellar and you won't have a drop."

"Who made you sheriff, asshole?"

"Nobody. But I sure as hell am not putting up with some young, drunken idiot for the next two months. Either wise up or take a hike."

Most of the others were nodding their heads in agreement with their eyes fixed on Randy.

"I'll second that," I said.

"I'll knock you on your ass," Harry said pointing at Randy.

"Y'all leave the booze alone," glared Randy. "I'll put a fix to anyone who touches it."

"You and who else?" questioned Peter. "You couldn't fix anything, let alone tie your own shoestrings right now."

Ada came from the kitchen. "Lunch is ready."

"Let's eat," Jessie said, seemingly anxious to break the tension.

Everyone got up and went to the kitchen.

"Peter, Stewart, Jessie, George, grab some bowls. The stew is on the stove and sandwiches on the table," Dorothy said as she stirred the pot.

"What about us?" Randy asked, leaning against the wall.

"Yeah, how come you didn't fix anything for us?" Harry questioned.

Dorothy shrugged her shoulders. "Hey, you guys said you were going to fend for yourselves. Start fending," she said with a smirk. "You don't want to help with anything, you're on your own."

"But you better not make a mess of things," stated Ada waving a kitchen knife she cut the sandwiches with, "I've no patience for anyone leaving messes to clean up—in the kitchen or the bathrooms." She slammed the knife into the cutting board and turned around.

"You're not my mother," Nicki said going to the pantry, "I'll fix something for us."

"I've got a couple loaves of bread rising on the stove. We only have one loaf here. If you three want any bread, now's the time to mix it. You have to give it time to rise and I'm going to bake tonight," Ada said. "I'll throw it in with mine."

"Nicki? You know how to make bread?" Harry asked.

"Who do I look like, Aunt Jemima? Your mother? You said you were going to fend for yourself. Like Ada said, 'start fending'."

"Aren't you the little bitch," Harry said.

"I'll show all of you once, but you're going to have to share among yourselves, we can't be wasting any food," Ada said. "Nicki, do you want to learn?"

"All right, I'll learn to make bread, but you two have to do the dishes," she said looking at Randy and Harry.

"All right," Harry said giving in. "You make the bread and we'll clean up."

"Soon as we're done here, I'm going to shut off the generator," Peter said. "We should have enough water in the pressure tank to make bread and wash dishes. Any objections?"

There were none.

"I'll turn it on again tonight for an hour and a half. Everyone needs to wash up then and do whatever they have to do until tomorrow morning. We'll fill whatever we can with drinking water before I shut it off."

Nicki fixed some canned spaghetti and meatballs, and peanut butter and jelly sandwiches for the three of them. Jessie and Stewart washed and dried the dishes for the six, then Randy and Harry for the three.

Peter went outside and turned off the generator. Once it stopped, he stood and took in the silence. The quiet was eerie. Only the distant sounds of the prairie and the low howl of the wind broke the stillness.

CHAPTER 10
Hair of the Dog

After lunch, one by one, we all drifted out onto the hotel porch. Some stood, most took a seat on the edge of the porch. A warm breeze wafted through the town blowing a few scraggly tumbleweeds down the center of the street.

"I guess we need to start writing our book," suggested Stewart who was sitting on the steps.

"And we need a schedule for the electricity," I said. "Peter, I'm recommending you be in charge of starting and stopping the generator. You just need to know what times to turn it on and off."

"I agree with that," Stewart said. "You want to do it, Peter?"

He nodded and stood up in front of everyone.

"Have any suggestions?" I asked.

"I'm going out on a limb here," Peter said as he lit his pipe, "but I propose we only turn it on twice a day instead of three times. An hour and a half in the morning and an hour and a half in the evening—say, seven in the morning to eight-thirty, and five till six-thirty in the evening. In the mornings we all rotate showers every-other day. One day shower, next just wash-up. Two shower in the morning, two in the evening. That way, hopefully we'll have enough hot water for everyone.

"This is awful," Dorothy stated. "A shower every-other day?"

Ada nodded her head in agreement with her. "That's it?" she asked.

"That's it," Peter replied. "Two people get to wash and dry their clothes each day after the showers, so everyone washes every five days; again, one in the morning, one at night. Hang your laundry in your room to dry or we can hang a clothesline out back if we can find a rope. Wash in cold water only. I'm going to disconnect the hot water to the washing machine to save electricity, so that won't be a problem. It's going to take a lot of juice to heat the water we need for showers and dishes. That's about all we'll have time for and it's going to be tight. If we find there's a problem, we can adjust, but that's my suggestion to start with. Everyone needs to agree and cooperate on this, even those who are fending for themselves. It's a matter of life and death for all of us."

"Sounds reasonable to me," Stewart said. "Make sure you all charge your laptops every time the generator is on. That's the only occasion you'll be able to do it."

Everyone else nodded approval except for Harry.

"Harry?" Stewart asked.

"I'll see. I'm not guaranteeing anything right now. But just for now, it sounds okay."

"What're we going to do about the book?" Jessie asked.

"I guess we just start writing about our experiences so far," Ada replied.

"I've only written some poetry and romance novels," Jessie said, "I don't know how to write about prisoners on a prairie."

Stewart laughed. "That sounds like a damn good title, Jessie, *Prisoners on the Prairie*."

"You shouldn't have too much trouble with the romance side, Jessie, hell, we've got a regular brothel going on here," Harry said looking at Nicki and Randy. "I wonder how much she's charging?"

"For you, Harry, no amount of money in the world would be enough. Why don't you just mind your own business," retorted Nicki.

"Oh, don't get your knickers in a knot," Harry replied. "That is, if you're wearing any."

"Harry, if you don't shut the fuck up...," slurred Randy.

"What are ya going to do, Randy, hit me with your bottle of booze? Have a showdown at high noon? You chicken-shit mother fucker..."

Randy lunged at Harry, but stumbled into Stewart, who held onto him, then stepped in front of him and pushed Randy back.

"Hold on there, Cowboy. You aren't in any condition to get into a fight." He patted him on the shoulder, and then turned, glaring at Harry.

"Anyway," Stewart said, "I wonder what was meant by collaborating on the book, but keep different manuscripts?"

I was impressed how Stewart handled the situation. He smoothly decompressed a pretty volatile situation.

"Maybe we should decide what each chapter is going to be about, but we write our own points of view?" Ada asked.

"Yeah, like the first chapter would be about meeting each other and our views on each person. It could include our flight here and how they lied to us about where we were going," I said.

"No, the first chapter should be about the offer to enter the writing contest," Dorothy said. "That's where it started. That damn letter they sent us, and how we got sucked into this whole stinking mess by that."

"I agree," Nicki said, "I should have never paid attention to that stupid letter. Now look where we are."

"But look who you're with, baby," whispered Randy to her in her ear.

"You want me to puke?" Dorothy asked.

"Is everyone okay with starting with the letter?" Peter asked. Several heads bobbed approval.

"Does anyone have a copy of the waiver we signed on the plane?" Ralph asked.

No one answered.

"That's great. I didn't think of it either at the time. I wish I had a copy of it now."

"I think we ought to title the first chapter, *The Offer*," Stewart said.

No one disagreed, and so it was settled.

"I'm going to go get started," I said. "See all of you this evening. By the way, who's cooking supper?"

"We made lunch, you four decide who is going to cook supper," Dorothy said.

"I'll try to make up a schedule this afternoon for everything," I said. "We can go over it tonight. I'll also volunteer to cook tonight; anyone want to help?"

"I'll help," Jessie said.

"Good, see you around five. Does anyone need to do laundry this evening?"

"I do," Harry said. "I was in a hotel for three days before we met."

"If no one else needs to, I'll start mine too, if there's time," I said.

"Okay, be ready at five," Peter said. "That's when the generator goes on."

***

At five that night, Peter turned the generator back on. Harry washed his laundry, Jessie and I prepared dinner, Dorothy baked three loaves of bread, and the kitchen and dishes were cleaned without an incident. Everything went like clockwork—even Randy had sobered up some and didn't insult anyone. He and Nicki shared a shower.

I'd spent most of the afternoon preparing a bathing and laundry schedule for everyone. In addition, a schedule for cooking, washing dishes, and cleaning bathrooms was also presented for the six who had agreed to work together. Cooking and washing dishes didn't seem to be a problem, but the bathroom cleaning immediately caused a conflict.

"I'm not cleaning up after any man," Dorothy declared. "I've done it most of my life and I'm not doing it again."

"Besides," Ada chimed in, "when do the other three clean?"

It was ultimately decided that everyone would clean up after themselves for now. If that didn't work, it would be brought up again later for discussion.

"Now, which one of you wants to take out the trash? We can't keep it in the kitchen; it'll start smelling by tomorrow," Dorothy said.

"Take it out yourself," Harry retorted.

"I'll get it," Stewart said. Where do we put it?"

"I saw a trash-pile around the back of the hotel when we checked on the generator," Peter said. "Looks like there's a pit. Just toss it in there."

"That's going to attract the coyotes," Stewart added.

"It's either that or burn it and I don't particularly like that idea with these buildings like tinder. Besides, who cares if the coyotes get to it?" I said.

The trash pit was determined to be the best alternative.

***

Peter, Stewart, and I took a walk through town after eating, talking about the day's activities, Peter puffing on his pipe. We watched as Nicki and Randy went into one of the old buildings on the opposite side of the street from the hotel. It looked like it used to be the town's general store.

"Hey!" Peter shouted. "Don't go in there. Those buildings aren't safe."

"Mind your own business, old man," Nicki shouted back.

"Those two are just asking for trouble," Stewart said.

"Those buildings look like they could come down any minute. The floors are rotted and parts of the roof could collapse any time," I said.

"I know, but they won't listen to us. They're still at the age where it's fun to be young and stupid—especially stupid," Stewart stated.

"I think Nicki's been acting a little strange since this morning. She didn't say much at dinner and her actions seem slow and careful, almost like she was drunk. Her pupils looked pinpoint, and, although she hasn't said much, when she did speak, her thoughts seemed disconnected," I said to Peter and Stewart.

After thinking for a minute, Peter said, "I think Nicki is on something or smoking some *wacky tobacky.*"

"You're probably right, but as long as it doesn't affect us, I don't really think it's any of our business," I replied.

"Shouldn't we say something to her? Maybe to Randy? I'd hate to see anything happen to her out here, there's not much we could do," Peter said.

"There's nothing we can do anyway, if she wants to take drugs, let her. She's a big girl and knows the consequences. I'm not going to stand in her way or interfere in anyone's personal life," Stewart added.

"You're cold," Peter said.

"You're going to say something to Randy about drug use? That's a joke. He's also probably smoking enough dope to stone an elephant," Stewart said defensively.

"How do you know that?" I asked. "I thought he was just drunk all the time."

"Hell, no. Can't you smell it all over him? Can't you smell it in the hotel by his room?"

"No, my I've been all stuffed up since we got here. I think I've got some grass allergies kicking up," I said.

"I just think we should do whatever we can to help keep them safe," Peter said.

"Part of what Dorothy is yelling about isn't Peter's pipe; it's Randy and Nicki smoking dope. And save her from what? Herself? She has her own choices to make—I have mine, you have yours. I can't save the world from itself, and neither can you. Besides, we have enough decisions to make here just to survive. If you bring up drug use, it's just going to inflame both of them and make them more difficult to live with. You heard Randy when he was told to ease up on the booze. What do you think he'll say if you bring up drug use? 'Oh, thank you, Sir Peter, for bringing that to my attention, I'll throw it all away right now?'"

The conversation was broken by an awful scream coming from the direction of the dilapidated building Nicki and Randy had gone into. It sounded like Nicki.

We ran to the building, me huffing and puffing, following Peter and Stewart at a distance. They recklessly swung open the dilapidated, worm-eaten door and went inside.

We came to an abrupt halt as soon as we cleared the threshold. The floor, what was left of it, sagged in places and was completely rotted through in others. Whole floorboards were missing from sections. Grass and weeds rose through the cracks and holes and a field mouse scampered across the room near the rear wall.

"Where are you?" Peter shouted.

"We're in here," yelled Nicki. "Hurry, Randy's hurt." The voice seemed to come from the building next door.

"How'd you get over there?" I shouted.

"Through the hole in the wall in back of the staircase."

We made our way over the unstable floor toward the sound of Nicki's voice.

As I made my way, step by careful step, I took in the sorry state of this building. The windows were all broken out, front and rear, jagged glass still protruding from their frames. Wrecked and hanging shelving lined much of the walls. A staircase to the second floor covered part of the back wall. It had so many missing steps; it reminded me of a meth-head's toothless smile. Dust and dirt covered everything. We still couldn't see Nicki or Randy.

Following Peter and Stewart, I headed for the opening. I heard a loud *crack;* I stumbled and fell to the floor.

"Shit," I yelled. My foot had broken through a rotted plank.

"You okay?" Stewart asked as he grabbed me, trying to pick me up.

"Yeah. Give me a sec." I kept trying to pull my foot out. I finally managed to yank it back through. The rear of my ankle burned. I pulled my sock down and found the skin had been scraped off, but otherwise I was okay.

"Hurry!" Nicki yelled from the next room.

"We're coming. Hold on," Stewart yelled back as he helped me up.

Slowly we inched our way across the rest of the room, testing each step. We had to get down on our hands and knees and crawl through the opening into the next building. As I entered, I saw Randy sitting on the floor with his leg through a floorboard up to his knee.

"Please, help him," pleaded Nicki, "He can't get his leg out."

"How in the hell did you do that?" Peter asked as he walked around Randy and studied the rotted boards he had broken through. Randy's other leg was folded under him.

"I just walked over here and it split open. If I try to pull it out, I'm getting large splinters poking into my leg." He tried to pull again.

"Damn, that hurts."

Stewart stood erect, his eyes widening. "Shhh. Quiet." Everyone went silent. "Listen." The noise was self-explanatory. "I've never heard that sound before, but I'm pretty sure what it is."

"Oh, fuck!" Randy exclaimed as he tried to pull his leg out again. "Owww! Get me out of here! Get me out!" he screamed. His leg wouldn't move.

Stewart pounded on the plank with his foot that was pinching Randy's leg, holding it in. It snapped, just enough to release him.

"Son-of-a-bitch! Pick me up!" Randy yelled. Stewart and I hoisted Randy off the floor as he jerked his leg free. His leg had spots of blood on his jeans in several places.

Nicki looked into the hole and screamed. "There're snakes down there!" She jumped behind me, screaming, jumping up and down. The floor cracked under the weight of both of us together.

"Knock it off!" I yelled at her. "You want both of us to fall through?"

She stopped jumping and gradually backed up, still whimpering.

"What the hell did you think that noise was, a baby rattle?" Stewart asked, rolling his eyes.

Randy looked at his leg. "Shit! A rattler bit me. *Son-of-a-bitch!*"

"Help him! Do something for him!" yelled Nicki.

Carefully, we shouldered Randy, and led him to the front of the room. The floor groaned and creaked, bowing under the weight of the three of us together. The front door to the building wouldn't open; it was frozen shut with age. The glass panes had long broken out from the top, leaving the rotted wooden frames, but the bottom was still intact. Stewart kicked the center of the door hard, splintering the center in several pieces. We both kicked out the rest. It fell apart like balsa wood. We helped Randy out onto the porch, and sat him down. Stewart pulled out a knife and cut the pants of the leg that was bleeding and examined the wound.

"There go those jeans," Randy said.

"There are different kinds of rattlers, some are more poisonous than others. Whatever it was, it looks like you got a multiple dose there, Randy," Stewart said. "There's not much we can do without a hospital."

"Just do something, it hurts like hell," he said, his face contorted with pain.

"There's several bite marks, Randy. Looks like you were hit by three snakes. Must have been a nest of them down there."

Stewart looked to Peter and me. Although I knew the look, I wasn't sure exactly what Stewart was saying.

"Let's get a tourniquet on the leg, at least it'll slow down the venom," Stewart said. He cut the pant leg completely off and then cut a strip of cloth from that, tying it tight around Randy's calf.

We helped Randy limp back to the hotel and hop up the stairs to his hotel room. We laid him on his bed and took off his boots and jeans. Nicki placed a blanket over him. The bites were just above the top of the boot. The fang marks in the back of his calf muscle still bled. One by one, everybody came to the room to see what the commotion was about.

Stewart motioned for me to go out in the hall with him for a moment. "He's probably done for. There's nothing we can do for him."

"Why?" I asked. "I thought most people survive snakebites."

"Without anti-venom there's probably no way he's going to survive, he got several doses."

"Holy shit," I said quietly as I leaned against the wall and scratched my head.

"There's a first aid kit in the kitchen, I'll go get it, for what it's worth," Stewart said, "but it's all for show, it's not going to help a bit."

I went back into the room.

"Should we cut the fang marks and suck out what we can of the poison?" Jessie asked.

"And who's going to do that?" Dorothy asked, looking around to see who would volunteer.

"Yeah, Nicki ought to be good at that," Harry said with a broad smile.

"Get him out of here," Randy yelled pointing at Harry.

Nicki pushed Harry out the door. "You're such an asshole." She slammed it shut.

"No, that's not done anymore, it just causes more infection," Randy said. "We'll just have to let it run its course, but it hurts like hell."

The door opened and Stewart came into the room with a first aid kit. "We can put some antibiotic on it and wrap it, but that's about it. We need anti-venom."

"What were you guys thinking of, Nicki? Weren't you told to stay out of those buildings?" I asked.

"We were just exploring. We went over to that next building to see what was in it and Randy fell through the floor. I didn't know there were snakes under it."

"You were told, but now it's a little too late. I fell through the floor in the other room coming to your rescue. I could have been bitten, too." The hair on the back of my neck stood up just thinking back on it.

Nicki sniffled. "I'm sorry."

Randy took a few swigs from a bottle of whiskey he had under his pillow. He poured some of the whiskey on the fang marks before Stewart applied the antibiotic and wrap. He yelled and his body stiffened as the pain rushed to his head.

"Like that's going to help," Stewart said to Randy.

Randy took a couple more drinks. "I'm going to need a few more fifths of this before it's over," he said holding up the bottle. "If I don't make it, bury me with one," he said to Nicki, smiling with a wink.

"What do you mean, *if you don't make it?*" she asked. "Of course you're going to make it." She looked at Peter. "Isn't he?"

Peter placed his hand on her shoulder. "Come with me," he said softly. I went out to the hall with them.

"We don't have any anti-venom," he said. "He may make it, he may not. Depends on how much venom he got and the kind of rattlers they were. You may want to stay with him, Nicki. He's going to run a hell of a fever and his leg is going to swell up and discolor pretty bad. We may have to cut it open."

"Try to keep him as comfortable as you can," I said.

We left Nicki with Randy and all went down to the lobby. There was mostly silence, but everyone was searching the eyes of everyone else. What do you do when someone is going to die and there's not a damn thing you can do about it? We were used to calling an ambulance or a doctor or hospital in an emergency; now we had to rely on ourselves and we had come up short. Not only did we not have anti-venom, no one knew exactly what to do for this situation. Was there anything we could do? Was it preventable? I don't know.

"The Lord works in mysterious ways. He's paying for his sinful habits," Ada said, breaking the silence.

"Oh, get off your high horse, better-than-thou bullshit," Harry said. "I'm sick of it."

"Ada, shut-up," Dorothy said. "We don't need your preaching right now, this isn't the time. Pray for him if you want, but keep your comments to yourself."

"He's going to get pretty sick," I said.

"I'll be surprised if he makes it," Peter said. "One bite he might survive; two bites is doubtful, but three bites is one hell of a lot of venom."

"Isn't there anything we can do?" Ada asked, looking at Stewart.

"Only thing I can think of is to cut his leg off before the poison gets to his heart. But, who would do it even if Randy would agree? And I know he wouldn't. I can't do it and we don't have a thing to operate with even if I could."

"We have some really big sharp big knifes in the kitchen," Dorothy said. "That would do it."

"That may cut the muscles and nerves, but we need a saw for the bones," Stewart replied. "We don't have any."

He looked around at the others. There were no other ideas.

"That settles it," he replied looking at the floor. "He's probably going to die."

CHAPTER 11
The Addict

Day Three

The next morning Randy was delirious. According to Nicki, he had been tossing and turning, talking and yelling in his sleep all night, having nightmares, dealing with his demons. He would wake up at times and Nicki would give him water and try to get him to eat some soup. He always opted for a few more drinks from his bottle instead. He was in serious pain and she had a hard time watching him go through it. His leg had continued swelling and it was now black and blue up to his thigh.

"Randy," she said to him in a low voice during one of his more lucid periods, "I have something that will help you with your pain, but you have to tell me it's all right to give it to you. I don't know how you will react to it, and I don't have much left, so we have to use it sparingly." She wiped the sweat from his forehead with a damp washcloth.

"What is it?" he asked, not even opening his eyes. His voice was labored.

She pulled the sheet away and looked at his leg. It was swollen almost twice its size and he couldn't even move it from the pain. Her face grimaced from the scene.

"It's...smack," she said.

"Heroin?"

"Yes."

"Where'd you get it?" He opened his eyes, searching her eyes for a clue.

Damn, I didn't want him to know. "I've got it. It doesn't matter where it came from right now. We can talk about it later."

"I guess so."

I should tell him, he deserves to know. "I brought it with me, but I didn't bring that much. I didn't count on getting caught here for two months; I thought we'd be in a city somewhere. I'm going to have to go through with-drawal myself soon, and it's going to be pretty nasty and painful; but I can do it. I've done it before."

"You're willing to give some up—for me?"

"You need it more than I do."

"Do it. This pain, I can't stand it anymore," Randy said, still partially delirious and barely able to speak.

Nicki went next door to her room and pulled a small black case out of her luggage. She came back and locked the door behind her. She didn't want anyone walking in on her while she cooked up a dose of the drug for Randy. Cooking the heroin in her spoon, she drew the drug into a hypo through a piece of cotton to purify it. She was careful to reduce the amount, as Randy was a first-time user and wouldn't have built up a tolerance like she had. He wouldn't need much. She carefully tied a rubber tube around his arm to bring up a vein, sterilized the needle with alcohol, and injected the warm narcotic into his arm. She sterilized the needle again, duplicating the cooking routine for herself, and shot herself up in her arm. She lay down beside him on the bed where they both fell into a deep sleep for the rest of the morning.

***

It took two more days for the venom to take its full toll. Randy's leg had grossly swollen up to almost three times its size. Gradually, the discoloration and poison worked its way up his leg to the abdomen. Nicki did what she could to make him as comfortable as possible, giving him a shot whenever he was in intolerable pain or some whiskey if he requested it. He had refused any food.

At two in the morning, Nicki awoke from her last shot, got up and used the bathroom. She wished the generator was on so she could take a shower, but was able to wet a washcloth and wipe her face and arms.

Lighting a candle, she searched her room for her computer. Finding it under the bed, she turned it on and found the battery was at half strength. She carried her laptop to Randy's room, pulled the pillow from the bed and sat on the floor where she could watch over him while she worked on her manuscript. She was the only one who had the first-hand experience and insight to Randy's pain and her special help; she would get it into her manuscript. It would be a blank spot in everyone else's. Even Randy wouldn't remember everything that occurred.

This was a hard task for her; she had fallen deeply in love. They had even talked about getting married when the contest was over and they would both return to New York to make a home. She adored Randy, and in the small time they had known each other, felt as though she had been with him all her life. Plus, the sex was great. They both felt an intense desire to write, but now it would involve their emotions and how they envisioned the world—especially in a little ghost town on the edge of the world that surely mirrored part of hell.

For two hours she wrote notes of what she had experienced so far and a brief personality description of the other contestants. She skipped several of the first chapters everyone had agreed upon, deciding instead to concentrate on her relationship with Randy and their final hours together, although she didn't know it at the time. Her computer screen warned it was shutting down; it had run out of battery power. She would have to wait for the generator to be turned on in the morning to recharge.

She silently cursed the computer, the hotel and the sponsors of the contest. She looked up at Randy; he was the only good thing these past several days had brought her. She went to him and placed her hand on his forehead to check his fever. Something was wrong. She couldn't hear him breathing anymore, couldn't *see* him breathing. She shook him and called his name several times. He didn't respond.

At four in the morning, Nicki's screams brought several of us running to Randy's room.

"He won't wake up," Nicki said sobbing. "I shook and shook him, but he won't wake up."

Peter felt for a pulse on the carotid artery on his neck; I felt for one on the wrist. I looked at Peter and shook my head.

"He's gone," Peter said.

I tried to pull the sheet up over Randy's head.

Nicki screamed, "No! No!" She threw herself on Randy and hugged him around the neck. "You can't go!" She fell to her knees along the side of the bed.

Randy was pronounced dead at four-ten in the morning by mutual consent of those present. We agreed to note it in our manuscripts.

The group knew there was nothing more we could have done but keep him halfway sedated with whiskey and bourbon. We hadn't known anything about Nicki's special help at the time.

"We can bury him later in the morning," Peter quietly said. "There's nothing we can do now. Take Nicki to her room."

Ada and I held Nicki's arms and guided her to her room as she cried uncontrollably.

CHAPTER 12
The Grave

Day Six

Later that morning, Harry, Stewart and I stood at the end of Randy's bed and pulled the sheet off him. He had turned an ashen gray as the blood had drained to the lower part of his body.

"Let's wrap him in his bed sheet and blanket," Stewart said as he started pulling Randy's body from the bed.

I helped lay the stiff corpse on the floor—rigor mortis had already set in. Stewart spread the blanket first and then the bed sheets on top. We lifted the body back onto the bed, wrapping it with the sheets and then the blanket.

"What are we going to do with him?" Harry asked as he flipped the sides of the blanket over the sheets, wrapping Randy's body up like a cocoon. "We need something to tie off the ends of the blanket. Tear one of the pillowcases into strips."

Stewart yanked the pillowcase off of a pillow, pulled out his pocketknife and cut it open. He tore two long strips and handed one to Harry.

"I guess we'll take him down to the southwest corner of town where they told us to bury anyone who dies," Stewart said. "That's always bothered me—why would they say that? I can't figure out what made them think anyone was going to die. It's like they were planning on some of us croaking."

"Beats me, makes you wonder if they've done something like this before," I said.

"It's possible, but you'd think someone, somewhere, would have heard of it and sent out a warning to other writers."

"You grab the shoulders, I'll get the feet," Harry said to Stewart and me, as he tried to get a grip on Randy's feet through the blanket and sheets.

"This isn't going to be easy," Stewart said, also trying to get a grip on the top end of the taut blanket.

"Just be glad it's not Dorothy," I said.

"Hell, I'm just ecstatic," Harry laughed, "but at least we could roll her down the stairs, out the door, and down to the end of the town. We have to carry this one."

We lugged him down the two flights of stairs struggling to keep a hold on the body, and met up with Jessie who was sitting at the table in the lobby drinking a cup of coffee.

"Jessie, could you give us a hand and grab the shovel on the side of the building?" Stewart asked. Then, looking around he asked, "Where's everyone else?"

"Most of them are in the kitchen eating breakfast, except Nicki. Haven't seen her this morning yet; maybe she's still in mourning."

"Probably just pissed she didn't get laid last night," interjected Harry.

Stewart rolled his eyes. Jessie gulped down the rest of his coffee and followed Stewart and Harry out the front door. He found the shovel and trailed us down the center of the decaying town.

As we arrived at the southwest end, we spotted a small cemetery with grave markers probably dating back to the late nineteenth century. Some had weathered wooden planks serving as memorials to past lives; now blank pieces of timber from the relentless sun and the shifting sands of time.

As we got closer, we saw a pile of fresh dirt with a *newly* inscribed board attached to a small post.

Here Lies Ralph,
He Should Have Gone South,
He Decided on East,
Now the Worms Have a Feast.

"God-damn it!" yelled Stewart. "What kind of sick fuck would write something like that?"

"Well, I guess we know now what happened to Ralph," I said. "So much for a rescue party."

"Should we dig him up and see if it's really Ralph?" Jessie asked. "See how he died?"

"I'm not, you can if you want," Harry said. "Digging up dead bodies isn't my favorite way to pass the time. And who cares how he died? If he's dead, he's dead."

"No, let him rest," Stewart said taking the shovel from Jessie. "It has to be him, who else would it be?"

"You know what this means," Harry said looking in the distance.

"What's that?" Jessie asked. "No rescue?"

"It means someone's been here. Again. We're being watched, maybe all the time."

We all turned and looked out onto the plains. Was someone having a laugh watching us dig a grave?

For the next two hours the four of us took turns digging a three-foot deep hole next to Ralph's grave—and scanning the prairie. He was probably out there somewhere, hiding, watching. Where is he? Who is he...or is it *they*?

Stewart and Harry lifted the body into the grave. Jessie started shoveling dirt back in.

"Hold up a minute, Jessie. Randy had a last request," I said.

"He did?"

"What, did he want his stash buried with him?" Harry asked with a sarcastic tone.

"No. Wait here."

I went back to the hotel and returned with a fresh bottle of rye whiskey. I placed it in the grave with Randy, just as he requested.

"That's a waste of good booze," Harry said.

"Well, if you run out, you'll always know where there's an extra one," Jessie added.

"I told Ada to notify everybody to come down for a small service. Whoever is coming should be here soon," Stewart said.

They continued filling in the grave. It was about fifteen minutes before everyone else arrived, including Nicki. The first thing they saw was Ralph's grave with the attached poem on the post. Dorothy let out a short scream and started sobbing.

"Now we're going to be here forever!" she cried.

"That right, Dorothy. Forever," Harry stated.

"That's great, Dorothy. Ralph's dead, Jessie's dead, and the only thing you're worried about is yourself," Peter said sarcastically. "Can't you at least pay your respects for a couple moments?"

"Who's going to rescue us now?" she asked.

"No one," I said. "We're on our own."

All the others were quiet and sullen while the reality sunk in. Maybe they were also disgusted at the morbid fun someone was having at our expense. I know I was.

After finishing the burial, we circled the two graves. Ada was asked to lead a small prayer for both of the departed.

Nicki stood like a zombie at the foot of Jessie's grave. She didn't speak, cry or talk to anyone; she just stood there. Her legs wobbled under her. Her eyes looked sunken. When we returned to the hotel, Nicki trailed all of us and went directly up to her room without saying a word to anyone. I wondered if she had completely lost it.

***

At lunch, everyone was quiet and no one seemed to have much of an appetite. It was hard to believe after only six days, two of us had already died, and I was wondering who was going to be next—if there would be a next. Would it be me? Nicki was still in her room and hadn't been seen since the burial.

"Does anyone know Randy's last name?" Jessie asked.

"I suppose if anyone does, it would be Nicki," Dorothy said. "Why?"

"Just wondering. Eventually we'll need it for that part of the manuscript we're writing. I don't even know where he's from. All I heard him say is a small ranch in Missouri."

"His death *is* part of our story," Peter said. "We need to find out if we can. Does anyone know anything about Ralph? We need to know his full name and where he lived."

"Why do we need that?" Ada asked. "We aren't using real names in the manuscript, are we? I haven't so far."

"I was using real names for now, but I was going to change them before submitting the manuscript," Dorothy said.

"Bullshit," I interjected. "We don't need any of that for the story. We can't use real names or home addresses in the final drafts, so why do we need them now? It's supposed to be a novel, not a true-life adventure."

"But it *is* true life. We may have to write a novel, but shit, this isn't fiction. It's real. We're like lab rats in the research center," Peter said. "They dispose of the rats that get out of their cages. They're contaminated and can't be used for the experiment anymore."

"Are you suggesting that's what we are?" I asked.

"Yeah, I think that's what we are—lab rats. They have us running in circles. They feed us and provide for our basic necessities, but that's it. If we get out of our cage, they get rid of us."

"You may be right," Stewart said, "but we still need the information for the authorities when we leave here. Someone has to pay for this."

Peter's voice became louder, "Aren't you listening to me? We aren't leaving here. They can't let us go. They can't afford to have us go to the authorities."

Dead silence ensued for several minutes. I don't think any of us believed him. I thought he was just blowing steam.

"Speaking of leaving here, any of you lab rats going to escape your cage and make another try for help?" Jessie asked, finally breaking the silence, looking around for a response. He was smiling. Either he didn't believe a word Peter said, or he didn't understand the significance of it.

There was no answer, no volunteers. No one even looked in his direction. Maybe now wasn't the time to be asking.

"What about all of us going?" he asked. "We can take whatever food we have and as much water as we can carry. We could make it."

"And what about skinny over there," Harry asked pointing to Dorothy, "just how far do you think she'll get?"

"I'm not going anywhere, asshole," Dorothy replied sternly, glaring at Harry.

"I'll go then. Beats hanging around here," Jessie said after moments of silence. "I'm having a hard time writing this kind of novel anyway, it's not my type of creative writing. Too confining. I never thought in my wildest dreams this would be the heart of the contest—seeing if you can survive out in the middle of nowhere while writing a novel. This seems to be a survivor contest, not a writing contest."

"When are you going?" Peter inquired.

"Probably in the morning."

"But, Jessie, aren't you scared? Look what happened to Ralph," Ada interjected.

"What happened to him?" he asked.

"You know what I mean."

"Which way do you intend to go?" Peter asked. "Ralph went east. We don't know how far he got or what killed him, but the poem on his grave said he should have gone south."

"I don't know; I haven't made up my mind yet." After a couple moments he asked, "Which way would you go?"

"I'm not going to suggest any which way," Peter said. "I don't want to be responsible for any outcome; but if I were to go, it would probably be west. I don't trust what a sick fuck who would write a poem like that would tell me."

"I'd probably go west also," Stewart said.

"Then, that's the way I'll head."

There was a period of silence. I didn't know what to say. I was really shocked. The person who I'd considered the weakest personality in our group was stepping up and volunteering to take the dangerous trek.

Six days and two deaths later—one by unknown means and the other from snakebite—I desperately wanted to go too, if everyone would go together, but I knew it would be too much. One part of me said "get the hell out of here," but the sane part said to stay put. Besides, with my blood pressure and weight, I don't know how far I would get. Dorothy wasn't the only one that had a handicap, and I knew it.

***

"We have to talk about our manuscripts," Dorothy said, "I'm well past the first chapter and ready for the next couple of titles. Any suggestions?"

"I'm ready also. How about, *The Plane Ride* and *Stranded?*" suggested Stewart.

"It should be about our flight, our meeting each other," I said. "What about chapter two titled simply, *The Flight?*"

"I like that, and the third chapter as *The Stopover*," Ada said. "They told us this was just going to be a stopover, which, of course, turned into being stranded."

"I like *The Flight* and *The Stopover*," Stewart said.

"Sounds good," Peter said.

I agreed.

***

Later that afternoon, I joined Peter out on the porch. I had a cold cup of coffee; Peter was smoking his pipe.

"Giving in to Dorothy?" I asked, grinning ear to ear, remembering their earlier confrontation.

"Yeah, right. That'll be the day." Peter took a few puffs on his pipe and sat on the porch step. "You know, as much as I hate being here, I rather enjoy the smells of the prairie and the clean air. The quietness and semi-solitude doesn't hurt either."

"I know. Beats the smog and smells of the city for sure. I'm also kind of enjoying the laidback atmosphere, not having to scurry here or there to have something done on time. But I'd still like to have a few more amenities." I sat down next to Peter. "You know, I've been thinking more and more about that damn electric fence."

"What about it?"

"Although it hasn't really held us back—we can get through it anytime we want, I was wondering what was powering it. It can't be the generator. We'd be able to just turn the damn thing off. We haven't checked it with the generator turned off though."

"That's simple enough. It's off now. Let's take a walk and see," Peter said.

As we walked to the fence by the main gate, I continued, "If it's not the generator, what could it be? If we are truly a hundred to two hundred miles from anywhere, there has to be another power source or else we wouldn't need the generator."

"That would make sense. The only thing I can think of is a solar array somewhere that would be hooked into a large bank of batteries and maybe converted to AC power. If it's not AC it has to be a very high voltage DC."

I stopped. "Where did that come from?"

Peter stopped and smiled. "I know a little about solar. We have a solar water heater at my parent's home. I've done some reading up on it, but I never really thought about how it might apply to the fence."

"You always surprise the shit out of me." We continued our trek.

"Maybe that's why they told us to stay out of the other buildings. Could be that's where the array is located," Peter said.

"Maybe the array is *outside* the fence somewhere."

"That could be. But does it really matter as long as we can get through it anytime we want?"

"It may matter if the power source could be used for our electricity. If we were to run out of gas, or the generator takes a shit, it might make a big difference. I don't know if we could use it to run the pump, but we would have to try."

"That's true, but I doubt it."

We arrived at the fence and found a piece of jagged, rusted metal lying on the ground. Peter picked it up and threw it at the fence. It crackled and popped when it hit the wire mesh and the ground.

"That answers that question," I said as we turned back towards the hotel.

"There has to be another power source," Peter said. "Where in the hell would it be located? If it's a solar array, and if it is in the town, it would probably have to be on a rooftop. And it would seem it would have to be pretty large to have that much juice. Of course it could be a smaller array with a large bank of batteries."

"The hotel is the tallest building in town, let's take a look," I said.

"You know, now that I think of it, there is another possibility," Peter said tapping his finger against his chin. "What if the generator is charging a bank of batteries somewhere? It wouldn't take much of the electricity from the generator, we wouldn't know it and would be almost impossible to track down. The wiring to a charger could come from anywhere and keeping the batteries charged would be easy with the number of hours we use the generator."

"Let's see if we can find some solar panels first before we go down that road."

"Okay."

"There is another question that keeps bothering me. Why would they surround us with an electric fence and then supply us with a shovel to dig our way out? It doesn't make any sense."

"I know. There're a lot of things here that don't make a lot of sense. They said the shovel was to bury anyone that passed away—but they had to know. You're right, it doesn't make any sense."

***

Harry and Stewart came into the lobby from the kitchen as Peter and I entered the hotel. We briefed them on our excursion to the fence and the results.

"Where've you guys been?" Dorothy asked as she came from the kitchen.

"Checking the fence," Stewart said, "Why? You writing a new chapter about us?"

"No, no. I'm concerned about Nicki. She hasn't been down all day. She didn't look too good this morning, I wanted someone to check on her."

"Well, haul your ass upstairs and check on her," Harry said. "I'm going to get something to eat."

"I'm on my way upstairs to see if I can find a roof access, I'll check on her," Stewart said.

"A roof access?" Dorothy asked.

"Yeah, there has to be a power source electrifying fence. One of the possibilities is a solar array and it may be on the roof."

Stewart headed upstairs and stopped on the second floor at Nicki's room. He knocked on the door several times, but received no answer.

"Nicki, open the door. I just want to see if you're all right." He waited a moment for an answer, but didn't hear anything. "C'mon, Nicki, just tell me you're okay." After waiting several more minutes, he decided to leave her to her grief.

Stewart climbed to the third floor and looked in every room, but could find no access to the roof. He went back downstairs. In the lobby, he reported his results to Peter and me. "There's just no access anywhere I could find."

***

Later, at suppertime, everyone was present except for Nicki. She still had not been seen since we'd buried Randy.

"I'll go up and check on her," Ada said. She's probably just depressed and doesn't want to talk to anyone right now."

"Forget it, Ada," snapped Dorothy. "She won't talk to you, even if she wanted to talk. I'll go up."

After supper, Dorothy slowly climbed the stairs and knocked on Nicki's door. Several knocks later and there was still no answer. She tried to enter. It was locked.

"Nicki, unlock the door," she yelled.

There was no answer.

"Nicki, if you don't open the door, I'm going to have the guys break it down."

There was still no answer. Dorothy went over to the stairway and yelled, "Peter, come up here and break the door down. I think something is wrong with Nicki."

Just then the door opened slowly, about four inches.

"What do you want," she barked.

"Forget it, Peter," Dorothy yelled back downstairs.

"I just want to talk to you. You've been in there all day and everyone is worried about you," Dorothy said as she walked back down the hall to Nicki's room. "It's not good to stay all by yourself when you're grieving. You need to talk."

"Come on in, I'm okay," she said with a sigh.

Dorothy entered the room, staying near the door; Nicki went and sat on her bed. She had been crying and Dorothy could see the red in and around her eyes.

"I'm...I'm responsible for Randy's death."

"Nobody's responsible, Nicki—he died of snakebites."

"Yes, but I'm the one who gave him...wanted to go exploring. Randy didn't want to go, but I made him."

"From what I could tell of Randy, nobody was going to make him do anything he didn't want to do."

"But I begged him. I wanted to get out of this hotel for a while. It was driving me crazy being cooped up in here all day."

Dorothy noticed the spoon and hypo syringe lying on the bureau.

"What the hell are you doing with those?" she said pointing to the items.

Nicki responded slowly. "I...had...to help Randy."

"What?"

"Randy was in so much pain, I had to give him something to help him. He asked me for it."

"You gave him what, morphine?

Nicki smirked. "You don't know shit, do you?"

"I know enough."

"You think you do. It's heroin. You know what heroin is?" Nicki picked up the syringe, her voice rising, she held it in her fist in front of Dorothy's face.

"Whose stuff is it, yours or his?"

"I thought you just wanted to talk, not interrogate me like a cop."

"I do, but..."

"Get out! Get out of here. Now!"

Dorothy turned to leave, but turned back around before exiting the room. "You're a junkie, aren't you?"

"Get out," Nicki screamed, pushing Dorothy towards the door. "Get out!"

Nicki slammed the door behind Dorothy as she left the room. She went downstairs as fast as she could, one step at a time holding tightly to the railings.

"Well, I didn't expect this," she announced to everyone in the lobby.

"What do you mean?" Peter asked. "What was all the yelling about?"

"We have a junkie on our hands. Nicki's been shooting up—heroin."

"How do you know?" Jessie asked.

"She told me. There was a cook spoon and a needle on her bureau. When I asked her about them, she freaked and threw me out."

"That explains why she's been acting weird lately," Stewart said. "I thought she was just smoking the funny stuff."

"She also told me she gave some to Randy to help him with the pain."

"I doubt it hurt him," I said. "He was probably lucky she had it."

"The way she's acted the past few days," Peter said, "she looked pretty ragged. I believed it was because of Randy's situation—I guess it wasn't just that."

"What are we going to do?" Ada asked.

"Do? I'm not going to do a thing. If she wants to kill herself, let her," Harry said munching on a cookie. "She's a big girl. That is, unless you want me to go up and spank her."

Dorothy couldn't listen to Harry anymore. "Harry, can't you be serious for one minute? Quit being such an asshole. You really know how to piss everyone off."

"But we can't just let her kill herself with that poison," Ada pleaded looking for a face that seemed as concerned as her.

"And why not?" Harry asked.

"Because she's a human being, we're human beings—at least I think we all are. Harry, you may be the exception."

"I tried to talk to her," Dorothy said. "She doesn't want any help and you can't help someone who doesn't want it."

"And you said she wouldn't talk to *me*," Ada said to Dorothy. "At least I wouldn't have talked down to her. She needs help, not someone condemning her. What'd you tell her, she's a junkie?"

Dorothy didn't respond.

Peter rolled his eyes. "I've got some writing to do," he said starting up the stairs. "I'll see all of you in the morning."

"If we ever want to get out of here, we better get our manuscripts finished," Stewart said. "I've only got about twenty pages completed—there's a long way to go."

CHAPTER 13
Westward Bound

Day Seven

The next morning dawned cloudy and overcast. Everyone seemed to be in a bad mood at breakfast. Nicki still hadn't come out of her room since yesterday morning.

"Are you leaving this morning, Jessie?" Stewart asked.

"I suppose," he replied, downing a piece of toast covered with grape jelly.

"You don't sound too convincing. Are you sure you want to?"

"No, but someone has to go. We have to get out of here somehow and I haven't heard anyone else volunteer. I don't see anyone raising their hands eager to walk a hundred miles through prairie, snakes and God-knows-what."

"No one's forcing you to go," Harry said, finishing up a bowl of cereal. "You can stay here and die with the rest of the rats."

"Don't talk like that," Dorothy said cutting into a pile of pancakes. "It's bad enough without thinking we're all going to die."

"I didn't say *I* was going to die, but I'm just being realistic. We've been here for a week and we still have almost seven and a half weeks to go. Look at our food supply. You're feeding your face pretty good now, but wait another couple weeks. We'll be eating snakes and bugs before we get out of here."

"Maybe *you* will, not me," she said with her mouth full.

"We ought to be rationing food now, the way we ration the fuel. Everyone gets the same amount. I think that is the only way we'll survive this. No more fifteen pancakes soaked in a gallon of syrup topped with a quarter pound of butter in the morning while we have a bowl of cold cereal."

"You can't do that," she protested, her cheeks bulging with breakfast. "And I don't have fifteen pancakes or...or a quarter pound of butter and a gallon of syrup."

"Yes, we can. And we may have to."

She swallowed the mouthful. "And just how are you going to do it? Divide up all the food and store it in our rooms? Then everyone brings their share of food down in the morning and night? That's crazy."

"I don't know yet. When I figure it out, you'll be the first to know."

"We are getting low on some items," Peter said. "We may not be able to eat all we want anymore; it might be we have to start some kind of rationing, or end up on bread and water later."

"Let's look at it again next week and decide then. There doesn't seem to be any crisis right now and I don't want to make it into one unnecessarily," Stewart said.

"Thank you," Dorothy said triumphantly.

"That doesn't mean we shouldn't conserve where we can," Stewart said sternly, looking up at Dorothy.

Jessie got up from the table and put his plate in the sink. "I guess it's time to go. I can't take all this bickering anyway."

"How much food do you need?" Peter asked.

"I figure at least five days worth if I travel twenty miles a day."

"Twenty miles a day?" I asked looking up at Jessie.

"No way in hell," Harry said. "Shit, that's ten hours a day at two miles an hour. A fairy like you, you'll be lucky to make twelve miles a day."

"Knock it off, Harry," Stewart barked.

"But, he..."

Stewart and I glared at Harry. He shut up.

"Pork and beans and some hash all right?" Peter asked.

"Yeah, and throw in a couple cans of peaches and pears, too."

"Take some of the kitchen matches and a small kitchen knife. I don't think we have any more flashlights. I'll get some more water bottles from the basement," I said.

"Does anyone have a backpack?" Jessie asked.

No one else had one.

"We'll have to tie up a bag of some type for you. Maybe one of those potato bags will do," Stewart said.

An hour later, we had gathered all the necessities and Jessie presented himself ready to go. We debated some more how much food he should take, and decided about six days worth should do it; any more than that would be too heavy and might slow him down. Along with two gallons of water, he all ready would be carrying over twenty-five pounds.

Goodbyes and good luck's were exchanged.

"Here's my key, keep it for me until I get back," Jessie said to Peter. "And if I don't get back, please mail this letter for me when you get out of here. It's to my parents."

Peter and I went with Jessie to the fence to help him under.

When we got there, the trench we'd dug for Ralph was still usable. We shook hands and I lifted the bottom with the old board so Jessie could crawl under. He inched under on his back, brushed himself off, and then dragged his supplies and water through. We stayed at the fence for several minutes until Jessie was almost out of sight. We saw him turn back towards us, waving one last time.

He had indeed decided to travel west.

"I wonder if we'll ever see him again," I said.

"I wish I could be optimistic, but the odds are against him."

"I know."

***

Peter and I walked back to the hotel and went to our rooms to work on our books. We had decided to meet later that afternoon to search for the solar panels.

After my battery died, I took a short nap to wait out the hottest part of the day. Around four, we met in the lobby. It had been a hot, dry day with the wind kicking up every now and then. Scattered clouds were starting to gather, partially hiding the unforgiving summer sun and cooling the evening.

"Where do we start?" I asked.

"I have a new theory," Peter said. "Whether there's a solar array somewhere, or there're batteries being charged by the generator, the thing similar to both is a bank of batteries. I think we ought to look for those."

"Before we do that, how about we walk the entire fence line to see if we can find where the connection is made from the power source. If we can find that we can see if the wire comes into the town or goes away from it. Maybe we can trace it."

"Okay, but I've got to be back in a half-hour to start up the generator."

"Shouldn't take that long. Let's get started. We should use the gate as a starting point and go from there."

We walked to the gate and then around the entire fence surrounding the town. Every eight feet was a wooden post with the chain-link fence secured to the post with heavy metal staples. We couldn't find any connection. It had been about twenty-five minutes and Peter had to get back to start the generator.

"I can't understand it, there has to be a connection somewhere," Peter said adamantly.

"I think I know where it's at," I said. I was so excited I was grinning like a kid who couldn't keep a secret.

"Where?"

"The gate. If you noticed, it had the only post in the whole damn fence that was different from the rest. We expect the gateposts to be different because they hold the weight of the gates. Instead of a solid wooden post, there is one that is made of four boards nailed together. It looks like it may be to hold the weight, but I believe it has the connection inside of it. We'll check it out after supper."

"I'll bet you're right!"

Right after supper a light rain started which finally brought some relief from the heat, dust and dry weather. I stayed in my room and worked on my manuscript.

CHAPTER 14
One More to Rest

Day 8

"That was a good rain last night," Peter said at breakfast the next morning. "We needed it."

"You ready to look for that connection this morning?" I asked.

"Soon as I'm done here."

Stewart joined us, asking about what we were doing the night before. I explained the situation to him, hoping he might be able to add to our assumptions. He couldn't.

"Has anyone seen Nicki?" Ada asked.

"Not since I was in her room," Dorothy said. "That was two days ago."

"I think it's time we checked on her again," Ada said. "She can't stay in there forever without eating."

"I heard junkies can go for days without eating anything, sometimes a week. Depends on how much they're shooting up," I told them.

"You ought to just leave her alone. If she kills herself, there's just more food for the rest of us," Harry said.

"You really are an asshole, Harry. You don't give a shit about anybody but yourself. Did you have a bad childhood? Did your wicked parents beat you? Or are you just naturally a prick?" Dorothy asked.

"I could ask you the same thing. What makes you eat so damn much, insecurity or something? Or did your last boyfriend tell you how fat and revolting you are? I don't know anyone who has psychedelic hair like yours that isn't fucked up one way or another."

"That's enough," Ada yelled. "Our Lord made us all different. We can't help who we are. Now stop it."

"We can't, huh?" Harry questioned. "Just how many junkies have you ever known, lady? How many fucked up people have you known with clown hair in your life? I'll bet you've led a sheltered life your, what, entire thirty-two years? Have you ever had someone threaten your life? Try to kill you? I know your type—it must be really nice to live in a sweet, protected world your whole life. Be lovable, kind; speak well of everyone you run into, but I'm going to tell you something, sister, one of these days you're going to run into someone who really intends to hurt you, and maybe they will. We'll see how forgiving you are then. We'll see if you hate them or if you still have that forgive-all attitude. We'll see."

Harry got up, wiped his face with his napkin while scowling at Ada, threw the napkin down on the table and left, leaving his dirty dishes.

"He doesn't know what he's talking about—my father— he was killed in the Twin Towers on nine-eleven. I forgave the terrorists who did it. Yes, it was hard, but I did it. I can never forget what they did, but I can forgive them. And I'm thirty seven, not thirty two."

Dorothy was sobbing again.

"Yes, I eat a lot, but I have a disorder, but it's none of his business."

Peter rolled his eyes and pushed his plate of half-eaten pancakes away.

"You ready to go look at that gate?" Stewart asked, obviously fed-up with the squabbling and blubbering.

I was too. "Let's go," I answered.

"I'm ready," Peter said.

The three of us walked down to the gate and checked out the one post that was different from all the rest—the column the gate was locked to.

"This may be it," Stewart said.

Peter picked up a large rock and started hitting the post, trying to separate the four boards that were nailed together. A separation started between two of them. He kept pounding at the boards. Soon there was enough of a gap to see inside the post.

"Well, there's the connection," Stewart said.

"Sure is."

"It goes down into the ground, just like I thought it would. Should we trace it?"

"Why not?" Peter asked. "I'll go back and get the shovel."

Peter returned and started digging around the post. He dug down about two feet exposing the cable, and it hadn't yet taken a turn. The post was becoming unstable, starting to move.

"Are we going to dig to China?" Peter asked, handing the shovel to Stewart.

"If that's what it takes," I said.

Stewart continued the digging. At about three feet the two-inch-thick black cable took a turn towards the town, heading directly down the middle of the street.

"Well, now we know it comes from somewhere *in* town," Stewart said.

"Now all we have to do is find the source," I said. "I'm still betting on a solar array somewhere."

We went back and notified the others of what we found. After discussions on the possibilities, the talk soon turned back to Nicki.

"I'm going up to check on her," Peter said.

***

Peter knocked on Nicki's door. There was no answer. He knocked several more times and yelled for her to come out. He put his ear to the door, but didn't hear anything.

"You have to come out sometime, Nicki. You've got to be hungry by now." He waited for an answer—nothing.

"Nicki, I'm going to have to break in to check on you if you don't open the door," he yelled.

Peter waited several seconds without hearing a thing. He tried the doorknob—it was still locked.

He went back down the stairs into the kitchen where everyone, except Harry, still sat.

"There's no answer from Nicki. I even told her I was going to break in if she didn't answer."

"She did the same to me the other day," Dorothy said. "She finally opened the door at the last minute after I yelled down the stairs for you guys to come up and break it down."

"I guess we're going to have to break in. Has anyone seen a crowbar?"

No one had.

"We'll have to use a shoulder," Stewart said.

"Great."

Peter and Stewart climbed the two stories and knocked on the door again.

"Last warning, Nicki, we're coming in," Stewart said. There was no answer.

"Let's do it," Peter said. "On three. One, two, three."

They both hit the door with their shoulder. The door-frame broke with a loud crack—the wood split and splintered around the latch. They hit the door again and it swung open.

There, on the bed—half covered up by a sheet, was Nicki, face up. She was pale, her blank, blue eyes wide open, and she wasn't moving. A syringe was hanging from her left arm, which was lying off to her side above the sheet.

"Well, I suppose this was bound to happen," Peter said.

He pulled the sheet partway down. She was naked from the waist down. He pulled the sheet back up.

"I don't know," Stewart said. "Not so fast. This doesn't look right."

"What do you mean?"

"Why would she be partially naked like that? Didn't you see the crusty stuff on her pubic hair and her stomach?"

Peter rolled the sheet back again. "No, I didn't see it. I do now. I see what you mean."

Stewart carefully raised her button down shirt. Her bra was pushed up over her breasts exposing the rings on her nipples. "I'll be damn, Harry was right. Pull the sheet all the way down."

Her pink, silk panties lay torn under the sheet at the bottom of the bed.

"You're right," Peter said. "Damn. What do we do now?"

"I don't know. Let me think a minute."

He walked over to the window and looked out over the town. "For the present, I think it best if we keep this quiet. Don't let anyone know what we know or suspect. There are only two others that could have done this, and I don't want it out yet. Maybe if whoever it is thinks he got away with it, he might say or do something and give himself away."

"My money would have to be on Harry. I don't think there's any way possible George would do something like this," Peter said.

"Oh yeah? How well do you know him? You know anything about his past? He could be a serial killer or a serial rapist and we wouldn't have the faintest idea. You're probably right, but until we're sure, we have to suspect both of them and keep this to ourselves."

"I just don't get the feeling he would do this. The door was locked, how did he get out? He couldn't have gone out the second floor window."

"Find her key," Stewart said. "Whoever it was, would have the key if they didn't throw it away. The door had to be locked from the outside. Maybe he kept it as a trophy. Rapists do that, you know."

Peter looked at him with a suspicious eye.

Stewart smiled. "Lots of cop television."

"I wonder how long she's been dead."

"Rigor has set in, I think it has to be over six hours."

"Could've been since yesterday then."

"Or last night."

"What now?"

"Take the needle out of her arm. I have a feeling whoever did this put the needle in there to make it look like an overdose."

"What makes you think that?"

Stewart picked up her left arm. "She doesn't have any track marks on this arm. If you remember, she was left-handed, so her left arm wouldn't be her first choice for injection. Look at her right arm, I'll bet she has a few marks on it."

Peter went over and inspected at her right arm. There were red marks and a few small scabs where she had shot up before. A couple of them looked fairly fresh.

"What else looks suspicious to you?" Stewart asked.

Peter studied the body for several minutes.

"I don't know, what?"

"You know anything about druggies or shooting up heroin?

"No, not really. Only what I've seen on television."

"She didn't have a band around her arm. It's over on the bureau. She would have had to use it to bring the vein up, make it visible. It gets harder and harder to find a vein the longer they shoot up."

"Just how do you know all this?"

"I've read a lot of murder-mysteries, Peter. I've written a few also. Maybe someday they'll get published. I had to do a lot research and I learned quite a bit. I spent a whole month with a friend of mine on a narcotics team and then a few days with a junkie that seemed like a week." Stewart smiled. "Why, do I sound like a suspect?"

"Yes and no. I was beginning to wonder."

"Think about it Peter, if I raped her, would I be pointing all this out? I could've kept quiet and you wouldn't have suspected a thing. You would've forever believed Nicki died of a drug overdose."

Peter nodded his head. He knew Stewart was right.

"Now, are you ready for the kicker?"

"There's more?"

"Not only was she raped, I suspect she was murdered, but it wasn't the heroin that did her in."

"What?"

"Like I said before, I think the needle was just stuck into her arm to make it look like she overdosed. See the red marks on her neck; the bruises on her arms? She must of put up a fight. She was strangled. Also, her eyes are open, I believe if she overdosed with heroin, she would go into a deep sleep and gradually die. Her eyes would be closed."

"You ought to be a detective."

"Yeah, well, I'd rather write about them."

"So, what are we going to tell the others? Do we need to tell the women to put something up against their doors at night?"

"We might tell Ada, I don't think we have to worry about Dorothy being raped."

"Maybe he has a fetish. You know—more bounce to the ounce."

Stewart laughed. "Stop it! If he did, do you really think he would've picked Nicki?"

"Let's put her clothes back on as much as possible and we'll wrap her up," Stewart said. "I don't want anyone else to see her and get suspicious about the murder. I want the person who did this to give himself away."

Ten minutes later they walked down the stairs to the lobby where everyone except Harry was waiting.

"Well, is she okay?" Dorothy asked.

"No, she's not," Stewart said.

"She's dead," Peter added.

"No!" Ada asked turning around in her chair. "How'd she die?"

Stewart looked at Peter.

"She had a needle sticking out of her arm," Stewart said. He knew they would assume she died of a heroin overdose.

"That poor girl," Ada said. "Her grief must have been overwhelming."

"She was a junkie," Harry said walking down the stairs. "She got what she asked for."

Stewart looked at Peter again with raised eyebrows.

"What'd she ask for? I take it you hate junkies, Harry?" Peter questioned.

"You bet. But I hate religious zealots even worse."

"Any particular reason?" Stewart asked.

"Yeah. A junkie killed my brother. The pastor of our church raped my sister when she was a teenager. There, now you know. Any other questions?" Harry looked at each person waiting for another question.

"You need to forgive, Harry," Ada said.

"I don't need to forgive anything. Don't preach to me, sister. You have no idea what I've been through or who I am—so just shut up."

There was dead silence.

"We have to go dig another grave, Peter," Stewart said.

"We dig any more graves and we might as well go into business," Peter said.

"I'll give you a hand," I added.

The next two hours the three of us took turns digging a burial place for Nicki next to Randy. About halfway through my turn, I had to stop when my face felt hot again and I overheated. I was sweating profusely.

"George, go sit down before you have a heart attack and we have to dig another hole," commanded Peter.

"I'm going back to the hotel," I replied. "I need some water."

After lunch, we retrieved Nicki's body. Peter and Stewart carried her down to the grave with Ada, Dorothy and I following along; a sorry ass funeral procession if there ever was one. Harry was conspicuously absent. Ada again led in a prayer, this time for Nicki's soul. In another hour the grave was filled in and a marker placed on it.

CHAPTER 15
Caught In The Act

Day 15

Another week passed with no major incidents—everyone was working intensely on their manuscript and cooperating on the assigned duties. Three more chapters had been discussed and the titles agreed upon. Chapters four, five, and six would be *Captive Audience*, *The Rescue Attempt*, and *The Addict*.

It had been over a week since Jessie left and we had given up any hope of ever seeing him again. There would be no early rescue, and no one volunteered to try again. We had resolved ourselves to settling in and staying the entire two months. Still, there was always a slight glimmer of hope that rescue would come and the police would show up and take us out of this prison.

In the evening, as the sun was going down and after the day started cooling off, I went for a walk to clear my head. I was having trouble writing about Ralph's death and Nicki being an addict. I never suspected that. She gave heroin to Randy before he died; was it a good thing as I thought earlier, or did it possibly weaken him and eventually kill him? Could it be she couldn't stand to see him in so much pain, overdosed him, and caused his death; a mercy killing?

I walked the length of town arriving at the graveyard before I knew I had walked that far. I was lost in my thoughts. Why I went that direction, I still don't know, but what I found staggered me—another grave with a sign attached to a post.

Here Lies Jessie,
His Death was Messy,
He Decided to go West,
Now He's a Permanent Guest.

"My God, not again!" I shouted. I cursed the person who would do such a thing to these good people, and to me. My heart sunk to my stomach—I now was positive there wouldn't be any help coming. Slowly, I walked back to the hotel. How and what was I going to tell them? I asked everyone to meet me in the kitchen.

I sat down at the kitchen table, sitting there staring at the surface, while one-by-one, everyone gathered around me. Looking up, I addressed the assembled group. They were waiting for me to speak, watching my every move. I cleared my throat. "I just walked down to the other end of town, by the graveyard." I stopped. I didn't want to continue.

"No. I don't want to hear this," Dorothy said. She put her hands over her ears.

"I'm afraid it's true. There's another grave. Jessie didn't make it."

"Oh my God!" yelled Dorothy as her hands covered her mouth.

"He also has a grave marker with another poem attached. It had to be put there the past day or so."

"What did the poem say?" Ada asked.

I told them.

"Whoever is doing this is one sick mother-fucker," Peter said.

"Please, watch your language," Ada pleaded.

"Sorry, Ada. It's just—"

"I'm really beginning to question this contest," Stewart said. "Did someone just put us all out here to die? This is making one hell of a story, but who's going to believe it? And how do they plan on getting away with it? We have to get out of here somehow."

"But how?" Dorothy wondered out loud.

"I'm about done playing this game," Harry said.

"And just what else are you going to do?" Peter asked. "They seem to have set up this contest, or whatever you want to call it, pretty well; there doesn't seem to be anything else we can do."

"If we're all going to die anyway, why do anything?" Dorothy asked.

"You have to believe we're going to get out of here, Dorothy. You have to believe, we can't give up," I said.

"I'm going to figure a way out of here. You can have my manuscript. I'm not writing anything else," Harry said. "They can kiss my ass." He got up from his chair and paced the floor.

"That's your option, Harry, but as long as you're here, you might as well keep up. Just in case we do get out," Stewart said. "Besides, they said *everyone* has to finish."

"Do you really think they are going to allow us to get out of here?" Harry asked. "We already have four bodies lying at the end of town. Just how do you think Jessie and Ralph died? Do you think they committed suicide? Someone watching us probably killed them. They can't let us out of here, we're witnesses to murders."

"And just which murder did you witness, Harry? We don't know for sure anyone was murdered. If you want to go dig up the bodies, you might be able to tell. Until then, we just don't know. They could have been snake bit, died of the elements, or any number of things. Let's not get too excited until we know for sure. We know how Randy and Nicki died, and those may not be considered murder," I said.

"You don't think holding us prisoners out here and denying medical attention until you die isn't murder?" asked Ada.

"Awful close to it, maybe manslaughter, but not outright murder," I responded.

"I call it murder," she answered.

No one had brought up murder before. We may have thought about it, but it was never stated. Now it was out in the open and would have to be considered that each of us might be targeted, but in what order? Was it random? Who would be next? Was it only those who disobeyed the rules? All of the deceased had violated the rules, one way or another.

"It's getting dark, see you all in the morning," Peter said. One by one, despair etched on their faces, everyone left and went to their rooms.

***

Several minutes later, I had a knock at my door. When I opened it, Peter and Stewart came rushing in.

"Close the door," Stewart said. "We don't want anyone to hear us."

"Why?" I asked.

"We don't want to unnecessarily upset the women."

"What's going on?"

"Look, there has to be someone out there that buried Jessie and Ralph," Peter said. "Who is it? Where is he?"

"I thought about it myself," I said, "but how would we find out?"

"He has to be camped out somewhere around here. Is he constantly watching us? " Stewart asked.

"What do you want to do?" I asked. "As far as we know, he's only been at the graveyard."

"As far as we know. What if he's checking on us all the time? What if he comes into the hotel at night?" Stewart added. "It's one thing to leave us out here, but what if we're not really alone?"

"How would we catch him?" I asked.

"Think about it, do we really want to catch him, or just find out who he is and find where he's camped out?" Stewart asked.

"Good question," Peter said. "If we do find him, maybe he has a way for us to contact help. Then the question becomes how we do that without him knowing."

"What if he's armed?" I asked. "We have nothing to defend ourselves."

That brought a moment of silence.

"We still don't know how Jessie and Ralph died. They could have been snake-bit or something, but they could've just as easily been shot. If we go snooping around, we could end up the same way."

"And if we don't, we could end up the same way, too," Peter added. "What if we take turns standing watch for a few nights—find out if we can see anything?"

I shrugged. "I guess that couldn't hurt. I'll take a turn. I can't stay awake all night, so we'll have to have shifts."

"How about we go from nine 'till six with three hour shifts?" Peter suggested.

"What about Harry?" I asked. "We could do two hour shifts for eight hours if we include him."

"Fuck Harry," Stewart said. "Leave him out. He's got a big mouth and he's an asshole."

"Okay, just asking," I said.

"What if we do spot someone?" Peter asked.

Stewart hesitated then said, "Wait until he leaves, then get the other two up. We'll try to follow or see which way he goes. We'll have to play it by ear. Just don't try to capture him by yourself."

It was agreed that I would take the first shift, Stewart the second and Peter the last.

***

At nine that night, I went downstairs and sat in one of the wicker chairs, placing it behind the hotel desk. Anyone coming in the front door would have a hard time seeing me without a flashlight. If he did have one, I would pretend to be asleep.

I was good for the first hour or so. It was so quiet and with nothing to keep my mind stimulated, I must have fell asleep for a little while. It was a half hour into Stewart's shift when I woke up. *Shit, Stewart's going to know I fell asleep!* I went to his room, softly knocked on the door. There was no answer. Thankfully, he had left the door unlocked. I went in and shook him. He got up, got dressed and I went to bed. He didn't say anything about me being late.

***

At three in the morning, Stewart went upstairs and woke Peter up. Stewart went to his room, undressed and got into bed. Amid the wind whistling outside and a pack of coyotes howling their nightly harmonies, he thought he heard muffled yells for help. He couldn't tell who or where it was coming from. *Could someone be having a nightmare? Could Peter be in trouble?*

He got out of bed, put his trousers on and silently slipped out into the hallway. He stopped and listened for what seemed like several minutes. Nothing. He turned around, heading back to his room when he heard a bed squeaking. He heard the muffled scream again. This time he also heard a male voice; not a whisper, but a coarse, lowered voice, *"SHUT UP, BITCH."* The sound of a slap followed.

He moved down the hall, stopping to listen every few steps. There it was again, the muffled cry for help. Now there was crying. It couldn't be a nightmare—there were two voices. *But where was it coming from? Where was Peter? Could it be the intruder?* The hair on the back of his neck stood up, adrenaline started pumping through his body. It was dark and he could barely see the outlines of the doors in the hallway.

A few more steps. Nothing. Two more. Stewart walked as close to the wall as he could. The floor didn't squeak as much there. He knew there were only four of us still on the third floor, himself, Ada, Dorothy, and me. But was it coming from this floor? It sounded like it, but he wasn't sure.

He arrived in front of Ada's room. The hotel was silent except for the steady wind pushing through the cracks in the building. He put his ear to Ada's door. He heard a few small squeaks from the bed. *Someone was stirring.*

"Help." There it was. He heard it, muffled, but it was coming from Ada's room and she was definitely calling for help. He tried the doorknob, turning it slowly. It was unlocked. He cracked the door open slightly. A grunt, a groan. He opened the door and peeked in. It was dark, but

from the moonlight coming through the window, he could make out a large bulge on top the bed.

"Ada, are you all right?"

A muffled scream. Stewart bolted in. As he got closer to the bed, a figure jumped off and stood up. Stewart lunged, tackling the intruder mid-body. The momentum caused them to crash into the wall and fall to the floor. Several punches were thrown from both men. They fought violently for what seemed to Stewart, an eternity. The attacker pushed Stewart off him and made a charge for the door. Stewart regained his balance and tackled the person again.

"*HELP—SOMEONE HELP!*" screamed Ada. She had managed to get the tape off her mouth. "*HELP ME—SOMEONE HELP!*"

Stewart continued to fight the intruder. He was strong, but Stewart had him in a headlock, beating his opponent's head with his fist and he wasn't letting go. They struggled relentlessly, one combating to get away, one fighting to keep control of the other. The brawl created a thunderous racket. Stewart yelled and kept punching the intruder steadily with blows to the head. Within a minute, others started pouring into Ada's room. Her screams and the fight had awakened everyone.

Peter was the first to arrive. I was right behind him. In the dark, we couldn't see who was who. "What's going on?" Peter shouted as we watched the two figures fall to the floor again, struggling.

"Peter...is that you?" yelled Stewart while continuing to throw punches at the intruder's head. "We've got him! Don't just stand there, damn-it! Give me a hand!"

We recognized Stewart's voice but weren't sure which person in the dark room was him. Peter took a wild guess, grabbed one of the men by the ankles, pulling them out from under him, bringing him down to the floor. I guess Peter had figured Stewart would let him know if he was wrong.

He had guessed right. The three of us were able to easily control the attacker.

"How'd he get by us?" Peter questioned.

"How'd he get by *you*? Stewart snapped.

"He didn't," he responded.

Ada was crying. "He raped me!" she screamed un-controllably between breaths. "He raped me!"

Dorothy made her way in the darkness to Ada's bed. She put her arm around Ada, wrapped a sheet around her and tried to comfort her. "You'll be all right now Ada, they got him. You're safe now."

"Peter, go turn on the generator," gasped Stewart. He was out of breath. "George and I can handle this for a minute."

It took a few minutes for Peter to get outside to the shed and turn on the generator. We had caught the intruder who was invading our little outpost. Dorothy flipped the light switch on as soon as she heard the hum.

There, on the floor, under Stewart and me, was Harry. Stewart threw another punch and hit him squarely in the mouth.

"That's for fighting with me," he stated, still breathing hard. He shook his hand, looked at it then balled up his fist again.

I grabbed his arm to keep him from throwing another punch. "Ease up, Stu. It's over," I said softly.

"It's far from over! You son-of-a-bitch!" yelled Stewart, his hand still balled into a fist, ready to throw another blow. "You're lucky he's here."

"Yeah, let me go and we'll see how lucky I am."

Ada's hands were still taped together at her wrists and the tape that had been over her mouth hung off the side of her face. Tears flowed down her cheeks.

"How could you, Harry?" yelled Dorothy. "You bastard."

Peter came back into the room. "Harry, huh? I'm shocked." There wasn't a bit of surprise in his voice.

"Find me some rope, Peter, I'm going to tie this rotten asshole up," Stewart said.

When I looked away for a moment Stewart threw another punch with his elbow, hitting Harry square in the nose. I heard a *thunk* and a scream.

"That's for Ada," he said.

I looked over and saw blood streaming from Harry's nose. I shook my head, but couldn't help smiling at Stewart. I could tell he was still hyped on adrenaline and wouldn't listen to anything I said.

"Let him bleed," he said.

"He... he told me if I screamed, he would kill me," Ada said between hiccups and sobs. "He said no one would believe me—that I could never prove it." She covered her head with her pillow, crying intensely.

Harry still had his trousers and underwear down around his ankles. He was also wearing a white t-shirt and sneakers. Why was he fully dressed?

"We'll take care of this, Ada," I said. "He won't be able to do this again."

Peter returned with a length of rope. Stewart went to his room, retrieved his pocketknife and cut some pieces. We tied Harry's hands in front of him and stood him up. I pulled his pants up and we led him out of the room and down the stairs to the lobby. Dorothy stayed with Ada and helped her unwrap the tape that was binding her hands together.

I was still in my pajamas and Stewart and Peter only had their trousers on. We took turns going upstairs one at a time to change clothes, while two of us remained on guard with our prisoner. When we were all dressed and downstairs, Peter confronted Harry.

"Why'd you do it, Harry?" Peter asked.

"That holier-than-thou bitch had it coming to her. Besides, she needed a good fuck to straighten her ass out— let her know who was in charge. She commands everyone to forgive, well; let's see of she walks the walk. She can talk her shit all day; see if she can live it."

"And you were just the one to test it, right?" Stewart asked.

Harry blew blood from his nose and shook his head. It continued to drip down on his t-shirt. His right eye was starting to darken. "You bet. Besides, like I told you, you're all dead anyway. I figured I might as well get a little satisfaction before you're all planted down there at the end of the street with the rest of them."

Harry talked about all of *us* being buried in the cemetery, but not him. It was beginning to make sense why he was fully dressed.

"You're going to be the lone survivor, is that what you thought Harry?" I asked.

He smiled.

"You weren't planning on sticking around. Were you?"

"What're you talking about?" Peter asked.

"This son-of-a-bitch was going to make his break tonight after raping Ada. That's why he's dressed. Check his room, I'll bet all his supplies are there ready to go."

Peter ran upstairs and returned in less than a minute. "You were right. He had food and water and a pack ready to go."

I grabbed Harry's shirt. "You know, Nicki said you were an asshole when we met. She just didn't know how big of one you really are. She had you pegged from the beginning." I thought about hitting him, but let him go.

Harry smiled up at me. "She was a real queen herself, wasn't she? Fuckin' junkie. I had a little piece of that too. Nipple rings and all. She was sweet."

Peter whispered something to Stewart.

Stewart nodded. "Get one of the wooden chairs from the kitchen first and help me tie him down. These wickers won't hold for very long."

"First, what?" Harry asked, looking around.

"Nothing," Stewart said, "none of your damn business."

We tied him securely to the chair. Peter motioned for me to follow him and we went out on the front porch.

CHAPTER 16
Inquisition

Day 16

Peter pulled a pipe from his shirt pocket and tapped it on the bottom of his shoe. "I have something important to tell you, George. It's probably going to anger you. I hope not." He pulled his tobacco pouch out and started loading his pipe. "I'm sorry we couldn't let you know earlier, but I think you'll understand once I explain. We *have* to keep this from Ada and Dorothy for now. If they find out, they'll go ballistic and be really angry at us for not informing them."

"Anger me? Find out what?"

"Nicki didn't die of a heroin overdose. She was raped and murdered."

Momentarily stunned, I just stood there looking at Peter. "What? How do you know? Are you sure?"

"She was strangled. She put up quite a fight. The bruises and marks on her neck were pretty clear. Whoever did it put the syringe in her arm to make it look like it was an overdose, but it was in the wrong arm. Besides, the rubber tubing she would have used to find a vein was still on the bureau. She wasn't shooting up at the time she died."

He lit his pipe, snapped the lighter closed and drew in a long puff of smoke.

"And," he continued, "her eyes were wide open. Stewart believes if she overdosed, she would have just gone to sleep. He's probably right."

"How do you know she was raped?"

"We saw what we believed was semen on her pubic area and her stomach, her underwear was torn as though they had been ripped off. We found them at the bottom of the bed under the covers. Her bra was pushed up above her breasts under her shirt. Everything indicated a rape or her having rough sex before she died. You figure it out. If it was consensual sex, I doubt she was fucked to death."

"Holy shit!"

"We didn't tell anyone, figuring the killer would give himself away sooner or later. Looks like he did, but we didn't expect it would happen this way. It had to be either you, Harry or someone from the outside."

"How could you think it was me?" I turned away from Peter looking towards the dark sky. I didn't know if I was more pissed off about Peter not trusting me, or steaming mad at both of them for keeping all this from me.

"We didn't know who it was, George. I'm sorry. But we had to do it that way."

"There's no way in hell you could have suspected me!"

"Calm down, George. I personally didn't suspect you, but I agreed with Stewart to keep it between us until some evidence pointed to the person who did it. We just never thought this would develop. We really didn't have a choice."

"You never suspected Stewart, but you suspected me? I can't believe this. Couldn't he have just as easily been the one?"

Peter thought for a moment. "I suppose it's possible, and I had my doubts at the time. I only knew it wasn't me. I guess I had to trust it wasn't Stewart. Besides, I wasn't the one that realized she had been raped and murdered. Stewart did, and he pointed out all the evidence to me. If he hadn't shown me, I would've just figured it was an overdose and buried her."

"I suppose you did what you had to."

"We really suspected it was Harry, but we couldn't be positive. Now you can see why we can't tell the women."

"Yeah, I do. You're right. They'd go berserk. Especially Dorothy. You have a plan?"

"I don't know yet. I haven't had time to think it through."

"Well, we can't just let him go. There's no telling what he'll do."

"I agree, George, but it's not up to me. It's going to have to be a group decision—everyone will give input and we'll have to arrive at something we can all live with."

He took a couple more puffs on his pipe and turned to me.

"Tell me, what are *you* willing to do—how far are *you* willing to go?" he asked, pointing his finger at me.

I thought for a moment. "Good question. I can't answer that right now either. I'll have to think about it. Poor Nicki though, now I feel bad thinking she was a junkie and killed herself."

"She was a junkie, it just didn't kill her. It may have later, but who knows, it may not have."

We went back into the lobby where Stewart was guarding Harry. He looked intently at me. I knew he was asking if I understood. I nodded to him.

Dorothy was just coming down the stairs.

"How's Ada?" Peter asked.

"She's been through a lot. I gave her a couple of my sleeping pills and I'm going to get her a glass of warm milk."

"Okay, why don't you see if you can get some sleep too. We'll keep this asshole down here tonight and watch him. We can decide what to do with him tomorrow morning."

"I'll try, but I doubt I can sleep after all this."

Stewart watched Dorothy go to the kitchen for a minute and then struggle back up the stairs. He waited until he heard her bedroom door close before he spoke.

***

"Why'd you kill her?" Stewart asked as he stood directly in front of Harry. "She make too much noise or did you just get carried away?"

"Kill who?" Harry asked with a puzzled looked.

"Nicki."

"I didn't kill Nicki. I thought you said she died of an overdose. You even said she had a needle sticking in her arm."

"I did, but I lied. She was raped and strangled to death. Were you planning on killing Ada too?"

Harry looked away. "I didn't have anything to do with Nicki."

"Right. I'm not asking *if* you did it, I just want to know *why* you did it. You already admitted having sex with her. What are you, some kind of serial rapist?"

Harry laughed. "You asshole, that was years ago. She was a little nymph...just loved to fuck."

"You're a liar," Stewart yelled.

"I didn't do it. Even if I did, what are you three stooges going to do about it, cut my balls off? Execute me?" Harry laughed.

"Maybe. That's up to everyone here, not just me," Stewart said. "But if it was up to me, yeah, I'd hang you. You piece of shit."

"You haven't got the balls. Have you ever killed anyone? Have you ever looked into someone's eyes, up close and personal, and watched the life drain out?"

Harry seemed to be taunting him.

"Not yet," Stewart replied, and slowly walked away.

"I'm telling you I didn't do it," Harry yelled as he struggled against the ropes binding him. The chair almost tipped over.

"Shut up," Stewart said. "And sit still."

"Even Ada wouldn't agree to that. She has to forgive me. Remember? That's what she believes."

"Is that what you think?" Peter asked.

"Yeah, she can't agree to kill me. It's against her religion. It's against what she believes."

"Maybe she won't have anything to say about it."

"Wadda' ya mean by that?" Harry looked disturbed by that comment.

"Never mind," Peter said.

"Shut up Harry. If no one else can do it, I will. I'll tie the knot around your mangy neck, throw the rope over a beam, kick the stool out from under you, and watch you swing and kick until your last breath. No problem," Stewart said almost gritting his teeth. "Nicki might have been a doper, but it doesn't justify her being raped and dying like she did, and Ada certainly didn't deserve to be raped."

"But I didn't kill her," Harry still protested.

"You mean you didn't get caught doing it," I said.

"No, read my lips. I-did-not-kill-Nicki."

Peter looked at Stewart and motioned him over to the front door.

"Remember the locked door? If he killed Nicki, he might still have the key to her room. We didn't find it in her room and the door could have been locked from the outside."

"I forgot about that. Let's go take a look. Maybe he kept it as a souvenir."

"George, can you watch Harry for a couple minutes?" Stewart asked.

"Yeah, sure. Where you going?"

"Let you know when we get back. We have to go check something."

***

Peter and Stewart went to Harry's room. The door was unlocked and they went in.

"Tear this place apart if you have to. If he has Nicki's key, that'll put the icing on the cake," Peter said.

Stewart started with the bureau drawers, taking them out one at a time dumping them on the floor and checking the contents. When he got to the bottom drawer and dumped it, he found a skeleton key hidden under the folded clothes.

"I think I found it," announced Stewart.

"Let's go to Nicki's room and try it," Peter said.

They went across the hall and tried the key. It locked and unlocked the door. They both looked at each other.

"I guess that settles that," Peter said.

"I'll say," Stewart said.

Returning to the lobby, Peter took me outside and told me they had just found Nicki's room key in Harry's bureau.

"Why don't you guys go get some sleep," Stewart said after we had come back in. "It's already after four o'clock. I'll take the first watch with dirty Harry."

"Oh, no. Don't you guys leave me alone with him. He'll kill me," Harry pleaded.

"He's not going to kill you tonight," Peter said as we walked to the staircase. "Maybe tomorrow, but not tonight." Peter stopped on the second step, turned, and looked directly at Harry. "Unless you give him reason to."

There was alarm in Harry's eyes.

"We'll see you in the morning," I said to Stewart.

Peter and I went upstairs to our rooms. I went to bed.

***

I couldn't sleep. I tossed and turned for an hour as my mind raced. What the hell were we going to do now?

Do we throw Harry out of the compound? With food and water, or without? Sending anyone out onto the prairie without anything to eat or drink would be the same as condemning them to death.

If we banish him, what would keep him from coming back and taking revenge?

Do we keep him tied up? What if he got loose?

Nothing sounded reasonable and there didn't seem to be any good answers.

Day 17

About seven in the morning, Ada was the first up; she had been in the shower for about a half hour. The generator was still humming; we had left it on all night. Peter and I were downstairs by seven-thirty followed by Dorothy a few minutes later. There'd be no hot water left this morning and no one said a thing. We understood.

"I need some water," Harry stated.

"People in hell want ice-water, too," Dorothy retorted walking past him. "So you better drink up before your get there."

"I'll get you some," Peter said.

"How do ya feel, Stewart?" I asked. "You look pretty ragged."

"The couch wasn't too bad, but I'd rather have slept upstairs in what they call a bed. It may not be much more than a cushion, but it's better than that thing," he said pointing across the room.

I pulled him out of earshot of Harry. "You want to go get some sleep before we discuss what to do with him?"

"No, I'm okay for now. Let's get some breakfast," Stewart said. "I'm starving."

"What about him?" I asked nodding towards Harry.

"He can eat out here. We'll untie his wrists enough so he can feed himself and I'll get him some cereal," Peter said. "You three go get something first, then I'll go."

"Dorothy, is Ada coming down?" Stewart asked.

"I don't know. I haven't talked with her this morning."

Stewart, Dorothy and I went to the kitchen and ate a breakfast of cold cereal. Peter ate after us, and when he was finished brought a bowl of cornflakes out to Harry.

Stewart partially untied Harry's hands keeping his legs and torso tied to the chair, as Peter brought out his breakfast.

"So help me if you try anything, I'll kill you where you sit," Stewart said, walking away.

"Yeah, sure you will," Harry scoffed.

Stewart froze in his tracks, his face full of restrained rage. He slowly turned around. *"Don't-try-me."*

Harry ate his breakfast without further incident. When he finished, Stewart retied his hands.

"What are we going to do with him?" I asked when everyone had returned to the lobby.

"See if Ada is coming down first," Stewart said. She has a right to be involved in this discussion if she wants to be.

"I'll go talk to her," Peter said. "She has to eat sometime too."

Peter walked up the two flights of stairs and knocked on Ada's door. She opened the door, but didn't look at Peter; she stared past him, as though captivated by something down the hallway. She had her toiletries cradled in her right arm, and a scrub brush in her left hand. She was fully dressed, but her bathrobe was wrapped tightly over her clothing.

"Where are you going, Ada?"

"I have to take a shower. I have to get clean."

"But you already took a shower."

"I'm not clean. I have to get clean."

Peter let her pass and she went to the bathroom, closing the door. A minute later he could hear the water running again.

He returned to the lobby and related to us what had transpired. "She's like an android."

"She's still in shock," related Dorothy, "If we were in civilization, she'd be in a hospital and sedated by now—and asshole over there would be in jail. I wonder how many others he's done this to."

Harry laughed, "Keep wondering, fatso, it sure wouldn't be you. Fat chicks don't turn me on, especially loud mouth, Bozo-haired ones."

"Wipe that smile off your face before I wipe it off you," Stewart said. "And keep your mouth shut."

"Untie me and we'll see about that," Harry challenged, sneering.

Stewart had enough. He wasn't going to hit a defenseless person, but he wasn't going to listen to Harry's bullshit anymore.

"George, would you run up to Harry's room and get me one of his socks and the pillowcase off his bed?" he asked.

"Certainly," I said. I had a good idea what Stewart had in mind—I had the same thought.

I brought the items down and Stewart attempted to stuff the sock in Harry's mouth, but he wouldn't open it; he kept turning his head from side to side. He grabbed and held Harry's nose until he had to breathe through his mouth and stuffed the sock in. Stewart then put the pillowcase over his head. Harry struggled, fighting the bonds tying him to the chair, almost turning it over.

"There, that'll shut him up," Stewart said.

Struggling, Harry muffled obscenities for a few more minutes, and then gave up.

"You knock that chair over, asshole, and you can stay there," Stewart told him. "It won't be nearly as comfortable as sitting."

"How's it feel, Harry?" Dorothy asked. "Now all I need to do is find something to stick up your ass, then you'll get a true experience."

There were a few muted laughs.

"Dorothy, you're brutal," I said, stifling a laugh.

"I've seen assholes like him before. I used to volunteer for a rape crisis center. I had to quit when it really started getting to me," she said.

"What do we do with Ada? Is there anything we *can* do?" Peter asked.

"All we can do that I know of is to treat her like a regular person and hope she comes out of it. In most cases, rape victims come out of their depression with counseling, antidepressants, and time. I don't know what else we can do. Time will tell," Dorothy said. "That's all we have."

"So, what are we going to do with him?" Peter questioned, nodding towards Harry.

"Let's go out to the kitchen and discuss it out of his earshot," Stewart said. "Place him where we can keep an eye on him."

We moved Harry's to where we could see him if we kept the door open. All of us retreated to the kitchen table.

"The way I see it, we have four options," Stewart said in a low voice, holding up his hand with four fingers raised. As he ticked off the options, he lowered each finger. "We can let him go; we can keep him tied up for the rest of the time we're here—and baby-sit him; we can banish him—

with or without food and water, or...and understand the implications of this, we can execute him."

"Well, we can't let him go," exclaimed Dorothy. "And if we banish him—I assume you mean just kicking him out the front gate or pushing him under the fence, what's to keep him from coming back?"

"Then I take it you're for execution—or, taking care of him?" Peter asked, staring at Dorothy inquisitively.

"No. I mean—how can we? He might have raped Ada, but execution for a rape? It just doesn't seem right."

"Seems it's either kill him or baby-sit him. That means feeding him, wiping his ass, washing him—everything," Stewart said. "We'd have to keep him tied up. There's no way we can let him free."

"Well I might feed him, but I'm sure as hell not washing him or the other thing," Dorothy declared.

"That means we all have to take turns watching him and all the other things that go along with the option of keeping him tied up," I said.

"What if he gets free?" Peter posed. "You know the first thing he'll do is go for a knife or other weapon to keep us from tying him up again. He might even try to kill us. We don't know what he'll do. He's fuckin' nuts."

"I know I won't be able to sleep very well as long as he's here," I said. "If we keep him tied up, it's only a matter of time before he gets loose. At a minimum, we still have five and a half weeks left in this place."

"I need to know something. How would we—I mean you—execute him?" Dorothy inquired looking down at the table. "I couldn't do it, one of you would have to."

"Probably have to hang him," Stewart said. "But leave that to me."

Silence enveloped the kitchen.

The vision of Harry hanging from a rope, kicking, swinging...it gave me a chill. Peter's eyes glanced toward me without moving his head. I believe he was thinking the same.

"Dorothy, would you go up and see if Ada wants to be a part of this conversation? She probably has an opinion on what she wants to happen. I know it's a chore for you to keep climbing the stairs, but she'll probably talk to you before she'll talk to us," Stewart said.

Dorothy nodded and slowly left the kitchen.

As soon as he heard her heavy footsteps starting up the stairs, Stewart addressed Peter and me, almost whispering.

"I don't think we really have any options here. Dorothy, and Ada, if she votes, will never choose execution. They haven't been told yet that Harry raped and killed Nicki, though I'd love to tell Dorothy. I'll bet she'd vote to do what is necessary if she knew, but telling her may cause more problems than it solves. I think we have to take the dog by the tail and decide among ourselves what we're going to do. I sure as hell ain't gonna wipe his ass for the next five and a half weeks. Now you know where I stand. Peter?"

"We can't tell Dorothy about Nicki. She'd want to kill *us!*" Peter got up and paced the floor and thought for a minute. His nervousness was obvious. "I don't like this whole situation. I've never been for the death penalty, but I don't want to live in fear of my life for the next five weeks either."

Stewart laughed. "Have an epiphany, Peter?" Not for the death penalty unless your own life is in danger?"

Peter gave Stewart a dirty look. "Fuck you. We have enough to deal with trying to survive here without worrying about him and looking over our shoulder every minute." He sat back down. Tapping on the table, he said, "The way I see it, he's already killed Nicki and raped two women; what else do we have to wait for? I don't think we can chance anything but..."

It was like he couldn't say the word.

After a moment he continued. "What I'm worried about is what might happen to *us* once we return. Will the police, or whoever investigates his death, see it as something we had to do, or will they prosecute us as murderers? We can't legally kill him, but we're all in serious danger if we don't."

"George?"

"I pretty much agree with Peter. We can't risk him getting free and we definitely can't let him go. I wouldn't like washing him either, but the question remains—what if he gets loose? There's always that possibility. If he kills another one of us, then I'd feel guilty for a long time for not doing something; and I'd really be pissed if he killed me! I already feel bad enough for not telling Ada and letting her take precautions. She might not have been raped if you had told her. There seems to be only one option left."

"Okay, it sounds like you're both in." He hesitated. "I have a plan," Stewart said quietly, looking intently at Peter and me. "If we stick together—nothing can happen to us. As a matter of fact, Dorothy and Ada will be witnesses that Harry died in a tragic accident. We'll have to wait a few days, so, until then, we'll have to take care of him. For now, we tell Dorothy we decided we are going to keep him tied up. That'll take the burden of making a decision off of her and Ada."

"What's the plan?" Peter asked.

"It's...probably better if I didn't tell you just yet. I still have to work out a few of the details. You'll know it's time when I call on both of you, but it'll be clean. No hanging, no blood. The women won't even know we killed him."

I must have looked like Dumbo, sitting there with a blank expression on my face. Peter's reaction appeared to mirror my own.

Stewart watched us. I think his intuition told him we weren't really ready to okay an execution.

"If the time comes and you want to back out, I'll understand," he said.

"I'm not going to do it," I said.

"Me neither," Peter stated firmly.

"Don't worry, I'll..." He went silent as Dorothy returned to the kitchen.

"I think she's losing it. I went into her room with her. She wasn't responsive—wouldn't talk to me at all. All she does is babble stuff I can't understand. She had taken a scrub brush with her to take a bath; she literally scrubbed some of the skin off her face. You should see her! She was dressed in several layers of clothes and in bed with the covers pulled over her. I asked her if she wanted to eat and she still wouldn't answer. I've tried talking to her and telling her this wasn't her fault. I don't know what to do with her."

The three of us looked around at each other, apparently not knowing what to say.

"I guess we'll just leave her alone and see what happens," Dorothy said.

"Have a seat, Dorothy. We need to talk to you," I said.

"What's your opinion on what we should do with Harry?" Stewart inquired, looking at Dorothy as she sat down at the table.

"I knew you were going to ask me that. I'm leaving it up to you guys. Do what ever you want. Just don't let him go."

"We've pretty well decided we'll keep him tied up for awhile and see what happens—if that's all right with you."

"That's okay with me. You guys are the ones who're going to have to deal with him. Just promise me he won't get loose."

"We'll do the best we can. We don't want him to get free either," Stewart said.

"I'll do the cooking for him, but everything else is left to you three."

"That sounds fair," Peter said, looking at Stewart and me. We both nodded agreement.

We walked back into the lobby and moved Harry back to where he had been before. Stewart pulled a chair over and turned it facing backwards in front of Harry. He sat down, his arms resting on the back.

"Pete, would you take the hood off and the sock out of his mouth?"

He complied with the request.

"Listen up, bigmouth," Stewart said, looking directly at Harry. "We've decided your fate. For now, we're going to keep you tied up and watch you. You make one move to escape—just one time, or give us any trouble and we've all agreed to march your ass across the street and string you up. Understood?"

Harry nodded his head—it looked as if he was beginning to believe Stewart. I know I did.

"We're turning you over to the police as soon as we get out of here—if you last that long. If we have to hang you, everyone has agreed that we'll say you left to get help, like Jessie and Ralph, and we never saw you again. We'll bury your sorry ass out on the prairie somewhere and no one will ever know the better."

"Will someone let me go to the bathroom?" Harry asked meekly.

I untied Harry from the chair, keeping his hands tied together.

Peter took him upstairs to the restroom.

"That was a pretty good speech you gave there, Stewart. I believed you," Dorothy said, smiling.

"I meant *every* word of it," Stewart replied.

She looked into his eyes, probably wondering if he was putting on a show, or telling the truth. I never did find out what she thought. *I* knew he meant it.

CHAPTER 17
The Escape

Day 22

Several days passed. We took turns watching and taking care of Harry while Dorothy held up her end of the bargain and did all the cooking. There were always two of us present whenever he had to be untied to use the bathroom, exercise or wash up. We fed him, let him stretch his legs with a walk a couple times a day, and let him sleep in his bed at night—totally tied down, of course. We took turns sleeping on a mattress in the hallway outside of his room. It wasn't the most comfortable setup, but it worked. For now, we suspended our nightly watch.

Whenever Stewart and I escorted Harry on the daily walk to the end of town and back, each time we passed the cemetery Stewart would remind him of how close he was to his eternal resting place. He had even started digging a grave, just to let Harry know he was serious. Everyday, the hole was a little deeper.

"See that empty spot next to Jessie's grave?" Stewart would ask. "That's reserved for you."

It must have worked on Harry's psyche. He never tried to escape.

Ada still wasn't speaking to anyone, but took food that was brought to her room. She showered twice a day, whenever the power was turned on, usually taking at least a half hour each time. Like clockwork, once she heard the hum of the generator, she calculated the minutes until the water would be hot enough for a shower and then shut herself in the bathroom. No one said a word about it and everyone worked around it. She was still scrubbing herself raw, but not as badly as at first.

On the twenty-second evening of our stay, a steady, light rain began to fall. Stewart came to my room first, and then to Peter's before the lights were turned out and told us to be prepared to get up sometime that night; he would wake us up when it was time. He wouldn't tell us his plans; he still said we were better off not knowing. He was probably right.

Stewart waited for Dorothy to go to bed and fall asleep. It was easy to tell; her snore rumbled like a freight train most of the time. He couldn't tell about Ada, but he felt sure she was asleep by around nine, and she never came out of her room anyway.

Around midnight, Stewart, who was in the hall on watch, came and woke me up.

"Go get Peter and wake up Harry, untie him from his bed and bring him downstairs. He'll ask you what's going on. Tell him we are going to turn him loose. We've decided he's to be banished. And tell him to be quiet, as we don't want the women to know what we're doing. They'll just think he escaped," Stewart said. "Keep his hands tied 'til we get to the fence."

"Are we really letting him go?" I asked.

"Of course not," Stewart replied. He gave me one of those looks that asked, "*Are you stupid, or what?*"

"I'll meet you downstairs. Put a jacket on," he said, "it's still raining."

I woke Peter. We went to Harry's room. I'd brought a candle and lit it once we were in the room and ready to wake him.

"Harry," Peter said in a hushed voice as he untied the ropes binding him to the bed. "Harry, wake up."

"Wha...what's up?" Harry asked confused and groggy.

He put his hand over Harry's mouth. "Keep quiet! Get up and let's go. We're turning you loose. Everyone's tired of babysitting you, but we don't want the women to know. Understand?"

Harry nodded.

When Peter told him we were going to kick him out, Harry didn't say another word and followed every instruction.

Stewart met us in the lobby with the food, water and supplies Harry had prepared for his own escape. Harry eyed the supplies, half-smiled, and seemed anxious to get out and be free of his bindings.

"How about untying me?" Harry requested.

"Not a chance 'til we get to the fence," Stewart said sternly.

"Can someone get my jacket upstairs?" Harry asked, seeing the rain on the windows.

"Where is it?" I asked him.

"On the back of the door."

I went upstairs, felt around on the back of the door for the jacket, and brought it down. I hoped the creaking floors didn't wake the women.

"Give it to him after he's on the other side," directed Stewart.

"But it's raining," objected Harry.

"Don't argue. We're not untying you until we get to the fence."

Harry fell silent. I threw the jacket over the top of his head. Stewart grabbed it off of him. He looked at me and shook his head, not saying a word.

We quietly walked out of the hotel in single file down to the gate where the others had crawled under. Stewart lit the lantern, handing it off to Peter. The rain had intensified during our walk, and I was soaked, even through my jacket.

"You go first and then I'll push your supplies through," Stewart directed Harry.

"You're not going to give me the supplies, are you?" Harry questioned. "You're going to turn me out without anything, let me starve."

"I've thought about it, and if it was up to me, that's what I'd do," Stewart said. "But the others wouldn't let me do it. So consider yourself lucky."

I untied the rope binding Harry's hands and Harry shook them vigorously. His arms were stiff and his hands probably ached from being tied for so long. Peter grabbed the board and started pacing it under the fence.

"Let me do that," Stewart demanded, grabbing the board. Peter just looked at Stewart inquisitively and then me. He gave him the board.

"Go, and don't come back," Stewart said to Harry. "If you do, things will be different and I don't think you'll like the consequences."

"You won't ever see me again."

"Don't be too sure of that," Stewart said. "You still have to pay for what you've done."

"Not likely. Not if I can help it," answered Harry, remaining obstinate.

The light rain had soaked all of us by now. Harry went down on his knees turning onto his back and started wriggling back and forth under the fence being careful not to touch any part of it.

He had shimmied through as far as his chest when Stewart said in a voice as cold as steel, "This is for Nicki."

Immediately, I realized what was about to happen. "Wait," I yelled.

Harry froze, his eyes almost popping out of his head. In that instant, he realized what was coming. "No! Don't!" he screamed.

Stewart pulled the board out, letting the electrified fence spring back down on top of Harry.

"Payment rendered," declared Stewart.

There were several loud pops. Every muscle in Harry's body contracted from the electrical current traversing through him to the ground. Harry's body jerked violently up and down. The fence sizzled and popped some more. Sparks flew. After about thirty long seconds Stewart put the board back under and raised the fence off of Harry.

"Pull him out," ordered Stewart. Smoke still rose from his body.

Peter and I looked at each other, grabbed a leg each and pulled Harry out from under the fence. There was no doubt—Harry had been terminated. Stewart checked for a pulse and shook his head.

"God, that was horrible to watch," I gasped as a chill ran up my spine. The smell of burnt human flesh filled my nostrils.

"I know, that can't be a pleasant way to go," Peter replied staring at Harry's body.

"He deserved every bit of it," declared Stewart. "Leave him, the supplies, and his jacket here. Everything will be in place in the morning when one of the women finds him missing. It'll look like he tried to escape and was accidentally electrocuted. Bring the rope from his hands and put it in his room along with the other ropes."

As we walked back to the hotel, Stewart explained to Peter and me, "We had to wait for a good rain. We could have tried it without the moisture, but I wanted to be sure it did the job the first time. Sorry I didn't let you in on the details, but I didn't want anyone backing out at the last minute. If you feel bad for him, think about what he did to Nicki and Ada. In the morning, you both have to stay in bed until Dorothy discovers his empty room. She has to be the one that discovers him gone. Have dry clothes on in the morning, hide the wet ones, and make sure you don't make any noise going back to bed."

I thought about how Stewart seemed to have it all figured out. I couldn't think of any loose ends.

We got back to the hotel and silently slipped back into our beds. Stewart went back to the mattress in the hallway outside of Harry's door.

Whether any of us slept the rest of that night was doubtful. I didn't. I was wide-awake for hours; I couldn't get the image out of my head of Harry twitching and writhing in pain under the fence. We were supposed to be civilized, yet we had acted like a mob— judge, jury and executioners. I'd never seen anyone die before, much less actually take part in a killing—and certainly not an execution.

***

About six-thirty in the morning, I was lying in bed wide-awake when I heard Dorothy get up and walk down the hall to the bathroom. A few minutes later I heard the stairs groan as she made her way down to the second floor. As she rounded the corner, she must have seen Stewart asleep in the hallway in front of Harry's open door. Stewart had left the door wide open, unlike the prior nights.

She probably slipped around Stewart and over to the door, looked inside and saw the ropes on the floor by the empty bed.

"He's gone! He's gone!" she shrieked, kicking at Stewart. "Wake up—he's gone!"

Stewart later told me he was actually awake and acted like he was jolted out of a sound asleep. He leapt up and looked into Harry's room.

"Son-of-a-bitch!" he yelled. "Get Peter and George up. I'm going to look downstairs."

She ran down the hall and banged on Peter's door yelling, "He's gone. Harry's gone—get up!"

I heard the whole thing. I smiled. It had worked. I then heard her make her way up the stairs to my room where she repeated the scenario.

I immediately answered the door and acted like it was an emergency. I quickly dressed and met Stewart, Peter and Dorothy downstairs.

"Would you put some coffee on while we look for him, Dorothy?" Peter asked. "I'll go turn on the generator."

"Okay, but are all of you leaving me? What if he's still around here? What do I do?"

"Kick him in the nuts," Peter said, wisecracking.

Stewart looked at me and winked. "George, why don't you stay here and guard the ladies while Peter and I search for Harry," Stewart said.

"No problem." I answered. "Dorothy, check the knives in the kitchen—see if they're all there. Get me one if you would."

"He's probably gone, but I guess we need to make a thorough search of the place to make sure. If I was him, I sure as hell wouldn't be hanging around here."

"But..., but what if he's in there?" she questioned, pointing towards the kitchen.

"Let me look." I bravely said. I cautiously crept into the kitchen as Dorothy watched. I made a show of checking the pantry and the laundry room and came back out. "It's safe. He's not there."

Dorothy, now confident Harry wasn't around the immediate area, carried out the request, rushing as fast as she could. She was keyed up. "There's a knife missing, George," she yelled. "It's one of the larger ones. Be careful."

She handed me a large serrated knife.

"We'll find him," I said.

"I hope not. I want his ass gone, and I hope he doesn't come back. The police can deal with him when we get out of this mess. I'll go make the coffee."

Fifteen minutes later Stewart and Peter arrived back at the hotel and came to the kitchen. They brought the bag of canned food and the bottles of water with them and threw them on the table.

"Well, do you want the good news first, or the bad news?" Stewart asked.

"The good news," Dorothy said. "I'm sick of bad news."

"It looks as though dirty Harry tried to escape. He had a bunch of supplies with him and tried to crawl under the fence. He didn't quite make it though. Looks like he got himself electrocuted. The rain last night made him and the ground wet. When he touched the fence, it was all over for him—he was French-fried." He looked at me with a short smile. "Pete, do you or Dorothy want to see him?"

"I don't," I said.

"Why would I want to see that son-of-a-bitch?" Dorothy asked.

"Sometimes seeing is a confirmation. I thought it might let you rest easier," Stewart said.

"Plant the asshole, that'll be confirmation enough for me."

"What's the bad news?" I asked.

"Now we have to drag his sorry ass from one end of town to the other, dig a hole, and bury him."

"Oh, yeah." I grinned. "But you almost have the hole finished!"

"You can breathe easy now, Dorothy. Here, I won't be needing this." I gave the knife back to her.

***

Later, Dorothy made pancakes for everyone—she seemed to be in an extremely good mood.

"George, if you'll get the sheet and blanket off Harry's bed...," began Stewart as he pushed his plate away and wiped his mouth with a paper towel.

"I know. I know," I interrupted, "we'll wrap him up and drag him down to the other end of town."

We all laughed. Everyone seemed relieved to be rid of a very large headache. It felt good to laugh; it'd been a week since anyone had.

Dorothy stopped eating and placed both arms on the table resting one on each side of her plate. "I want to thank all of you for taking care of everything this past week. I know it hasn't been easy," she said. "I told Ada what happened. She didn't say anything, but she closed her eyes and I suspect she was satisfied."

"You can thank us by making these pancakes every morning," I said.

"Don't push it, George," she said with a smile. "I'm grateful, but I'm not going to be your maid. Besides, we're running short on syrup. We might have enough for a few more days."

"Why, I was ready to get you a kimono and let you massage my feet." Then, on a more serious note, I said, "Dorothy, I know going up and down the stairs is wearing on you. Why don't you move your things down to one of the empty rooms on the second floor?"

"We'll help you move if you want," Peter said as he placed his dirty dishes in the sink.

"In which room? Nicki's? Randy's? Harry's? No thanks. I'll stay where I am. Those rooms will be haunted for sure."

We all laughed.

After breakfast, while Dorothy cleaned up the kitchen and washed the dishes, I bundled the sheets and blanket from Harry's bed and Peter grabbed the shovel. Together, we walked down to the gate area where Harry lay, and wrapped the body. Peter and Stewart half-carried, half-dragged the stiff to the other end of town.

Stewart had already dug most of the grave taunting Harry. I continued where he left off, giving them a well-earned breather.

"Seems everything is going as planned, just like clock-work," I said as I shoveled more dirt.

"Dorothy didn't seem to suspect a thing," Peter said.

I stopped digging and looked up at Peter. "I know."

"We're lucky Dorothy didn't go look at the body," Stewart said. "We fucked up."

"Why's that?" I asked, now leaning on the shovel.

"Because if Harry had tried to escape and was electrocuted, he'd still been under the fence. I wonder if she would have caught on to that?"

I grinned. "Oh, shit. You're right! And here I thought we had the perfect execution! I guess we wouldn't make very good criminals." After thinking a few moments I said, "Naw, it would have been okay. You could have just told her you and Peter pulled him out this morning."

"How about his jacket? We left that next to him with the food and water. It was raining, why wouldn't he have his jacket on? Didn't want to get it dirty?" Peter asked.

"We might've left a few loose ends, but I don't think it was anything we couldn't explain away. He was kind of in a hurry to get out of here, remember?"

We returned to the hotel a couple hours later after burying Harry. This time, there was no ceremony, no prayers, just a one-finger salute.

CHAPTER 18
Ada's Plight

Day 30

"I can't believe we've only been here a month and we're stuck eating this shitty, cold-ass cereal," Peter complained.

"Yeah," Stewart chimed in, "they promised us everything was taken care of; all our needs would be provided. I'm surprised they didn't leave us a crib full of cattle corn. This is bullshit!"

"I can't take this much longer," Dorothy stated throwing her spoon down on the table and wiping a tear from her eye. "This isn't civilized. We can't even get enough hot water anymore. I can't blame Ada for using it all; I'd probably do the same if that slime had been on me. What are we supposed to do?"

It was hard to believe thirty days had passed since we had arrived in this broken-down place. It's so desolate out here, now I know why it's a ghost town. Everyone seemed to be feeling the strain from cold cereal in the mornings to beans and whatever we could throw together at night. With Ada taking two long showers each morning and evening, the three hours of electricity a day put the five of us on a tight schedule for bathing, washing clothes, dishes and cooking. We tried to turn everything off whenever possible in order to conserve fuel. Even though our conservation did reduce usage, we realized we were not going to make it another thirty days. There was less than a half tank of gasoline left. We were going to have to cut the generator time even more.

***

It had been a week since we executed Harry, but we never spoke of it. The women accepted that he died trying to escape, and that's the way we wanted to keep it. I was still having second thoughts about the execution, and sleep brought nightmares to life that I'd have to live with. I still tried to convince myself we had no other options. As distasteful and objectionable as it was, I suppose we had to do it.

Ada still took her meals in her room, and Dorothy was getting tired of going up and down the stairs playing nursemaid. I wondered if Dorothy had let Ada know how hard it was for her.

***

Later that afternoon, I was with Peter on the front porch of the hotel while he enjoyed a few puffs on his pipe.

"Thanks for smoking that outside," Dorothy said as she joined us. Her tone was almost apologetic.

"No problem. It's a nice evening. I enjoy being outside when it's like this."

"Look, I've been trying to snap Ada out of her depression. I haven't taken any food to her today, trying to get her to come downstairs to eat, but I'm not having any success. She just won't eat if I don't bring it to her."

"What do you want to do?" I asked.

"Do you think I should just let her go hungry until she comes down?"

"You can give it a try. See what happens," Peter replied thoughtfully while exhaling a cloud of smoke. "She's not going to starve to death if she doesn't eat for a couple days."

"I'm going to have to. My knees aren't going to take much more stair-climbing."

***

Since the rape, Ada still took two showers every day. During the day we would often hear her singing in her room followed by several hours of mumbled speech—which Dorothy believed was praying. As much as she tried to reach her, Ada seemed to be sinking deeper and deeper into a world of her own. She declared to Dorothy each morning and evening when she got her food that she had to get clean—she still felt dirty. After talking it over, we agreed we had to stop her from taking the two showers a day in order to save on fuel. It was a matter of survival.

We had Dorothy tell her. When she tried to take a second shower that evening when Peter turned the generator on, we turned the water off at the pressure tank. We all felt bad about it, but there was nothing else we could do.

Day 31

On the thirty-first morning, we were all treated to a great breakfast. Dorothy, at everyone's request, had fixed another large batch of pancakes and all were enjoying them with plenty of butter and maple-flavored syrup. It was a welcome change from cold cereal, but there wouldn't be many more mornings like it.

"I haven't seen Ada yet this morning. I heard her go into the bathroom and turn on the water, but I haven't heard her come out," remarked Dorothy as she sat down to eat.

"You probably just missed her," Peter replied while shoving in a mouthful of syrupy soaked pancake.

"Are you taking pancakes up to her this morning?" I asked.

"Maybe, if there's any left. She hasn't eaten anything since the day before yesterday."

Stewart patted his stomach, "Well, I guess she's eating cereal then."

That brought a few chuckles.

"On second thought, I'm not going to take any food up to her today. I'm trying to get her to come down and eat. She needs to start associating and socializing with everyone again, come back to this world."

"Think she'll come down?" Stewart wondered.

"We'll find out pretty soon," answered Dorothy, stuffing her mouth with pancakes.

After several minutes of silence, the conversation turned to what we believed had to be done.

"Where are you guys on your manuscripts?" Dorothy asked.

"I'm ready to pen a few more chapters," Peter said.

"I've already started," I said. "I just need the titles we're going to use and how we're going to section it."

After about a half hour of discussions, we settled on names for the next three chapters, *The Grave,* for when we found the first grave, *Westward Bound,* for Jessie's jaunt westward, and *One More To Rest,* for Nicki's burial.

***

Stewart washed the dishes while Peter went to turn off the generator. Dorothy and I went upstairs to work on our manuscripts. When we arrived on the third floor, we could hear water running in the bathroom at the end of the hall.

Dorothy looked in Ada's room. "She's not there."

We went to the bathroom and knocked on the door. There was no answer, only the sound of running water.

"Ada, turn off the water," Dorothy yelled.

Still no answer. She knocked on the door and repeated the demand. After knocking several more times and calling for her, Dorothy tried the door. It was locked from the inside.

"Ada. Ada, are you all right?" yelled Dorothy.

"Not again," I groaned as Dorothy gave me an exasperated look and stood back.

I hit the door several times with my shoulder, but it wouldn't budge. I stood back and kicked it hard a couple more—it still didn't give.

"I'm going to have to get Peter or Stewart to help me."

I hurried down the two flights of stairs and yelled for Stewart who was still in the kitchen.

"What's the problem?" he asked, drying his hands as he came out of the kitchen.

"Ada's locked in the bathroom, the water's running, and she's not responding. I can't get the door open."

We went back up the stairs, me huffing and puffing by the time I reached the third floor. I had to stop and catch my breath at the top of the stairs.

"Come on, George—it's just a little farther," taunted Stewart.

"Give me a minute." My face was hot, probably beet red. I gasped for air as I held on to the banister.

After several moments, I slowly shuffled the rest of the distance down the hall.

"Ready?" Stewart asked. "On three. One. Two. Three."

We both hit the door with our shoulders. The door-jamb split with a loud crack; the door opened. We fell into the bathroom.

***

Downstairs, Peter had just come into the hotel after turning off the generator when he must have heard the loud crash coming from upstairs.

"What the hell is going on up there?" he yelled.

Stewart ran over to the top of the stairs and shouted down, "Get up here."

Ada was under water in the bathtub, dressed in her nightgown, her yellow robe lying next to the tub on the floor. The bath water was a light pinkish color. The holding tank must have emptied since the generator was turned off, causing the water to stop running. I pulled Ada's head out and put my fingers to her neck to check for a pulse. I shook my head. There was no use trying to revive her.

Ada had not only slit her wrists, but also continued cutting halfway up her arm. She was pale—a grayish-white color from losing so much blood. A broken dispos-able razor lay on the floor next to the tub. I didn't know if she died from loss of blood or she passed out and drowned.

"Poor Ada," Dorothy said sobbing. She fell to her knees next to the tub and stroked the top of Ada's head. "She really did lose it. It's my fault. I shouldn't have tried to make her come downstairs. She was probably starving and thought she had lost her last friend."

"Don't beat yourself up, Dorothy. I don't think there's anything we could have done. We did all we could for her under the circumstances," Peter said.

"You did more for her than all of us combined, so don't feel like you caused this. She completely changed after the rape. Maybe she's better off where she is now," I said.

"Are you sure she's gone?" I guess Stewart also felt obligated to check for a pulse. He then turned to Peter and shook his head.

"I know, I know. Get the sheets and the blanket," Peter said.

We gently pulled her limp, drenched body from the tub and laid her on the floor.

"Dorothy, can you dry her off some before we carry her downstairs?" Stewart requested as he made his way to the door.

"Okay," she mumbled. Tears flowed down her face.

"God, I hope this is the last body we have to bury," I said. "This is really getting so morose as to be unbelievable. It's just plain bizarre."

We went downstairs while Dorothy prepared Ada for burial.

***

"This place is cursed," Dorothy exclaimed as she came down the stairs. She paced back and forth, still in tears. "We have to get out of here somehow. We're short on food items and we don't have enough fuel to make it another month. What else could go wrong? What more can they throw at us?"

"That reminds me, Peter, we still have to check on the power source to the fence," Stewart said. "We may need that power sooner than we thought."

"Tomorrow, it doesn't make any difference today." Peter went over to Dorothy and put his arm around her. "We've thought of every possible escape, Dorothy. There just isn't any way out of here right now, short of burning the whole place down and hoping someone spots the smoke."

"But then if no one does, we're completely shit out of luck," I said. "No hotel, no water, no nothing."

"Why don't we try making a huge bonfire at night down by the gate or outside the fence? Perhaps a plane flying over will see it and report it," Peter said. "Or during the day— maybe someone will see the smoke."

"It's worth a try," I said. "It's going to take a pile of wood. I know we have a whole town of scrap to pick from, but it's going to be a lot of work taking things apart and hauling it down to the gate."

"Do we have anything that'll create smoke—like tires?" Peter wondered.

"We'll have to search the town. I haven't seen anything yet," Stewart said deep in thought. "What would happen if we started a prairie fire?"

"I wouldn't care if it brought help," Dorothy said.

"What would we do if it ends up blowing back on us and burning the town down?" I responded.

"As long as it brings help, I don't give a damn," Dorothy repeated.

"And if it doesn't?" Peter asked.

No one said a thing.

***

Peter and Stewart wrapped Ada's body, carried her down the stairs and out to the end of town. Again, I followed with the shovel. We dug another hole next to Nicki. When it was finished, I went back to the hotel and escorted Dorothy down to the gravesite. She carried Ada's Bible with her. She read a few passages, and then we stood for a few minutes of silent prayer. Afterwards, we gently placed Ada's body in the grave with her Bible. An hour later it was filled in and over with. A marker was placed on it with Ada's name and the date.

There were now six graves in an unknown, rundown, dusty, dirty town out in the middle of nowhere. Where in the hell were we? What did we get ourselves into?

***

We four remaining captives returned to the hotel and mostly worked on our manuscripts until about four when it started cooling off, or when our batteries ran out, whichever came first. We started gathering any wood we could find for a signal fire while Dorothy prepared supper.

CHAPTER 19
The Storm

Day 38

During the cooler evening hours of the days that followed, Stewart, Peter and I gathered wood for a large signal fire. We decided to locate it by the gate where we had entered, but off to the side of the main road by the hole under the fence. We cleared all the brush and tumbleweeds from the area hoping it would keep the fire from spreading. We'd have to light the fire when there was no wind and hope someone would see the smoke. It was a gamble, a huge one. If the fire got out of hand, or blew back on us, we could lose everything and die. With this crazy scheme, we could be writing our own death warrants. We thought about locating it outside the fence some safe distance away, but decided it would be too difficult to get all the wood either under or over the electrified fence.

Dispersed throughout the pile of scrap wood were sheets of tarpaper we'd torn off walls from inside the other buildings. It would create a thick black smoke that, hopefully, would attract either a plane or someone who would spot the signal. It wasn't easy carrying all the wood through the town, and then almost a football field's distance out to where the fence was located. There were hundreds of rusty nails to watch for, and the only tool we could find was a rusted crowbar to rip out the walls and floors of the old buildings. We took turns at the crowbar while the other two hauled it down to the gate.

Snakes. I couldn't believe the hordes of rattlers hiding under the floors we pulled up. I wouldn't get near them. I don't know where my fear of snakes came from, but I hate the damn things. Every time I found one, I called Stewart. He'd laugh at me, but I didn't give a shit. He killed most, but several slithered away before he got to them. They weren't particularly big, most no more than eighteen inches, but we learned the hard way, through Randy, how deadly they could be.

Peter drained about a gallon of gas from the generator's tank to pour on the wood. We'd need it to start the fire quickly if we spotted a plane, or to signal someone. The whole thing was a crapshoot. We debated how much fuel to draw off, as we knew it was precious and life giving.

***

Towards the latter part of the evening, Peter was the first to notice dark clouds gathering in the west. These weren't regular clouds, but tall, black, boiling ones. There was a definite edge to them indicating to me that a large weather front was moving in. A light breeze had picked up. Within a short while, tremendous volleys of rolling thunder resounded seconds apart, accompanied by multiple bolts of brilliant, spectacular lightning that lit up the evening sky. It came closer and closer.

"I think we're going to be in for it tonight," Peter said as he sat resting between loads of wood. "Looks like we better batten down the hatches."

"It does look threatening," I said.

Stewart yelled to me as he tossed an armload of wood, piece by piece, on top of the eight-foot high pile, "Is it coming our way, or do you think it'll skirt us?"

"I don't know. It came in rather fast. I haven't looked to see which way it's moving yet."

"Well, we better get back anyway. It looks like a huge front, and those clouds are black as hell. I don't see how it can miss us unless it completely dies out," I said. "And that's not likely. These plains storms along with the lightning can be really nasty. I hope we don't see any tornados."

"Tornados?" Peter raised an eyebrow.

"Yeah," I said. "If we're anywhere near where I think we are, we may be in a tornado belt. There are lots of them this time of year on the plains. Remember *The Wizard of OZ?* That was in Kansas. We may not be that far from it and we're probably on the same high desert plain."

"Oh, that's encouraging," Stewart said under his breath.

"Yeah, and we've even got Dorothy with us; all we're missing is Toto," Peter said with a smirk.

I had to laugh.

By the time we returned to the hotel, the wind had increased in intensity and was swirling large dust devils down the center of the street. The storm front appeared to be moving in quickly. Thick clouds of dust and sand blew through, blanketing the town.

"Let's get all the windows closed," Peter shouted above the noise of the wind. "It looks like this thing is going to hit us a lot faster than I thought."

We ran room to room in the hotel making sure all the windows were closed and locked. Stewart took the third floor, Peter the second, and Dorothy and I the main floor. The single pane glass windows were old and loose in their frames. They rattled and shook violently as the wind velocity picked up even more. In no time at all, the sky had blackened; it looked like nighttime in the light of a half moon.

We all met up in the lobby after everything was checked and secured.

"Do we have candles anywhere?" Stewart asked.

"There's a box in the pantry," Dorothy said.

"Grab them, we may have to go into the basement pretty soon. The kitchen matches too."

"I'll put some water in jugs just in case," Peter said.

The wind now blew at gale force. The wood and tar-paper we had labored so long and hard at for the bonfire, blew and scattered down the middle of the street. Pieces of salvaged boards pounded the side of the hotel and the front porch.

"It's only a matter of time before we get some broken windows," yelled Stewart. "Best everyone stay away from them."

No sooner had Stewart finished warning us, a two-foot long broken board with large splinters protruding from both ends crashed through one of the front hotel windows. It sent shards of glass scattering across the hotel lobby. I turned away from it just in time as pieces sprayed my back. Golf ball sized hail fell, pounding the sides of the hotel and the front porch.

"Shit! Let's get outta here!" I shouted.

"Downstairs," yelled Stewart.

Peter had just come up from the basement with four plastic milk containers. "Let me rinse these first and get some water."

"Forget it! Go back downstairs," I yelled. "It's too dangerous."

Dorothy brought the candles and matches and started to follow us down the rickety wooden stairs. She was shaking as she negotiated the top two steps. The handrail she tried to hold onto was virtually unusable. It slapped against the wall as the screws that secured it had long since come loose in several places.

"I...I can't go down there," she yelled down the stairs, staring into the abyss of the dark cellar.

"Why the hell not?" Stewart yelled up to her. He was in no mood and there was no time for discussions.

"I'm clau..stro...phobic," she said between hyperventilating breaths.

The wind was now howling so hard it was shaking the old building. The windows that were still intact were rattling, the frames pulling at their restraints.

"You'd better get down here. The building may not hold up much longer and the rest of the windows are going to blow out any minute."

The wind sounded like a phantom train, careening out of control down the center of town, screaming, rumbling, and tearing at the buildings as it announced its impending collision. The pressure had dropped and my ears started to pop.

"There's a tornado coming, Dorothy, get the hell down here," Stewart yelled from the bottom of the stairs.

"I'm going to my room," she yelled as she threw the candles and box of matches down into the void, turned and stepped off the stairs, out of the basement.

I started upstairs to get her, "Dorothy, there's a tornado coming!"

There was no answer.

I waited a moment and then climbed the stairs two at a time. The door was still open and was swinging wildly with the wind. Yelling for Dorothy at the top of the basement stairs, another loud crash and the sound of glass shattering captured my attention. The other front window of the hotel blew out sending more shards flying across the room, some sticking into the far walls like daggers this time. The wicker chairs in the lobby slammed against the inside wall and the table turned over. Glasses and cups that sat on the table went flying, breaking against the walls. Baseball sized hail now battered the hotel, some flying through the broken windows into the lobby.

The noise was deafening. Everything outside that wasn't tied down became deadly projectiles, flying through the air with the force of a gunshot. I closed the basement door. Dorothy would have to fend for herself.

As I got to the bottom of the stairs, I thought I heard Dorothy's footsteps coming back down the stairs, but I wasn't sure. I went back up and forced open the basement door a couple of inches and peeked out hoping she had come to her senses and was ready to join us. She was nowhere to be seen. The side windows of the lobby blew in, sending everything flying in different directions. A large shard of glass pierced the center of the door next to my head. Two inches over and it would have been lights out. There was nothing I could do now. I shut the door again.

In the cellar, Peter had collected the candles Dorothy had thrown down the stairs and lit several. The glow cast eerie shadows on the antique stone foundation. The bottles of amber and clear liquor sitting in an old hutch in the corner must have called Stewart's name.

"How 'bout a little nip?" He motioned to Peter and me.

"Not for me," Peter said. "I don't need another head-ache."

"Me neither," I said, waving him off.

"George, look at your hand." Peter pointed to the one I had just waved with. "You're bleeding."

"Shit!" I shook the blood off and grabbed a candle. I could see a clean cut right across the top of my hand. "A piece of glass must have got me when the window blew out. I didn't feel a thing."

I took off my shirt and tore a section off the bottom. "And this was my good shirt."

Peter laughed. "Yeah, right. I'd hate to see your worst."

Stewart unscrewed a bottle of bourbon and took a swig. "I hope Dorothy's going to be all right. We still need a cook."

Peter rolled his eyes, but he didn't say anything. Neither did I.

Stewart walked over to me. "Let me see that hand."

I held it out so he could see the cut. Without saying anything, he poured the bourbon over my hand.

"Owww. Fuck, that hurt!" I shook my hand.

"Don't be a baby. You have to keep that cut clean and that shirt sure as hell ain't going to do it."

"You could've told me you were going to do that."

"And that would've made it hurt less?"

"What a waste of good bourbon," Peter said with a smirk on his face.

I wrapped my hand in the strip of shirt. Damn, that stung.

Water started dripping through the ceiling of the basement from the torrential rain and hail. It dripped into Stewart's hair as he took another drink from the bottle. He shook his head and brushed his hair with his hand to wipe it off.

"How long do you think we'll be down here?" I asked.

"Till it's over," Stewart said sarcastically. "Who the hell knows?"

I was worried. Peter looked it too.

***

I picked up a candle and looked around the basement. I'd never been down here before. The dirt floor and stone walls looked like a medieval dungeon. All it needed was a massive wooden door with an iron bar window and chains hanging from the walls to complete the scene. Large oak beams crisscrossing the ceiling were held up with massive wooden posts, which were partially rotted at the base where they came into contact with the dirt. Old two-wire type electric wiring paralleled the beams, held by antique white porcelain insulators. Part of the insulation had rotted off the wires exposing the bare copper. Galvanized pipe routed water to the kitchen and bathrooms from the well's pressure holding tank. I walked back and forth along the sidewall, inspecting the foundation. Something wasn't right, but I couldn't put my finger on it.

The continuous thunder, the relentless wind, and the cracks of lightning pounded our auditory senses. The storm was right on top of us. The flying debris beating the building outside made it sound like the whole hotel was being attacked with sledgehammers wielded by an army of men. The rain was still coming down in torrents. With no windows on the first floor left to deflect the rain, the water poured through the floorboards into the basement creating pools that soon turned the dusty, dirt floor into thick, sticky muck. The quicksand-type mire stuck to our shoes, which picked up the dry dirt, weighing down our feet. It felt like I was walking around with lead weights on.

"Great, now there's no place to keep dry," Stewart said kicking the thick mud off his shoes against one of the wooden posts. "I wonder what our bedrooms look like. My laptop is probably trashed by now."

"You looking for something, George?" Peter asked as he watched me pacing the length of one of the walls.

"There's something funny here." I tapped on the stone wall.

"Like what? It's part of the foundation."

"Maybe. Maybe not. Look at the top, there's nothing sitting on it."

"What do you mean?"

Stewart walked over to the wall with a candle, studying the top. "He means there's no partition on top, no beams sitting on it. The beams and wiring pass over the top. It's like a false wall, or an interior wall, but it's certainly not part of the foundation." He pushed on it, as if trying to move the stone partition.

"Exactly," I said.

"So how do we get to the other side?" Peter questioned.

"That's what I'm looking for," I said. "There has to be some way to get over there, unless it's accessed from upstairs or outside.

We inched slowly down the wall until we came to the hutch containing the liquor. I held the candle towards the back of it.

"Look here," I yelled. "Help me move this monstrosity."

It took all three of us to move the large oak hutch away from the wall, heavy with the weight of all the liquor.

Behind it was a five-foot high, two and a half foot wide solid plank door with a black, rusted, wrought iron pull-chain latch at the top. The massive hinges creaked as we struggled to open it. After several tries, and a few cuss words, the door opened enough to admit each of us in single file.

"Looks eerie," I said. "I'll bet that door hasn't been opened in twenty years."

"Would you look at that," remarked Stewart, holding the candle high as he entered the hidden room. "It was under our noses all the time."

"Jezzuss," exclaimed Peter. "Those things are huge."

Inside the room there must have been fifty large batteries, stacked on shelves from the floor up to the ceiling, the type used with large diesel engines, stacked on shelves from the floor up to the ceiling. Thick wires connected each battery to the next, and then to a large metal box mounted on the opposite wall.

"Someone's been in here recently," I said. "Some of these batteries are pretty new."

"That's probably an inverter," Stewart pointed to the metal box. "It would convert this DC current to AC. I'm willing to bet there are solar panels on top of this building charging these batteries."

"Seems to solve part of the mystery of the fence," I said. "The generator could be what is charging them. They're close enough; the generator is right outside."

Just then a large bolt of lightning cracked. It sounded as if it hit right on top of the hotel, followed immediately by a deafening clap of thunder that shook the hotel. It made all of us jump. A loud crash from somewhere upstairs followed several seconds of what sounded like baseballs hitting the hotel. Smoke poured out of the large steel box Stewart had said was an inverter.

"Holy shit! That was close!" yelled Peter.

The wind was still howling. Upstairs we could hear doors slamming, items crashing to the floor, and glass breaking. We retreated to the main part of the basement. I looked for a place to sit down and wait out the storm. The only place was on the stairs, which I quickly claimed.

***

As rapid as the storm blew in, it abruptly ended. The water was still dripping into the basement through the overhead floorboards, and the majority of it had flowed to the lower part of the earthen floor where it pooled to several inches in depth.

"Think it's safe to go up?" Peter asked as he eyed the top of the stairs.

"We can give it a try," Stewart said.

I led the parade up the stairs and tried to open the door. It wouldn't budge. "Shit, not again," I said. I hit the door with my shoulder. The top part moved and then bounced back closed.

"Let me at it," Stewart said. I retreated back down the stairs and Stewart took my place. He hit the door three times with his whole body before it finally opened enough to let him pass through. I followed.

As I entered the lobby, I turned back to Peter who was halfway up the stairs, "Don't forget to put out the candles," I reminded him. "We don't need a fire on top of all this."

Peter went back down and collected the candles, blowing them out as he came up the stairs. We gathered in the lobby and stood around with our mouths agape. I couldn't believe the destruction.

"First order, we have to find Dorothy. I hope she made it to her room," Peter said.

To say the hotel was heavily damaged would be the understatement of the year. It was completely trashed. All the windows were blown out, the furniture was strewn about, and the whole place was soaked. A light wind blew in the lobby through the broken windows.

Peter and Stewart headed up the stairs to Dorothy's room.

"I'll check the kitchen—see how much damage we have and how much food was affected," I said.

I entered the kitchen and found it in remarkably good shape. One window was broken, and that was only the upper half. There was some water on the floor from the rain, but no food or appliances had been destroyed or affected. I was relieved; at least we would be able to fix meals.

***

Peter and Stewart climbed to the third floor and found all the doors shut. Water was puddling into the hallway from under several of them. They knocked on Dorothy's door.

"Dorothy!" yelled Stewart. "Dorothy, are you okay?"

There was no answer.

"If you don't answer, we're coming in."

They opened her door. She was lying on the floor amid a thin layer of water between the bed and bureau; face down, with her arms next to her sides.

Peter ran over and shook her vigorously, "Dorothy, are you all right?"

He could see the water was dark red around her upper torso with a heavy pool of blood around her head.

"Let's roll her over," Stewart said. "Give me a hand."

It took both of them to turn her. There was a large shard of glass sticking out the front of her neck. It had embedded deeply, severing her carotid artery. Smaller pieces of glass were stuck in her abdomen, arms and legs.

"Looks like she bled to death. In the wrong place at the wrong time." Peter shook his head. "Who's next?"

"Well, we warned her," Stewart said.

"Yeah, but still..."

They covered her body with a wet blanket.

"I'm getting out of here," Peter said heading for the door.

"Let's go check my room," Stewart said. As he started to leave, he hesitated momentarily, looking back at Dorothy. They exited her room and gently shut the door.

***

I climbed the stairs and joined them in the hallway. "You find Dorothy? How is she?"

"She's dead. She caught a piece of glass in the neck when her window blew out," Stewart said. "Severed an artery."

I looked at Stewart, despair sucking the energy out of me. "Son of a bitch!" I exclaimed. "Not her, too!" After several moments I looked at Peter out of the corner of my eye, "Now who's going to make pancakes for us?"

"You're one sick fuck," Peter said poking a finger at me, but he, too, was smiling.

I was joking, but in my heart I felt bad. What else could I do? Cry? Scream? What good would it do? There didn't seem to be any end to the madness of this place. A few minutes later I felt bad for cracking the joke, but I didn't want Peter and Stewart to know.

We walked down the hall to Stewart's room. It was a mess. The floor and carpet were soaked, the mattress was half off the bed and wet, and everything he had on the bureau had been blown off. The mirror on the wall was broken and all the windows were blown out.

"Where's my laptop?"

"Is that all you care about?" Peter asked.

"Right now, yes. After all this crap we've gone through and endured—the only thing that would make all this worthwhile is to win the contest and get paid a huge chunk of money."

"Well, if that's all you're worrying about—don't. I've got it tied up. You don't stand a chance in hell." I smiled as I gave him a quick glance. He flipped me the finger.

"Where did you leave it anyway?" I asked.

"Hell, I don't remember."

We searched until Stewart found his computer in the bottom bureau drawer, dry and working.

"The battery is about dead. It needs recharging."

"Yeah, you can do that—if we have any more electricity. I need to inspect my room," I said as I headed out the door. Peter accompanied me.

We went down the hallway and entered my room. Everything seemed to be in place, no windows were broken, but the area was drenched in several locations. Water still dripped down through the ceiling plaster. I felt around my bed. It was saturated—there'd be no sleeping in it tonight. I pulled out my computer, which I'd tucked under the mattress. Turning it on, it still worked. I looked at some of the other rooms on the third floor and found most to have similar damage.

"Let's go check out my mine now," Peter said.

We went down to the second floor and entered his room.

"Well, how about that?" exclaimed Peter. The room was in almost perfect condition—untouched by the storm. There were only a couple of small puddles where water was dripping by the door and the outside wall, seeping through from the saturation upstairs.

We went back down to the lobby.

"How the hell are we going to carry Dorothy all the way downstairs and out to the cemetery?" Peter posed as we neared the bottom landing. "That's going to be one hell of a load."

"I know, but what else are we going to do? Leave her here?"

"Not likely."

"Yeah, tell me that after we lug her ass down the street and dig a hole big enough to bury her. I can hear the jokes now. You better start thinking about how we're going to haul her down there," I said.

"Worry about it tomorrow. We've got plenty to lose sleep over tonight. How's our food supply?"

"The kitchen is in pretty good shape. No real damage except an upper window blown out and a little water on the floor."

"I need to turn on the generator," Peter said. "It's getting dark."

CHAPTER 20
The Aftermath

Peter went out to the generator shed. Moments later he returned.

"Get more candles out," he announced as he came back inside the hotel.

"Why?" Stewart asked.

"The generator is trashed."

"Trashed? How bad?" I asked.

"Totaled, toast, caput. The whole shed's gone; probably took a direct lightning strike. Only a small part of one charred wall remains. The generator and motor are still there, but the motor's fried—I couldn't even get it to turn over. I'm betting that really close lightning crack we heard was what did it in. The noises we heard right after that were probably the pieces of splinters raining down on the hotel. There won't be any electricity from it tonight—maybe never."

"Great." Stewart rolled his eyes upward. "What else can go wrong? We just found the batteries and now we can't use them."

"Why not?" I couldn't figure out what he was trying to impart.

"The generator is what was probably charging the batteries. No generator, no batteries."

"That's possible, Stu, but those things are huge, they'd probably keep a charge for quite a long time. We haven't discounted the possibility of solar panels either."

"We'll have to check it out tomorrow. For now, anyway, we don't have a thing."

"We better start thinking about how much drinking water we have," I said. "No generator, no pump, no water."

"I would guess about twenty gallons in the pressure tank and whatever else is in the lines," Peter said.

"That's not going to last us all that long," Stewart said. "We'll have to gather as much water as we can for all our other necessities. Save the water in the lines strictly for drinking."

"What are we going to do about the lobby? We don't have any windows. It's certainly not habitable anymore."

"Take the chairs and whatever we can use and put them in the kitchen. We can board up the one window that's broken out and at least make the room weather-tight. We may have to live in there for a while," Peter said.

"I'm going to see if I can find a dry mattress and pillow and bring it down to the kitchen," I said. "I can't sleep in my room tonight. I'll open the windows tomorrow—maybe things will dry out in a couple days, but until then..."

"Me too," Stewart said. "My room's a mess."

"I'll give both of you a hand. Mine's fine for now. Let's get going though, it's getting dark."

In Ada's room we found a completely dry mattress, but the window was broken and small pools of water were on the floor. Her room had made it through the storm without much damage. Although it was on the third floor, it was opposite the wind. Jessie's room had a broken window, but the rain didn't get to the mattress.

We wiped up the wet spots in the kitchen, hauled the mattresses and some blankets downstairs, and found a couple of dry pillows. I would normally refuse to sleep on another person's pillow and sheets. But we were in survival mode now. Those things didn't matter anymore.

Cold beans and stew were warmed up over the glow and heat of several candles. We drank water sparingly. Twilight had come by the time we had finished eating.

"What are we going to do now?" Peter asked while we sat staring blankly at the kitchen table.

"Let's take a look at everything in the morning. Then we can see what we're up against," suggested Stewart. "I'm tired, I'm pissed, and I can't think straight right now."

"We're going to have to go outside from now on. We can't be using any water to flush toilets," I said.

"Yeah, you're right," Peter said. "As a matter of fact, give me one of those candles. I'll be right back."

"How many candles do we have left?" Stewart asked.

"There's a few more downstairs in the basement— in the drawer of the liquor cabinet. We'll have enough for a little while," I said. "Use them sparingly."

Peter came back in from outside and threw a partially used roll of toilet paper on the kitchen table. "I'm going to bed. I'll see you guys in the morning."

Stewart and I put the sheets and blankets on the mattresses and settled in for the night. I wasn't looking forward to the next day.

CHAPTER 21
Truth or Consequence

Day 39

The next morning brought a bright blue, cloudless sky with just a whisper of a warm breeze. The humidity still hung in the air; it looked to be a very hot and muggy day. While eating a breakfast of cereal and powdered milk, it was decided that burying Dorothy was the first order of business. We didn't want her getting ripe on us, and with the coming heat it wouldn't take too long.

"How are we going to get her down to the cemetery?" I wanted to know.

"We'll probably have to carry her as much as possible. We might even have to drag her part ways," Stewart said.

"Drag her?" Peter asked.

"Yeah, why, do you think she'll feel it?" Stewart smirked with a mouthful of cereal. "You find a wheelbarrow and we can roll her down."

"Let's wait a while until the street dries up a bit. I don't want to drag her through the mud," I said.

"We can dig the grave," Stewart said. "That in itself is going to be a job and I don't want to do it at high noon."

After finishing breakfast I went outside for the first time since the storm. Peter and Stewart followed a few minutes later.

"My God!" Stewart said. "Look at this place."

Several of the old buildings were flattened; debris was strewn all over town. Any quaintness it held as an old western town had been obliterated. Almost every window that had survived through the decades in the old town, was now gone. It was going to be like maneuvering through an obstacle course just to walk down the street.

The shovel was still alongside the building, although not where it had been placed. The winds had moved it about twenty feet to the rear, near the remnants of the generator shack. We walked down to the cemetery avoiding the hundreds of boards, large splinters, tarpaper, and wreckage strewn about the street.

"All that work we did for a bonfire sure was a waste of time," I said.

"Yeah, if we would have waited a week, the tornado would've given us all the scrap we needed," chimed in Peter. "We wouldn't have had to tear all those buildings apart."

When we arrived at the cemetery, we all took turns as usual digging the grave. Morose as it was, the activity had almost become routine. We didn't have to discuss anything; we just dug. And dug. The hole had to be almost twice the size of Ada's and Nicki's. To our relief, the soaking rain made digging a little easier. It must have been noon when we finished. Our clothes were soaked with sweat. The heat and humidity took its toll.

"Let's wait till around six to move her," I suggested still trying to catch my breath. I had exerted all the energy I could muster for now.

"Sounds good to me," Peter said. "We'll have do it then for sure though."

"We might as well go ahead and bring her downstairs. That's going to take some doing in itself. At least then we'll have a break before we have to take her down the street," Stewart said.

"Okay." I sighed. "I guess we should."

Back at the hotel, we revived ourselves with a couple sips of water before going up to the third floor.

We stood in Dorothy's room, looking at the large blanket-draped form on the floor trying to figure out how to get her down two flights of stairs.

"How much do ya figure she weighs?" I asked.

"Three-hundred to three-twenty," guessed Peter.

"I'd say three-twenty-five to three-fifty," Stewart said.

"Anyway you put it, that's over a hundred pounds a person," I said.

"This is going to be like moving a beached whale," muttered Peter.

"Spread out and find all the bedspreads and sheets you can," directed Stewart as he slowly walked out into the hallway. "I don't think we can carry her, so let's make this as easy and clean as we can."

Ralph's bed was stripped, and even though damp, the sheets and bedspread were brought to Dorothy's room. We wrapped her in several layers of the sheets and then rolled her onto the spread-out blankets. Rigor mortis had already set in, which helped us with our task.

"Okay, lets see how easy she slides," Stewart said. "Grab hold."

Stewart and Peter each grabbed a leading corner of the blankets, with me taking the two back corners by her feet. I pulled up my end as much as I could to take some of the weight off the load, but it probably wasn't much. We wedged her out the door and slid her down the hall to the staircase doing a duck-walk.

"We'll have to be careful going down these stairs. There's close to nine hundred pounds between all of us and Dorothy. I don't trust this old staircase to hold that much weight. If you hear anything start to crack, back off and spread the load," instructed Stewart.

"Wait," Peter said. "Let's think about this a minute. Let me get a rope to tie around her feet. George can stay at the top of the stairs and anchor the rope, letting her down easy while we guide and pull from the bottom. That way we won't lose her coming down."

"Sounds better," I said. "I think there's still some rope in the basement."

"I'll look," Stewart said as he went down the stairs.

He returned in a few minutes with about twenty feet of rope.

"Wrap the blankets around her and I'll tie this around her ankles. Take her down head first," Stewart said. "George, if you don't think you can hold the weight back, wrap the rope around the base of the ball at the top of the banister and let it out gradually. When we get to the second floor landing, we can do the same thing again."

"Got ya," I said.

"We should have let her have a room on the second floor," remarked Peter as he lifted Dorothy's legs to get the rope under her.

"Wasn't an option at the time," I said.

Peter and Stewart pulled the corners of the blankets towards the downward side of the stairs while I wrapped the rope around the base of the ball. I started letting out the rope as we eased the body down the stairs. She was almost half way down to the second floor landing when it happened.

"If this doesn't look like three monkeys fucking a duck, nothing does," remarked Stewart with a straight face.

I started laughing and stopped letting the rope out, which caused more tension on the ball the rope was looped around. It started tilting, coming loose.

"Hurry up! The ball is coming off!" Peter shouted.

It suddenly popped off the top of the banister. Dorothy's body slid down the stairs, ramming Peter who tripped and fell backwards onto the landing. Stewart tried to hold on, but the body kept sliding down the last several steps, ending up with Dorothy's head in Peter's crotch.

"God-damn it, George!" yelled Peter.

Stewart bent over, reeling with laughter, pointing at Peter. I broke into a belly laugh, tears streaming from my eyes.

"Peter, I always thought she had a thing for you," I said, trying to catch my breath.

Peter finally cracked a smile as Stewart and I continued laughing at his predicament.

"You two are assholes." He got up from the floor.

"I know," Stewart said.

Several minutes passed before we regained our composure. I stepped down to the second floor landing and wrapped the rope again around the ball at the top of the banister. They pulled Dorothy's body to the top of the last flight of stairs and started easing her down to the first floor. Before we could even get the body halfway down the flight of stairs, the ball again broke off with a sudden "crack."

"Watch out," I yelled.

Peter and Stewart jumped out of the way this time and watched the body thump its way to the bottom, coming to rest half on the floor of the lobby, half still on the stairs.

"Shit, I hope this isn't a prelude to the rest of the day," Stewart said.

I couldn't help myself as I went down the stairs with a big grin plastered on my face. "At least we have her down now."

I untied the rope; they picked up the corners of their ends of the blankets, and we slid the body to the front door. Even in death, Dorothy was still a pain in the ass.

***

We had peanut butter and jelly sandwiches for lunch.

"Good thing Dorothy took the time to make these loaves of bread before the tornado." Stewart cut another piece from the loaf.

We went to our rooms to try to clean up and dry things out. Stewart and I took our mattresses and bed linens outside. We stood the mattresses up against the side of the building facing the sun and the sheets were spread out on the porch railings.

"I thought this contest was going to be more of a vacation than a third-world survival mission," Peter said to me as he swept the water out of his room. "I haven't even had time to write for several days."

"We're going to have to figure out what to do about the water situation soon. We don't have a whole lot left," I said.

"I'm thinking we all may have to leave this place," Peter said. "We can't stay if we don't have water."

"Any chance of you fixing the generator?"

"I don't think so; I'm not a mechanic. Maybe you or Stewart can look at it."

"It wouldn't do any good for me to look at it. I don't know shit about that kind of stuff. I wouldn't know the motor from the generator."

A while later all three of us were in the kitchen.

"You know anything about gas engines or generators?" I asked Stewart.

"No, can't say I do. I've done a little wiring, but I don't know anything about engines and that stuff."

"Well, we're kind of screwed then. We've got less than twenty gallons of water left. It's not going to last us very long."

"I'll look at it. Maybe we can hook the batteries up to the well pump through the inverter. I doubt they have matching voltages, but it's worth a try."

"I think we all ought to leave and try to find our way out of here," Peter said. "I'm betting the inverter is fried too. Remember the smoke that poured from it after the lightning strike? There's probably not enough electricity flowing through it to light a candle."

"We'll have to leave if we can't get the pump working. Without water, we haven't got a chance in hell to survive out here." Stewart paced the floor.

"I can't go with you," I said.

He turned towards me. "Why not?"

"Shit, you've seen how good a shape I'm in. I can't even help you dig a grave without gasping for breath. If the heat didn't kill me, the hike would. I'd do nothing but hold you up, and that's not what you need if you're going to make time. Besides, I hate snakes. I get the jeebies just thinking about them crawling around out there."

"You want to stay here by yourself?" Peter asked.

"No, *I don't want to*, but I don't see any other options, do you?"

He thought for a few moments. "No."

"I'm not going to have you two babysitting me, constantly urging me on, holding my hand. Look, if I go with you and I run out of steam, you'd have to leave me, and I'd die anyway. If I hold you up out on the prairie, and you don't leave me, we'd probably run out of water and food, and we'd all die. If I stay here and you two make it, I'll make it. If you don't, then I'll die here. The way I see it, any way you cut it, all three of our fates are tied together."

No one spoke for a few moments.

"He has a point." Peter tapped on the table, staring at Stewart.

"I suppose," Stewart said. "But I still don't like it. I think we should all stay together."

"You guys talk about it between yourselves. I'm going to work on my manuscript." I got up from the table.

"What?" Stewart asked sarcastically. "You still think this is a contest? You gotta' be nuts! How could you believe that?"

"I don't know if it is or not, but, just in case, I'm going to keep writing. I need that money."

"If you live to see it."

I knew he was right. "Anyway, I'm going to work on it this afternoon. Besides, what else have I got to do? I can't use the computer anymore; I want to save the rest of the battery. I'm going to have to write it out. I have pens, but do we have any paper?" I asked.

"There were a few pads in the hutch in the lobby. They're probably wet, though," Peter said.

"I need more chapter titles," I said "Anyone have any suggestions? My next chapter brings us to where we caught Harry raping Ada."

I didn't think Peter would want to write anymore either, but I wanted to keep a positive attitude. They were going to leave, possibly to their deaths, but I didn't want them thinking about it; anything to distract from the moment.

"*Caught in the Act* might be a good name, followed by *The Trial*," Peter finally suggested.

"I like the first one, but how about *The Inquisition* for the second?" Stewart asked. "We sure as hell didn't have any trial."

He was smiling. I was glad he decided to contribute to the conversation.

"Yes we did," Peter said. "Harry just wasn't there."

Stewart laughed.

My eyes widened. I knew he had exactly what I wanted. "That's a good one," I said. "I like that. How about the next one? That'll bring us up to Harry's death or execution, however you want to portray it. I kind of like, *The Escape*. It doesn't really make you think either way."

"I could accept that," Stewart said wryly, "if I was going to write anymore. By the way, which way are you guys going to write about Harry's death?" He looked at both of us. I didn't volunteer an answer; neither did Peter. "Come on, how do you propose to write it, execution or accidental death?"

Stewart continued looking inquisitively at both Peter and me. Neither of us seemed to want to state our intentions first.

"I haven't decided yet," I responded. "I know we're supposed to write about our circumstances and real life situations here, and it does add drama, but we may really be screwing ourselves if the authorities don't see it the way we did, if and when we get out of here."

"Who says the manuscript has to be marketed as a true story? Can't it be published as a novel?" Peter questioned.

"You could publish it as fiction," Stewart said, "but it probably won't sell as well. Hell, after everything we've been through, and after all the bodies we've buried, this would be a huge seller as a real-life, non-fiction, with or with out the execution of Harry. I think we have to protect ourselves first. It'll be just as exciting with Harry electrocuting himself while trying to escape."

"You know that's bullshit, Stu. An execution would be shocking to the average person. An accidental electrocution is a yawner," Peter retorted. "Why do you care anyway? I thought you weren't going to write anymore."

I broke in. "I might write it both ways and decide when it's time to turn it in. I still don't think we had any options with Harry and I don't feel bad about what we did. Yeah, I've had second thoughts, but hell, we're prisoners here. We're isolated. We made a decision that had to be made. It's like we're on a ship, the captain is in charge and he's the final authority. Combined, we're the Captain, and we made Harry walk the plank."

Stewart's demeanor suddenly changed. "Fuck both of you! That's not the point." He was unyielding, angry. "You can feel good about yourself all you want. I set the electrocution up as an accident so we wouldn't get caught up in legalities by some over-reaching, do-gooder prosecutor and end up being charged with murder. It's not just your ass on the line—it's mine also. You want to go to prison for the rest of your life? I don't, and whatever you write will affect all of us. I don't want some district attorney, who needs to make a name for himself, cutting my balls off to get elected next time. I can see the headlines now, *Captives Turn On One— Executed By Mock Judge and Jury*. This isn't just about you; it's about the future of all three of us."

Silence followed Stewart's tirade.

"I have to agree with Stewart." Peter rubbed his chin and folded his hands on the table. He spoke slowly. "We can't take a chance like that, and we don't have the women to back up our story anymore. They were our witnesses, our alibis, but they had to go and die. I don't want to have a great book and enjoy the profits in the crowbar hotel with Bubba as my cellmate, or have to spend every dime on defense lawyers. There's no good reason to take that kind of risk."

"There are only three people in the world that know the absolute truth, and we're all sitting right here," Stewart said tapping heavily on the table with his index finger.

He was talking directly to me this time.

"Don't put our butts in jeopardy just to sell a few extra books. Believe me, if you write it as an execution and publish it as non-fiction, you won't want to be my cellmate if we get prosecuted and convicted. I'll arrange another *accident*, or beat the eternal crap out of you."

I had to relent. "Okay, okay. I'll go the non-fiction route and leave out the execution. Harry died accidentally while trying to escape."

Stewart sighed. "Thank you.

"I'm going to find the paper." I got up from the table and headed for the lobby. Peter thought he was being discrete when he spoke in a low voice to Stewart, but I heard them both.

"I hope he's telling us the truth," Peter said. "He's a good guy, but I don't know if I trust him on this. What do you think?"

"His butt's on the line too. He'll come to his senses."

CHAPTER 22
The Dead Speak

Six o'clock rolled around and it was time to take Dorothy's body down to the cemetery. It had cooled off slightly, but the sun still heated the prairie to what felt like a hundred degrees. We didn't have a thermometer, but it was hot. Peter and Stewart took the front corners again, with me pulling up the rear.

"George, your face looks like a ripe tomato, let's stop and rest a minute," Peter suggested after we had traveled only about a hundred feet.

I was sweating profusely again. We stopped several more times as we dragged the body down to the gravesite. We tried placing Dorothy in the hole as gently as possible, but that wasn't to be. As we pulled her over the opening, the blanket ripped and she did a belly flop into the hole, landing face down. It wasn't pretty or dignified, but we weren't about to try to roll her over.

I was physically drained. Peter and Stewart took turns shoveling the dirt back in over Dorothy's body. An hour later she was fully covered. We stood silently together for a few moments next to the grave.

"As much as a pain-in-the-ass Dorothy started out to be, she came through for us when it counted," I said.

"And she made great pancakes and bread," Peter added.

Stewart nodded. "Yes, she did."

As we walked back to the hotel, I broached the topic that hung in the air, but no one seemed to want to bring up. I didn't want to sound as though I was pushing them to go, but we needed to discuss it. I knew Peter was having reservations.

"Have you guys decided to leave, or stay here with me and stick it out?"

"We haven't talked about it yet," Stewart replied. After several moments he continued, "I don't think we really have a choice though, there's just not enough water. If I'm going to die, I'd rather it be quick than die of thirst, although I don't particularly enjoy the thought of a snakebite either after watching Randy die."

"I've been thinking it over," I said. "The last two guys who left, Jessie and Ralph, ended up buried down in the cemetery. By whom, we don't know, and how they died, we don't know. I don't believe they were gone long enough to die from a lack of water or food. If they died from snakebite or were attacked by coyotes it's one thing. If they were murdered, we need to know that, too. I think we ought to find out how they died."

"What do you want to do?" Peter questioned. "Dig them up?"

"You got a better idea?" I asked. "How else are we going to find out?"

"Oh my God. Do you know how bad that's going to smell?" Peter asked. "Not *my* favorite activity."

"It's probably not a bad idea," chimed in Stewart. "We do need to know how they died. Maybe we could be more careful, do things differently. There'll be two of us this time. It might make a difference if they were attacked, but it's possible they died of snakebite, scorpions, or whatever else is out there."

"I'd still like to know who buried them," I said.

"All right, all right" Peter said as we got back to the hotel, obviously disgusted, but outvoted. "When do you want to do it?"

"How about now?" Stewart replied.

"How about tomorrow morning?" I asked. "I've had enough of playing in the dirt for today. I'm hot and I'm tired."

"Tomorrow it is," Peter said.

"I'm going to check on the pump and see if I can rewire it to the batteries," Stewart said. "It's probably a waste of time, but it's worth a try. Either of you want to give me a hand?"

"I will," I said.

We went into the basement with the candles again. We traced the wires from the inverter, which crossed the basement near the pump. They were thick, unlike the wires going to the pump from the generator. It took hours, but Stewart masterfully cut the cables, continuously sawing with a serrated kitchen knife for what seemed forever. He then connected some smaller wires we'd cut away from the ceiling, wrapping the wires tightly around the cable. The air was stale and humid, and even though the basement was probably the coolest place for miles, sweat poured off us. Stewart then began connecting the smaller wires to the pump, using his pocketknife to turn the screws. He attached the first wire.

"When I touch this next wire to the pump connection, the pump should start," Stewart said. "If it works, we can stay, if not..."

I held my breath. I desperately wanted the pump to work. I didn't want to stay here by myself and I knew this final act would determine whether they stayed or would have to leave. I said a silent prayer.

He touched the wire to the connection. Nothing.

"Fuck!" he yelled. He looked back over all the wiring, tracing everything, making sure he had it just right.

"It should have worked," he said. "The inverter has to be burnt out."

"Let's get out of here," I said. "There's nothing else we can do."

"At least we know."

Upstairs, we gave Peter the bad news. We gathered in the kitchen and worked on manuscripts by candlelight during the evening. Even Stewart. I didn't say anything to him; maybe he just wanted something to keep him busy. I don't know why I continued working on it, I knew in my heart this wasn't a real contest—but maybe, just maybe... It was probably also good therapy; besides, I now considered it more of a journal than a manuscript. If we didn't make it, hopefully someone would find our notes and give them to the police. The assholes that put us here needed to be captured and prosecuted.

Day 40

The next morning, after another tasteless breakfast of cornflakes, we returned to the cemetery. We decided to dig up Jessie's grave first to see how he had died. The dirt was still loose and it only took about an hour and a half of digging between the three of us to get to the body. Whoever had buried him hadn't dug too deep. It was wrapped in a heavy, clear, plastic tarp, secured with gray duct tape.

"Who in the hell would have a plastic tarp out here in the middle of nowhere?" I posed.

"Someone who was ready to bury bodies," Stewart said.

The body had definitely decomposed and the stench was overwhelming. Peter ran off a few dozen yards, bent over, and heaved his breakfast. Stewart and I also had to stop and get away from the area for a few minutes.

"Breakfast taste better the second time around, Pete?" Stewart asked with a laugh.

Peter coughed. "Didn't taste that good the first time."

"Anybody got any bright ideas how to get past the smell?" Stewart asked.

"We can't get rid of it, but if anyone has any cotton, we can put some in our noses. Maybe put a little aftershave on the cotton to hide the smell," I said.

"I've got something," Stewart said. "Be right back."

He strolled back to the hotel, in no particular hurry. I didn't blame him; I don't think any of us were very anxious to continue. Peter and I found a seat up-wind and several yards away from the grave until Stewart returned.

"I didn't have any aftershave, but I found some perfume in Dorothy's room, and these." He held up a box of cotton swabs.

We unraveled the cotton from the ends of the swabs, wadded it, splashed a little perfume on it and stuffed it up our nostrils to help conceal the rancid smell.

We continued digging until we had removed enough dirt to uncover the body. Stewart jumped down into the grave and lifted the plastic end that held Jessie's feet. Peter and I grabbed it and pulled Jessie out.

"Your turn to go back and get a knife," Stewart said to Peter. "I didn't bring my pocketknife."

Peter went back to the hotel, returned with a kitchen knife. He sliced the plastic open from the head down to the shoulders. When we opened the plastic there wasn't any immediate indication of how he died. Stewart continued cutting and unwrapping the plastic down to the waist. There, in the middle of Jessie's chest was an unmistakable gunshot wound.

"Guess we know now," Peter said.

The gunshot wound was a hole almost the size of a fist.

"That's an exit wound," Stewart said. "Turn him over."

We did and found a small hole in his back where the bullet had entered.

"He was shot in the back with a high-powered firearm. My guess is a rifle," Stewart murmured as he examined the wound. "He most likely didn't even know what hit him. Probably died instantly."

"Kind of throws a new light on things, doesn't it?" I posed.

"Should we look at Ralph also?" Peter asked.

"No, I don't think it matters. We know Jessie was definitely killed by a gunshot. Whether Ralph was or not, isn't going to change a thing," Stewart said.

I wanted this over with. "Let's get him reburied."

No one said a word as we gently placed him into the grave and then shoveled the dirt back in. We walked back to the hotel in silence and gathered in the kitchen.

"Why would someone go to all this expense, all the details of getting us out here, just to see all of us killed?" Peter inquired.

"Doesn't seem to make any sense, does it?" Stewart asked.

"It may. Think about it," I said. "Whoever survives all this probably has a publishable manuscript; it's going to be a great story, possibly worth millions. That's why we were told we had to write about our experiences here; everyone had to write the same story. Now, whether anyone will believe it really happened, I don't know. Could it be an agency or publisher who *needs* a great selling book? But how in the world could they think they could get away with killing everyone and still go free? It would seem that they'd need one of us to confirm the details of the story. In many ways it still doesn't make sense."

"Why would they need one of us? If they have the resources to conduct this contest, they could pay someone to say they were one of the contestants, to confirm the story," Peter said.

"Even if they didn't mean for any of us to die or be killed, they virtually kidnapped and imprisoned us without any medical aid and no way to obtain any help if needed," Stewart said. "There has to be a reason."

"We should start thinking like them...criminals; think out of the box," I said. "Let me throw a couple of possibilities at ya. Why does the book need to be marketed in the U.S.? Wouldn't it be just as big a seller in Europe or Australia for example? And what if they changed the names? We changed them; they could too. Why does it have to take place in Wyoming or Colorado? Couldn't they change the place to Australia, somewhere in the outback? That would throw anyone off the trail. There're all kinds of possibilities, but the one thing they can't have is witnesses."

I must have hit a nerve or something. Neither said anything for a few moments.

"I never thought of any of that. Do either of you know of an agent or publisher that demented?" Peter asked.

"They were all assholes," I said. "I only had contact over the phone with jerks and I always ended up yelling at them. Never met any of them in person."

Stewart just shook his head. "Me too. We have to assume we're being watched all the time. Ralph and Jessie left during the day; maybe that was their downfall. Whoever is watching us could easily have seen them leave, followed and killed them at his leisure. I don't intend to get shot. If we leave at night and only travel at night, maybe whoever killed them won't spot us. We just might be able to make it."

"Sounds like a plan," I said.

"I still don't like it," Peter said. "What chance do we have against someone with a high-powered rifle who intends to kill us?"

"What chance do we have staying here?" Stewart asked, his eyes fixated on Peter. "We're almost out of water. We have to take the risk."

"Remember, Peter, your destiny is also mine," I said. If you don't survive, I won't either. I can't stay here very long with just a few gallons of water. You two have to make it—I'm counting on you."

"I still don't know if I want to try," Peter said.

"I understand what you're thinking. I'd go with Stewart if I thought I could make it, but I know I can't. I'd just hold him up. But it's entirely up to you whether you go or not. We can both stay here if that's your decision."

"I'm going no matter what," Stewart said.

"When are you planning to leave?" Peter asked.

"Either tonight or tomorrow night, I haven't decided yet."

Peter drew a deep breath. "Okay, count me in. This shit really sucks, but I guess we really don't have any other options."

Stewart pounded his fist on the table. "That bastard ain't going to get us. We just have to be a little smarter than him and not play his game."

"We'll play the game, but we'll play it our way. What if we both go in different directions?" Peter suggested. "He wouldn't be able to follow both of us at the same time."

"No, but he has a better chance of getting one of us. Maybe he won't try anything if we stick together," Stewart said. "He hasn't taken on two of us at a time yet."

"Is there anything I can do to help you get ready?" I asked.

"Not that I know of. We'll need a couple gallons of water each and canned food," Stewart said. "Maybe some matches, candles and a knife."

"And a lot of prayers," Peter said under his breath.

"Let's wait until tomorrow night, Stu. Give me some time to do a couple things."

"What's that?"

"Pray. Work on my manuscript. Write a will."

Stewart chuckled.

"Okay, I suppose one day isn't going to make a hell of a bit of difference."

CHAPTER 23
Double or Nothing

Day 41

The next day, I helped gather enough food for Stewart and Peter for five days' travel. They each filled two gallon jugs with water. The matches and candles were wrapped with their food and spare clothes in bedrolls to be draped over their shoulders. Stewart retrieved a couple of steak knives from the kitchen and gave one to Peter. They were ready to go by noon. The remainder of the day they rested and prepared for the trip.

Peter wrote a last will and testament, had Stewart and me witness it, and then gave it to me.

"If you don't hear from me again, make sure the person on the envelope gets this."

"Don't count on it, Peter. If you don't make it, I won't either. Like I told you, my friend, my fate is in your hands."

"Well, if I don't make it and Stewart does, take care of it for me."

"All right, if I ever get back to civilization, I'll see it gets to the right person."

He then gave me another envelope.

"This is the letter Jessie gave me to give to his parents. Would you take care of that too?"

"Sure."

***

That evening, as a farewell, I built a campfire right in the middle of the street and cooked a hot meal from our meager supply of canned goods; corned beef hash, canned potatoes, corn and, for dessert, canned peaches. I brought out the few remaining chairs and placed them upwind of the smoke. We had an honest-to-goodness cookout. I should have thought of it earlier as it kind of helped raise everyone's spirits. I wish we had some beer; it would have been perfect!

"George, I didn't know you could cook this well," Stewart said with his mouth full of hash. "Hell, if Dorothy would have known this, she'd have made you queen of the kitchen and demanded you cook every night."

"Yeah, and she'd have probably gained another fifty pounds." After a short laugh, I asked, "What time you guys planning on leaving tonight?"

"I'd like to leave about an hour after sundown," Stewart said. "We ought-a make some good distance before sunrise. I figure we can find a gully or wash to camp in, that way it'll be hard for anyone to find us."

Peter was tapping nervously on his plate with his fork. "Peter?" I asked.

His eye had developed a twitch.

"I still don't like it. I've never been a survivalist, and I haven't camped out since I was a kid. As a matter of fact, I fucking hate sleeping outdoors. I guess I'm what you'd call a city slicker; I only camp out at hotels. But I'd rather go walking through the prairie *during the day*. At least then we can see the fucking snakes before I step on them, and I could see any assholes coming to kill me before they get to me. I keep getting these mental pictures of someone sneaking up on us at night and sticking a rifle up my ass."

"Now there's a real vision." I laughed, trying to lighten the mood light.

"I'll just have to follow Stewart's lead. That's why I'm so hesitant—I have no knowledge about the outdoors, no control over anything, and we have no way to defend ourselves. I'm really nervous about this."

"If I were you guys, I'd take several changes of socks. You'll be more comfortable and you can toss them after you use them," I said. "And take a hat, the sun gets pretty damn hot. You'll get burned if you're not undercover during the day."

"Both good ideas," Stewart said.

"By the time we get anywhere, if they don't see us coming, they'll smell us," Peter chuckled.

"I was going to mention that," I said.

"Which way do you want to' go?" Peter asked as he turned to Stewart. "Let's try south this time—see if he's actually telling us the best way."

"I was really thinking 'bout going north," Stewart replied.

"That's what I was originally thinking. I know this asshole wants us to go south, but is he keeping us from going south by suggesting it?"

"Good God, Peter, you're thinking too much again. We might as well toss a coin for all we know. Which way would you go, George?"

It was a good discussion, but ultimately they had to decide, north or south. It was bending my mind trying to figure out what kind of psyche game the author of the signs at the gravesites was playing. And who was it that was watching us? How did he find out when and where Jessie and Ralph left? Was there just one of them, or several?

"I'd probably have to vote on north, also. I suppose there's only one way to actually find out. But, since I'm not the one sticking his ass out..."

"North it is then," Stewart said. "We can second guess ourselves to death, we just have to pick a direction and go."

"Whoa," Peter yelled, sticking up his hand. "What about going south? What about my vote? George isn't going with us."

"Peter, I'm going north. You can go south if you want, but I'm going north. Decide for yourself which way you want to go."

No one said anything for a few minutes.

"One more thing," I suggested. "Think about going under the fence in a different place. Whoever is watching this place knows where Ralph and Jessie snuck out. He's probably keeping an eye on that spot. Go out on the north side, behind the old general store."

"I concur," Stewart said looking over at Peter who had his arms folded, kicking at the dirt. He appeared to be pouting.

"Okay," he finally said.

"Done," Stewart said.

***

At about ten that night, in the light of a quarter-moon, Peter and Stewart gathered their gear and walked around the wreckage that was once the general store. I brought the shovel. Peter was already sweating from nervousness.

"Peter, after we go under the fence and out a couple hundred yards, let's find a place and sit still for a few minutes and see if we can hear anyone following us," Stewart whispered. "We'll take our time and hopefully not make any mistakes. If we hear anything, get back to the town."

"Okay."

When we arrived at the fence we were stunned to find several sections were flat on the ground, the wooden posts snapped like toothpicks.

"Must have been the tornado," I said.

"Is it still live?" Peter asked.

"I doubt it," Stewart said. "It should be grounded out sitting on the ground that long. That's probably why the pump didn't work. The batteries are drained. I'll test it though."

He looked around for a piece of wire or metal to throw on the fence, but couldn't find anything. He took out a can of beans from his bedroll and tossed it in the middle of the fence. It rolled about without any sparks.

"It's dead," Stewart said. He stepped on the chain-link fence and quickly removed his foot. He took a step onto it, and then another.

"Let's go."

Peter and Stewart shook my hand, and then we gave each other bear hugs.

"Goodbye and good luck," I said. I had tears in my
eyes as they left. I hoped they didn't see them in the
darkness.

"See you in about five days," Stewart said.

"I hope so. When you come back, bring me a cheeseburger and a chocolate shake!"

As they went to leave, Peter turned back to me.
"Look," he whispered, "if anything takes place where you
happen to find me tits up in the graveyard, dig my ass up
and look in my back pants pocket. I'll keep a journal of our
trip so you'll get a good idea of what happens to me or us, if
anything does. It might help you survive."

I nodded my head. "Hope I won't have to."

"Me either." We shook hands again.

Balance of George's Day 41

I waited until the two were out of sight then returned
to the hotel. My thoughts were on what Peter told me.
What I didn't think of at that time was, *if they don't make
it, what good is it to know how they died?* I didn't know if I
would see either of them alive again and I could barely
keep my eyes open. Emotionally, it had been a long day. I
was tired; more mentally exhausted than physically, and
decided to go to bed.

***

I didn't sleep very well that night. Every little sound
woke me up. The coyotes howling in the distance didn't
sound like a song anymore. It sounded more like a threat;
a taunt from the wild. The breeze blowing against the
hotel and the whistling through the cracks wasn't inviting.
I was constantly reminded of the tornado. Knowing the
fence was down made me fearful of what could wander into
the hotel while I slept. I was going to have to get back to
the third floor.

During my fitful sleep, my dreams were disjointed,
frightening. I dreamt the angel of death walked me down
to the cemetery where I found two more graves. He

brought me back to the hotel and showed me that the water was completely depleted; all of a sudden I was dying of thirst. I ran into the kitchen and found the pantry empty. A pack of coyotes chased me from the hotel to the cemetery and back, then sat outside and waited for me. Their fiery red eyes glowed in the dark. I could feel their hot breath.

Then the hotel was full of rattlesnake nests. They came out of everywhere and slithered after me into whichever room I fled.

The coyotes left and I was brought back to the cemetery. Another grave had been freshly dug. The angel pointed to it. I looked into the hole. It was empty but a wooden cross had been erected at the head of it. It had my name on it—*HERE LIES GEORGE*. I woke up hyperventilating, covered in a cold sweat, and realized I was having a nightmare. I'd never felt so all alone.

George's Day 42

For the next several days, I enjoyed the solitude and worked on my manuscript. There was no one to bother me and interrupt my thoughts while I wrote. I didn't feel much like eating and I was losing weight. My belt had moved two notches. At least this forced captivity-vacation might be good for something.

I inventoried my water the best I could; I estimated about fourteen gallons remaining. The dishes in the kitchen had piled up due to lack of water. My clean clothes were all used up; I would have to start recycling—wearing my cleanest dirty clothes.

I set all the bowls, pots and pans outside in case it rained. I wanted to collect all the water I could, boil it, and save it for drinking. If I could collect enough, I might be able to wash a few clothes.

The nightmares didn't end and haunted me every night. The same dreams of the graves, snakes and coyotes played over and over like a bad trailer at the movie theater. The restless nights made me so tired I started taking naps every afternoon. The rest of my day consisted of writing and editing, there wasn't anything else to do and if there was a prize to be had, I figured I would have it wrapped up. I was soon caught up to date with my story— I was the only one left in this God-forsaken ghost town. What a retreat it turned out to be. I always wondered, would anyone believe a story like mine? The final chapters were yet to play out and *possibly* be written.

CHAPTER 24
On The Prairie

Balance of Peter & Stewart's Day 41

Peter and Stewart walked out about five hundred yards from the fence and stooped down. A slight breeze sent a shiver down Peter's back. He buttoned the top half of his shirt.

"Let's have a seat for a few minutes and concentrate on listening for anyone," Stewart whispered.

"All I hear are coyotes," remarked Peter in a low voice. "You don't think they would attack us, do you?"

Stewart didn't really know if the coyotes would attack or not, but he wasn't about to let Peter know that. He tried to make light of the situation. "They're probably more scared of you, than you are of them. Anyway, in a few days our stink will deter them more than anything else. They won't even want to come near us."

Peter wasn't amused. "Good thing we have a partial moon. I'd hate to step on a snake. I don't know if I can see one as it is."

Again, Stewart tried to allay Peter's fears. "Snakes are mostly out during the day and go underground at night. It's too cold for them without the sunlight to warm their body. They're cold-blooded."

"Cold-blooded. Just like the son-of-a-bitch snake that killed Jessie and Ralph. But, I hope you're right."

They waited about another ten minutes in silence, scanning the distance. Stewart stood up and grabbed his pack. "Let's go. I don't hear or see anything."

They started their journey, but it was slow going avoiding the brush, cactus, and prairie dog holes by moonlight. The night was cool and the dry air parched their mouths. They walked for about two hours before taking their first break. By sunrise, both were exhausted and they had each consumed about a third of a gallon of water.

Peter & Stewart's Day 42

"We're going to have to do better with the water," Stewart said. "We have to ration to make it last for five or six days travel at the least."

"You drink your water and I'll drink mine," Peter fired back. He spun around and faced Stewart, confronting him directly. "How do we know where we're going? How do we know we're not walking in circles?"

Stewart was taken aback by the sudden change of demeanor. "I've been guided by that bright star up there. It's the North Star. Have a better idea?" Stewart didn't really know if he was following the North Star, he'd only heard about it when he was a kid, but it sounded good and he didn't want Peter to know he didn't know where the hell he was going.

"Who me? City boy? We can't even see the stars in the city. We only see them in pictures."

"We may have to travel a few hours during the day so we can maintain direction. That's the only other suggestion I can think of."

Peter was tired and had enough wandering for the night. "Let's get some chow and some sleep."

Stewart looked around at their surroundings. "Sounds good to me. How about that wash over there? It looks deep enough to hide us."

"As long as it doesn't rain and carry us away. Can we find anything to build a campfire and warm up some food?"

"Why don't we just send up a flare?"

"I thought you said they wouldn't be able to find us in a gulley or wash."

"I doubt they can if we're quiet and *don't build a fire*! If someone is following us, they 'd be able to smell the smoke even if they couldn't see the fire."

After sharing cans of cold corned beef hash and beans, Peter wrapped himself in his blanket and tried to get some sleep. Stewart soon followed.

"Let me give you some advice," Stewart said as he rolled over towards Peter. "Scorpions will be out, so button your sleeves and the collar of your shirt. Take a rope or shoestrings and tie them around the bottom of your pant legs. You don't want the little critters wandering in and snuggling up against your balls."

"You didn't tell me about them before."

"Didn't want to scare you," Stewart replied as he rolled back over.

"Thanks a bunch," Peter mumbled as he threw his blanket off. "Guess you don't mind it now."

"Wake me up if you hear anything strange."

Peter & Stewart's Day 43

They slept sporadically most of the morning and woke from the heat around mid-afternoon. Peter worked on his journal for George and his manuscript until about an hour before sunset.

Stewart whittled on a piece of wood. "I don't think we covered enough ground last night. We have to do better or we'll run out of food and water. We might find some water, but unless you like to eat prairie dogs and snakes..."

"Well, just what do you suggest? I can only go so fast when I can't see shit. We aren't going anywhere quick if one of us breaks or sprains an ankle in one of these damn prairie dog holes."

"We travel during the day."

Peter poked the ground with a stick for a while. "Your suggestions suck."

"Then you come up with a plan."

After several minutes of silence Peter said, "I don't have one. I suppose we don't have a choice."

"Let's get going then. We need to make as much distance as we can before sunset, but we'll have to keep traveling 'til around midnight, then sleep until sunrise."

They packed their food and supplies in their bedrolls.

"I wish there was a better way to carry this water," Peter said. "The rope is digging into my shoulders."

"You only have to start worrying when it's not digging into your shoulder," Stewart replied.

"Yeah, thanks. I know that too."

Peter & Stewart's Day 44

The next morning, after six hours of sleep, they traveled for about an hour keeping the sun to their right. Stewart kept looking to his rear. He suddenly stopped and held his hand up toward Peter.

"Listen."

He ducked down.

"Get down."

Peter hit the ground beside him.

"What is it?"

"I'm pretty sure I heard a horse."

For several minutes there was nothing but the sound of the wind and crows cawing in the distance. Peter took off his backpack and sprawled out on the ground. Then Stewart heard it again. He motioned to Peter and pointed toward the south, from the direction they had traveled from.

"I heard it this time," Peter said.

Stewart was up and down trying to see where the whinnying was coming from. "Sounded like it came from behind us," he whispered to Peter. "I don't see anything, but it's out there." They both stood up gradually, looking for any movement in the distance. "It wouldn't bother me as much if it came from up ahead, but from the south..."

"What should we do?" Peter asked.

"Let's keep moving. If we can't see whoever it is, maybe they can't see us either."

"What if it's someone who could help us?"

Stewart stared at Peter. "How would we know?" He received no answer. "Do you really want to bet all your marbles and risk it? I'm sure as hell not going to."

"But, maybe..."

"Peter, this is life and death. I'm not ready to throw in the towel just yet. Grab your stuff and let's get out of here."

They started traveling again, this time a little faster. Stewart kept checking the rear.

Both froze as a gunshot rang out in the vastness behind them. A slight rumble could be heard which seemed to be getting louder as the seconds passed. A cloud of dust rose in the distance.

"Whatever it is, it's coming our way," Peter said.

"Let's find some cover," Stewart directed.

"Why? What is it?"

"Not quite sure, but it sounds like a herd of something."

Peter turned and looked out over the expanse of prairie. "Cover, what cover? There's nothing out here but sand, rocks, cactus and buzzards."

"Quit complaining and let's go." Stewart took off, looking for a place that would conceal them.

Peter followed several paces behind. "I *knew* this was a bad idea."

The rumble increased to a thunder as the cloud of dust also grew. Then, the noise stopped. The prairie was again silent.

"Antelope," Stewart stated looking back at the diminishing dust cloud. "Must be two to three hundred of them."

"Why'd they stop?"

"How the hell do I know? Maybe nothing is chasing them any more. Go ask 'em."

"An antelope burger sounds pretty good to me right now."

Stewart smiled. "Yeah, you go sneak up on one and I'll kill it and cook it for you. Let's go. Whoever is back there must have shot one. He'll have to take some time to gut and dress it. Meanwhile, we can put some distance between us."

***

They picked up their pace until dusk when they had to slow down. Again, just after sunset, in the solitude of the high plains, they could hear the whinny of a horse.

"I wish I knew who that is and where he is," Peter said trying to pinpoint and gauge where the sounds were coming from.

Stewart turned and looked with Peter. "Noise can travel quite a ways out here, especially at night. I can't tell how far away that horse is."

"Aren't there wild horses out here?"

"Yeah, that's always a possibility, but they're usually in herds. I'd think we'd hear several of them. And, I don't think they'd know how to fire a rifle."

Peter chuckled. "I guess not."

They traveled until around midnight. Worn out, they decided to rest for the hours of darkness. They ate cold corned beef hash and beans again with a can of pears and prepared their bedroll. Stewart had just wrapped himself up in his blankets when Peter sounded an alarm.

"Stewart! Look!" he said in a loud whisper.

Stewart got up and looked in the direction Peter was pointing. "Looks like a flashlight." The light was cutting the night like a laser beam, moving side to side.

"That's what I thought."

"Probably about a half-mile away."

They watched the light for several minutes. It was not stopping and was coming closer. Barking could also be heard from the same direction.

"Shit, he's got a dog. That's how he's tracking us. Let's get going," whispered Stewart.

They packed their supplies in the bedrolls and headed out away from the light, picking up the pace.

"You got a plan?" Peter asked.

"Not yet."

"Seems like a good time to come up with one."

"I'm thinking. I'm thinking."

Looking over his shoulder several times, Stewart could see the light gaining on them.

"Whoever it is, he's on horseback with a dog. Sooner or later he's going to catch up with us," Peter said.

"I know. I'm working on it."

About an hour later Stewart stopped and looked around. The light was nowhere to be seen.

"He must have stopped for the night," Stewart said. "We can stop, or we can go on and put some distance between us."

"Let's keep going."

"Good, I've got a plan, but we have to make it at least one more day without being found."

"What's that?"

"Instead of being hunted, we become the hunters."

"Oh, great. Just what I wanted to hear."

CHAPTER 25
Alone

DAY 46

A few days after Peter and Stewart left, I took to walking to the cemetery to see if any fresh graves had been dug. I dreaded each trip, not really wanting to know, yet feeling elated whenever I found nothing new. I felt a sense of deja vu, my nightmares adding a dose of reality. Maybe they were going to make it after all.

It was a beautiful day, but the mid-morning was hot. Clouds were starting to move in and the high humidity indicated it might rain a little later in the day. As I walked, my thoughts turned to what I would have to do if I *were* about to run out of water. I didn't want to die of thirst; that would be a horrible death. But could I kill myself? Would I have the will to do it? How would I do it? Would it hurt much?

As I approached the cemetery, my heart dropped to my stomach. Another grave. A cross had been erected at the head of it with a board attached to the top, just like the others. As I inched closer to the fresh pile of dirt, I saw Peter's name and another poem. My knees buckled and I sat right there in the road and cried. I'd lost a companion, who through adversity had become a good friend. I crawled on all fours closer to the grave and through my tears read the poem.

Here Lies Peter,
He Walked With a Teeter,
He Was Part of a Team,
Now It's All a Dream.

"Why, why?" I cried out as I looked around, pounding the dirt with my fist. "Who's doing this? Why are you doing this? Is this your idea of entertainment?"

Thoughts raced through my head. Had Stewart made it? Did he get away? Maybe Peter died of injuries or some other hostile action. That's what I wanted to believe. My mind was awash with scenarios of what could have happened. I wanted to know how Peter died. I needed to know. My stomach started churning—I lost my breakfast.

I suddenly remembered what Peter had told me about a journal before he left. After I pulled myself together and could stand up again, I went back to the hotel and retrieved the shovel and a knife from the kitchen. My anxiety and despair had turned to a raging anger. I spent the next several hours digging up Peter's grave, turning my anger to sweat. I dug furiously; I could only excavate ten minutes at a time before running out of breath and overheating. Several times I made a trip back to the hotel to sip some water. I suppose I should have brought some with me, but I found the break more beneficial. I finally had to stop and rest for a few hours and get something to eat.

The afternoon clouds brought dry lightning, but no rain. With the cloud cover, the day cooled down several degrees and I went back to digging. When I finally got down to the body, I cleared the dirt from around the upper torso and cut away the milky white plastic tarp; I didn't want to see Peter's face. There it was, just like Jessie, what Stewart had described as the unmistakable hole from a high-powered bullet that had blown a hole in his chest. It appeared Peter had also been shot in the back.

I had to find the journal. Had the shooter gone through his pockets and found it? I had to dig more and uncover the whole body to turn it over. Cutting away the plastic in the area of his pockets, I felt for some papers. There they were, the left pocket, just like he said! I pulled out the documents and unfolded them. Three pages of notes!

The anger swelled in me and boiled over as I sat on the side of the grave reading his notes. The hair on my neck stood up as I read that someone on horseback pursued them with a dog. I knew then they didn't have much of a chance when he said the man had a rifle, as that is how the others died. The notes ended with Stewart having a plan to bushwhack the rider. I had no idea what happened to Stewart. I hoped he got away, but at the same time, I hoped he hadn't sacrificed Peter. I don't think he would have done that, but you never know how people may act when it comes to saving their own ass.

I stayed and spoke to Peter for almost an hour, swearing to him I'd get revenge for his death. I'd find and kill the sick son-of-a-bitch who murdered him. By sunset I'd covered the body back up and returned to the hotel. I vowed I wouldn't forget my friend. Someone would pay.

***

My only salvation now rested with Stewart. My life was in his hands. It hadn't rained at all and I had less than twelve gallons of water left. Should I start cutting back even more? Would it ever rain? Should I start out on my own and hope for the best—maybe going south after all? A bullet in the back would be quicker and less painful than dying of thirst. Maybe Peter had found the easy way out.

I lay down and tried to sleep. The nightmares came back; only this time there was one more grave alongside Peter's. Were my dreams premonitions of what was to come?

I couldn't sleep and needed something to occupy my time. I decided to read one of the other contestant's manuscripts; maybe I could gain insights I didn't possess that would improve my book. I went to Dorothy's room and found her computer in a bureau drawer. I hoped the battery wasn't dead as I clicked the power button on. It started up and the manuscript appeared on the screen. I felt like I was eavesdropping, intruding into her life. I asked her to forgive me and not haunt me.

I first checked to see how she wrote about Harry's death. She had indeed believed it was accidental while he tried to escape. I smiled—the ruse had worked after all. I also found the description of Harry quite entertaining, definitely from a woman's perspective.

Her take on Randy and Nicki's activities were nothing less than two rabbits locked in a room for several days. The writing was eloquent, to say the least, but Dorothy's prose left no doubt she was sexually starved, or hadn't much experience, about which I had several chuckles.

The males in her manuscript, including me, were nothing but dirty, trashy, bossy, Neanderthals. Dorothy definitely had a problem. She had changed the names of the individuals, but they were unquestionably identifiable.

Her description of Ada was the gentlest—described as a caring, shy and introverted woman, but hardheaded with no understanding of the world. She was out-of-time and out-of-place.

Dorothy's description of herself was as a motherly type; a steel-willed, outspoken individual trying to maintain her privacy among the slobs and the commune-type lifestyle she was forced into. Her resolve to keep absolute cleanliness while surrounded by all of us goons was constantly being tested.

This was great stuff and I had several good belly laughs. I needed it. I turned off the computer and went to sleep.

When I awoke, the thought hit me; *why not copy the manuscripts from all the other computers? It would surely enhance my own, and I would have the point of view of all the other contestants! What a narrative that would make!*

I retrieved a flash drive from my room and went to each room in the hotel. To my non-surprise, several of the computers were password protected, but I did manage to copy Dorothy's, Peter's, Stewart's and Nicki's.

CHAPTER 26
Thoughts

DAY 47

When I awoke the next morning, a light rain was falling. I had no idea what day or date it was. I'd lost all track of time.

It was hard to get up, but I needed to gather the water from every cup and saucer I had set out. My depression was growing and knew I had to break out of it somehow. My back and arm muscles ached from all the shoveling the day before. I had to find something to do besides sit around and feel sorry for myself. After breakfast I was determined to start editing the first draft of my manuscript. I usually didn't edit until months after finishing, but this was different.

After the rain stopped and the clouds dissipated, I poured all the water I'd collected from the pots, pans, cups, bowls and saucers into one large pot. I'd accumulated about a gallon. I carried it into the kitchen, careful not to spill the liquid gold. I'd boil it later and use it as a last resort, but I'd have to start a campfire first.

I skipped breakfast. I couldn't take my mind off Stewart; was he still alive or planted in the graveyard with the rest? I dreaded the thought of the walk down to the cemetery to find out; but I had to know. I really didn't want to know, but how could I not? Again, I had to find out. Would there now be nine graves, or was there still hope for a rescue on the horizon?

Halfway to the burial ground, I stopped and turned around. I slowly started back to the hotel. I didn't want to know. Stopping again, I held my head as I fought to bring myself to go back. This was it. This was the moment of truth. Was Stewart going to be my savior or was I... a walking dead man? I couldn't get the image out of my head— my name on a board above a grave. I turned and walked slowly back towards the cemetery.

I closed my eyes as I neared. I was afraid to look. I turned around and walked backwards. Opening my eyes a slit, I twisted towards the graves.

Son-of-a-bitch! I felt as if I'd been punched in the gut, the air vacuumed from my lungs. There were now nine. The one thing I was deathly afraid of...had come true. My premonitory dreams were almost complete; maybe now they would stop.

Again, there was a marker with a poem.

Here Lies Stew,
He Thought He Knew,
He Also Went North,
Now He's the Fourth.

I turned around and walked back to the hotel screaming, crying, stomping my feet, and swearing at the top of my lungs. The hatred I felt towards whomever was killing my friends erupted in me. The burning desire to see the person roast in hell for his crimes, no, have their eyes gouged out, one-by-one, even have him drawn and quartered, was now tempered by my fear of being totally alone, having to contemplate my own demise. There would be no one to come to my rescue.

I reasoned there could only be one outcome to this nightmare. The two big questions were...how would it happen and when? Would I succumb to thirst and hunger, or would I set out on foot as the others had, tempt my fate, and probably be shot? Would *I, George Russo,* be strong enough, have the intestinal fortitude to make the final decision, or would someone else have to do it for me? I had to decide. My destiny was now in my hands, and my hands only; the one place I didn't want it to be.

I didn't want to have to make that decision. If I had a gun, I could take the easy way out. I had some sharp knives; maybe I could ceremoniously take the way of the Samurai, commit seppuku, hara-kiri. It would be quick and efficient. Hell no, I thought, that would hurt too much.

Maybe Ada had the right idea, except, now I didn't have any water to fill a tub, let alone hot or warm water.

As a matter of fact, with the rain I collected, I only had about eleven gallons total, and that wouldn't fill the bottom of the bathtub. My mind was a blur; it was on a merry-go-round, traveling in circles a hundred miles an hour. I could hang myself, but I'd heard that's also a horrible way to die—but was it worse than dying of thirst?

Lunchtime came and went. I couldn't eat. I felt a sense of finality set in. I questioned the many decisions I had made in my life, my past and present relationships. How did everything lead me to this point? How did my life get so screwed up? Was it just greed, or a real desire to become a great writer? One would be seen as good, the other bad. How would my sister, and her family, remember me? Would they even miss me? Would they even know if I died? If I'd taken a different fork in the road anywhere in my life, would I have still ended up here? Should I give up, or should I fight till my last breath? I figured time would probably give me the answers I sought.

I had enough food to last a long time, if I were frugal, maybe even a year. Not necessarily what I enjoyed eating, but it was nourishment. Water was the big problem. There was enough for at least a couple weeks if I used it sparingly, maybe more if it rained. No medicines and no prescriptions, except for a bottle of aspirin and a couple band-aids. Could I survive an infection, a heart attack, or a stroke? What if I broke an arm or a leg? Could I continue? How would I survive a winter out here with no heat? Buffalo was cold enough; this would be ludicrous, if not deadly.

I realized how easy life really was back in New York, how fragile it was. I longed for a double cheeseburger with the works, a double fudge sundae and a banana split with chocolate, pineapple and cherry toppings. A beer; how I longed for just one cold beer. In New York, everything I *needed* was within an arms reach, a telephone call, or a taxi ride. Here, everything I *had* was within an arm's reach—but it was all too miniscule.

My thoughts turned to the contest. How could I have been persuaded so easily to go somewhere, anywhere, with people I didn't know anything about? In Buffalo, I was miserable, hungry, cold, and my apartment house was filthy, but I would go back to it now in a New York minute.

I lay in my bed most of the day feeling sorry for myself. Twilight came and went. Could this all be a bad dream? Maybe a little Scotch would help clear my head. I'd rather have a beer, but Scotch would do, and do what I needed a lot faster.

I went down to the cellar and brought up a fifth of my favorite, Johnny Walker Black. Ahhh, tomorrow would be another day.

CHAPTER 27
Surviving

DAY 48

The only medicine I did have was aspirin, and without a doubt, I needed about five of them early the next morning along with nearly a quart of water. My head pounded and my mouth felt like a rabbit had run through it, shedding his fur while hibernating overnight. I looked at the nearly half-empty bottle of Scotch. I still couldn't eat. All I wanted to do was sleep. With really nothing to do, that's exactly what I did.

Waking about an hour later. I needed to get something to eat, but my stomach told me to wait. I fixed half a cup of cold, black, instant coffee and went outside and sat on the porch. God, the coffee tasted terrible, but I continued to sip it. There was no one to talk to except the birds. No one to listen to; only the breeze gently gliding by and the few crows circling, looking for food. Maybe they thought I was their next meal. I knew they were waiting for me to die so they could pick my eyes out and feast on my innards like some rotted road kill.

One landed on a hitching post across the street from me. He was a big son-of-a-bitch, black as coal. He stared at me with his beady eyes, intermittently cawing, looking away and then staring again. I got up, picked a rock off the ground and threw it at him. "You'll have to wait a little longer, you bastard," I yelled.

Water. That was my main concern now. I needed to know how much I had—how long I could go. No more booze. That only made me drink more water. I couldn't wash or shave. There were about ten more empty milk containers in the basement. I gathered them and drained the holding tank, gallon by gallon. There was far less than I thought, only five and a half gallons. How could that happen? The tank had to hold more than that. I only had half of what I thought.

I should have drained the tank earlier. I found a wet spot on the side of the tank; it had a leak. It had to rain soon.

I also had to inventory the remaining matches and candles. I had to boil any water I collected; I didn't need dysentery. I scoured the kitchen and the basement, finding a half box of kitchen matches, three whole candles and four partials.

I didn't have a way to keep a continuous fire going. There was plenty of wood around, but without a stove to contain it, it would go out during the night. The wood was much too dry to burn for six or seven hours.

My thoughts soon turned again to rescue. The only idea we could come up with before was to build a signal bonfire. Should I try it again? I'd have to collect all the wreckage scattered throughout the town and rebuild the mountain of debris. I had plenty of gasoline since the generator was now trashed. The gas! That's how I could keep a fire going. I still had at least a hundred gallons.

I went to the rear of the hotel where we had our trash dump and found an empty coffee can. Draining some gas from the tank into the coffee can, I lit it. It burned for hours. I was able to heat my food and I could boil water. I could finally have some hot coffee! A small win for me, but a welcome one.

DAY 52

For the next four days, I picked up the tornado-splintered remains scattered throughout the town. I started a new woodpile for the bonfire in the same place as we had planned it before. I only worked in the evenings, when it was the coolest, to conserve water, but it was still plenty damn hot. I grabbed several more cans out of our dump and filled them with gas. My plan was to keep them close to the mound of wood to light a fire if I heard a plane anywhere. Otherwise, I would light it and hope for the best when my water was about gone—it would be one of my last acts of desperation.

I ate heartily, as my appetite was increasing due to the work I was putting in. I probably lost a few more pounds and the physical activity also seemed to help with my sleep; I wasn't having as many nightmares as I had before.

There was one downside to all the work; I was drinking more water. I also had to start washing my plates and utensils as I ran out of clean ones.

Since I didn't know what day it was, I wasn't sure how much time was left of the two months. I was sure it was getting close, but would this nightmarish hell actually end? Would they really come and get me? In the back of my mind, in truth, I doubted it; but I tried not to think about it. I had to stay positive.

I'd used two of the five and a half gallons. I needed rain. I needed rescue.

DAY 55

As I'd nothing to do but write and eat, the next several days seemed like an eternity. Still no rain. By now, I thought I was past the two-month mark.

I took a walk down to the cemetery. I don't know why—maybe it was just to see if anything had changed. It hadn't. I talked to Peter and Stewart for a while. I cried. I prayed. I couldn't help it; my loneliness was intolerable. As I was walking back, I heard a sound in the distance; one I'd been waiting for—an airplane. I couldn't see it, but I could definitely hear it.

I ran to the hotel for the matches. Out of breath as I came back out, I scanned the sky. I could barely see it, but as I watched, it headed straight for me. The altitude worried me. Would he see the fire? I half ran and half jogged to the woodpile. I had to pour the gas on it, get it lit, and hope it smoked like hell before the plane passed over. I had gas in five different cans and threw them on the pile of wood. I was so excited I broke the first match trying to light it. The second one did the trick and the pile of wood exploded into flames. Within a minute, it was fully engulfed.

The tarpaper did its job creating a thick black smoke that rose high into the air. I was lucky; there wasn't much of a wind. I backed off and watched the fire mature.

The plane banked away from me in a small turn just as I lit the fire. I watched it intently, waiting to see if the pilot would see the fire and turn back. Seconds seemed like minutes. The plane slowly banked, turning back! *He saw me! He's coming my way!*

Within another minute, the plane had dropped in altitude and was almost over me. I jumped up and down waving my arms like a madman. As he flew over he dipped his wings several times in acknowledgement. It was a single engine plane with fixed landing gear. I knew he could land on the road coming into town. I'd seen it done on television before. I was going to be rescued!

As the plane passed over, I watched it regain altitude and then turn back onto his original course.

"No, no, no," I screamed waving my arms again as I chased him down the center of town. "Come back!" Could it be he was just going to report the fire and someone else would come?

I knew there was a landing strip about a half-hour away where we set down when we arrived at this hellhole. I wondered if he was going to land there and how long it would take for someone to appear.

The fire was raging, sending embers and smoke high into the air. The dry wood burned hot and the pile soon started to settle, sending up more ash and embers. The breeze that had dissipated earlier now came back and shifted towards the town, but the embers settled back down before going very far. There was nothing I could do but watch. I didn't know what I would do if the wind became stronger. I had no plan. I'd no water to spare.

I went back to the hotel to wait. Hopefully the pilot had called in the fire. He had to, I thought. What else could the fire be but a signal for help out here in the middle of nowhere?

Opening a can of pears, I started lunch. As I finished, I smelled a strong odor of smoke. Had the wind shifted that much towards the hotel? I walked out on the front porch, still chewing the last slice of a pear. What I saw horrified me. The building on the opposite side of the street was on fire! The wind had picked up and the embers had reached the town. Ashes and embers were falling all around, some reaching the hotel!

I raced back inside and grabbed the blanket off my mattress. Grabbing the pitcher of water I had collected from the rain, I soaked part of the blanket and began beating embers that reached the hotel porch. I couldn't do anything about the ones that landed on the roof. I raced up and down the street stamping and beating out the hot ashes. I had to use another gallon of water to keep my blanket damp.

Later, the wind shifted again and began pushing the embers to the other side of the street. This time, I remained on guard on the porch as the building across the street was consumed. My rescue scenario with the bonfire had almost become a disaster and cost me dearly.

Now I only had about a gallon and a half of water left.

***

I waited on the porch until sunset for someone to arrive. The fucking pilot never sent for help. How could he not? Here I was with a huge bonfire, I was waving and screaming at him like an idiot. What more could I have done? Yeah, I should've spelled something out on the ground, but still, he had to know.

I went to bed that night wondering what to do next.

Day 59

It's overcast today, but it doesn't feel like rain. The past few days I paced the floor and tried to stay positive. I'm going to have to leave. I have no other choice. I drained the two toilet reservoirs and got about a gallon of rusty, foul-smelling water out of each.   I boiled it, so it should be okay, but it tastes like I'm chewing on a rusty nail.

There was more in the bowl, but I couldn't bring my-self to take it. Maybe that'll change too. I'll decide that before I leave. I can't take more than two gallons with me anyway; it'd be too heavy.

I gathered some food and one change of clothes, stuff-ing them into a pillowcase. Nothing was clean and every-thing stunk, so it really didn't matter much which ones I took. I grabbed a small knife to open the cans of beans, peaches and pears. I had my computer and the small pile of paper I'd been writing on, plus Peter's notes. By now, I was sure I looked like an old forty-niner who had been up in the mountains mining for a year. The only difference was—I was the mule. All together, everything must have weighed over thirty pounds. I'd probably scare the shit out of anyone I came upon.

As I prepared for my departure, I wrote a letter to leave in the hotel that detailed the horrors of the last two or so months.   I gave the name of the business that brought us here, places and dates we were picked up and all the names and hometowns I could remember of those who rested here. Signing my name and adding my sister's address to it gave me some hope that maybe someone would be caught and prosecuted for what they did to us. I left it on the kitchen counter where I hoped it would someday be discovered.

My gear was packed and ready to go. I knew I was walking into certain death, but I couldn't bring myself to do the final deed myself. Someone else would have to do it. I was prepared. I'd made peace with my Maker and I no longer feared the inevitable. Strange how that happens. Maybe it's the same for the soldier on the battlefield. Once I accepted I was going to die, there came a strange peace within. I just concentrated on what I had to accomplish.

There was only one thing left to do. I'd made up my mind to get drunker than a hoot owl that night. I knew I would pay for it the next morning, but what the hell. I had no one but myself to answer to.

CHAPTER 28
Rescue

DAY 60

I woke the next morning to what I thought was an engine running. I sat up and opened my eyes just a slit. The sun was up, but I'd no idea what time it was. It could've been seven; it could have been noon. I didn't have the stomach to finish the bottle last night and my head wasn't pounding quite as hard as it did the last time, but it still throbbed.

No, there wasn't any engine noise, just some crows screaming somewhere outside. I must have imagined it. I swallowed the four aspirin with the cup of water I had prepared, lay back down and tried to go back to sleep. My trip would have to wait until I was good and ready.

Minutes later, as I lay in the kitchen on the bare mattress trying to coax myself back to sleep, I thought I heard footsteps on the wood plank floor in the lobby. This time I sat up in bed, as still as a cat alert to his prey, listening. There *were* footsteps! It sounded like boots and he was scuffing his feet. But who the hell could it be? Was I hallucinating?

My thoughts raced. Could it be the pilot actually sent for help? Had someone finally come to rescue me; or were *they* here to finish me off? Of course they were going to finish me off— there were nine bodies they would have to account for. They couldn't leave any witnesses!

The manuscript. They were here to kill me and steal my manuscript, my soon to be, real life *bestselling thriller!*

"Hello!" came a voice from the lobby. "Is anyone here?"

I heard his footsteps starting up the stairway to the second floor.

I looked at my computer and the pile of notepaper that sat on top of it. I looked for a place to quickly burn the manuscript and destroy the computer. I could always rewrite it later if I had to. *Where the hell were the matches?* If they were going to kill me, they sure as hell weren't going to profit from it.

"Hello! Anybody! I'm here to take you home," came the shouting from the lobby. "The bus is outside, pack your things and let's go."

I got up and peeked around the corner. He was standing on the staircase hollering up the stairs. *Holy shit! It was the pilot who brought us out here; the son-of-a-bitch who tricked us and lied to all of us!* The bastard never came back—he had to have known we were being left behind in this God-forsaken place. What the hell was going on? Why him?

I silently eased across the kitchen in my bare feet and underwear and grabbed a knife from the drawer—a large, sharp butcher knife. It had a large handle—one I could hold onto tightly. I grabbed a second, and a third knife—I might have to throw one or two, even though I had no idea how. Anyway, I wanted to look like I was ready for anything. I opened the oven, and quietly placed my computer and the papers in it. *Where did I put those damn matches?*

The voice sounded familiar, more than just the pilot's voice. I slapped my forehead. *Think. Think. Where have you heard that voice before?*

"Who are you?" I yelled from the kitchen.

His footsteps came closer to me.

"Stay where you are," I yelled.

The steps stopped.

"I'm the pilot. I'm here to take you home."

"I know you're the pilot—Captain Rogers, but *who* are you really?"

"That doesn't matter right now.

"Look asshole, I'm in no mood for..."

"You've won the contest. Now it's time for you to go home and enjoy the rewards. Do you remember the prizes?"

"Yes, of course I do. I just have a hard time believing this is a real writing competition."

"Well, it is and this is the first part of the award, *the prize of your life.* You, my friend, get to live. I also have checks for you in the amount of sixty thousand dollars as a retainer on your book, once you sign the contract of course."

Sixty thousand dollars? Think, George, Think. Who is this guy? You know that voice!

"How do I know I can trust you?"

"Why wouldn't you?"

"Is that supposed to be a joke?"

"Well, you can distrust me and stay here and probably die, or you can go with me and enjoy the fruit of your experiences. I'll gladly leave if you want me to."

"What about all the others?"

"What about them?"

His footsteps started again.

"Stay where you are!" I yelled.

The footsteps halted.

"Are you armed? Do you have a gun?"

"No, no. That's not necessary. Why do you ask?"

"Because half the people you dropped off have been shot dead, that's why," I screamed.

"I don't know anything about that. I'm just here to pick you up. That's what I was hired for. I've told you what I know and what I've been told to tell you. What else can I do?"

"Are you saying I've won the contest because I'm the only one left?"

"I surmise since you're the only one left, you've won by default. There doesn't seem to be a reason to continue, does there?"

I cautiously showed myself, knives in hand. I must have been a sight standing there in only my boxer shorts. I was dirty and smelly, and hadn't shaved or bathed for weeks.

"You won't need those," the pilot said pointing at the knives. "I'm not armed." He put his arms above his head and turned around.

"Forgive me if I don't believe you. You lied to us before. I don't know what to believe anymore."

"I didn't lie to you. I thought someone was going to pick you up. That's what I was told. Get your things together and let's get out of here. Your bus awaits."

I looked out towards the front of the hotel and saw the same bus we had arrived in.

"I'll get my things. You wait outside."

"Gladly."

The pilot walked out the front door, lit a cigarette, and stood by the bus.

I got dressed, then took my time and went room-to-room collecting an ID from each of my deceased friends' effects. I couldn't find Ralph's, Jessie's, or Stewart's identifications, they were probably with them in their graves. I skipped Harry's room; I didn't give a flying shit about him. It took nearly a half hour to find and collect every one else's. I silently chastised myself for not having done it earlier. I should have planned to take them with me. I packed my bags, went to the oven and grabbed my computer and other papers, and went outside to the waiting pilot. As I stepped from the porch, I turned around and went back inside.

"Where you going?"

"Be right back," I yelled.

I returned with the rest of the fifth of Scotch in my hand. I'd also tucked one of the large knives in my computer bag—just in case.

"I may need this. It's a long flight," I said holding up the bottle.

"Boy, this place is a wreck. What happened?" asked the pilot. "It's sure not the same place I brought you to."

"Tornado and fire." He acted like he didn't hear me.

"You look like hell. Your clothes are a mess, you're a mess, and forgive me, but you stink."

"A tornado," I yelled. "It hit us and a lightening strike destroyed the generator. No lights, no water, no nothing. Part of the town caught fire when I lit a signal fire."

He snickered. "Too bad. Looks like I got here just in time."

Now he was pissing me off. "Maybe for me. For everyone else, you're about two months too late."

I got on the bus and set my bags on the seat next to me. The pilot climbed on, closed the door, turned the bus around, and drove through the now unlocked gate.

I felt a strange sense of relief, grief, remorse, and guilt, all wrapped up in one. I was the only one leaving; I was the only one who had survived the gauntlet. Why was I was the only survivor? Would the contest still be continuing if I weren't alone? I thought about what the pilot told me, the first part of the award was, "you get to live." The pilot said that's what he was told. Would he have really been told that if he was just the pilot? It didn't make sense, but what the hell did make sense these past two months?

Twenty minutes later we were at the dirt airstrip, probably the same one we had arrived on over eight weeks ago, but I couldn't tell. Nothing I saw could be used to identify where we were. Prairie surrounded us wherever I looked, just a dirt landing field in the middle of nowhere. We boarded the aircraft and he shut the door.

"Got the engine fixed, huh?" I asked.

He ignored my question.

"You can sit in the co-pilot's seat if you'd like," he said, "or sit in the cabin. The way you smell, I'd prefer you stay back here—maybe a little more towards the rear."

"I'll stay in the cabin. I may want to enjoy a little sip of my buddy here," I replied patting my bottle of scotch. "Johnny will keep me company."

"Suit yourself."

The pilot went through his preflight and started the engines. As we took off, I looked out the window over the vast expanse of prairie. Still nothing to make out the area we were flying over.

We passed over the old ghost town—my home for the past eight and a half weeks. Smoke billowed from the hotel. A large bulldozer was being unloaded from a trailer at the edge of town near the formerly electrified fence. I couldn't believe what I was seeing! I unbuckled my seat belt and fought my way up to the cockpit as the plane continued to climb. I was due an explanation, and I sure as hell was going to get one.

"What the hell is going on down there? The town's on fire. There's a bulldozer there!"

There was no answer from the pilot.

"Tell me what's going on," I demanded.

"I'm sorry. You weren't supposed to see that."

"What do you mean?"

"The town is going to disappear."

"They can't do that! I have to go back and get my friends' stuff, their I.D's, their computers! I have to notify their families. I promised!"

"You'll never go back. You don't even know where you are."

"How do you know that?"

"Trust me. I know."

This asshole knows a lot more than he's telling me. I sat dumbfounded. *Trust me. I know.* The phrase played over and over in my head. I'd heard that somewhere before. *Think, George, think.* Suddenly it hit me. I now knew where I'd heard the pilot's voice before. It was now all coming together and becoming clearer, but it begged a lot more answers.

CHAPTER 29
Disclosure

We continued climbing to an altitude above the clouds.

"Paul, did you ever read my book?" I asked as I sat down in the co-pilot's seat and watched the pilot out of the corner of my eye. I wanted to see if he would answer to that name.

"Yes, I...." Paul stopped short and looked over at me with a smile. "That was clever. I guess you know."

"Know what?" I asked angrily. "I know your real name. I know you're a literary agent. Other than that, I don't know shit. What's this all about?"

"You're better off not asking any questions, George. Just take the money and walk away."

I strapped myself in the co-pilot's seat.

"Answer me!" I yelled.

Paul didn't respond. He just sat there looking out the windshield, smiling.

I grabbed the controls in the co-pilot's seat and pushed down. Hard. The plane nosed down into an immediate dive. I held it there, stiff-armed, against Paul's vigorous attempts to pull back.

"What the hell are you doing?" he yelled. "Are you trying to kill us? Let go!"

The plane stayed in a steep dive. The engines started screaming; the plane vibrated, and then shook violently.

"We're exceeding the airspeed. It can't take much more!" Paul cut back on the power. "Let go!" he demanded. "You're going to kill us!"

"Yeah, we're going to die unless you tell me what's going on," I yelled, staring out the windshield. I imagine my eyes were wild and bugged-out, like I was in a drugged-out trance. "*Death is with me! I am death!*" I yelled above the scream of the engines. I was determined to get an answer. At that moment I don't think I cared what happened. I had prepared to die so many times in the past weeks; I think I almost lost my expectation to live.

"Okay, okay, I'll tell you! Let go of the controls! We're going to crash!" he screamed.   Paul desperately pulled back against me.

We were below the cloud cover; the ground was getting closer and closer.

I hesitated another moment and then removed my hands from the yoke.   Paul strong-armed the controls, pulling back as hard as he could.

"Help me," he pleaded.

"Do it yourself."

The G-forces pushed me down in my seat; I could hardly raise my arms.   He gradually brought the plane back to level a couple hundred feet above the ground. Reapplying power, the plane regained altitude, and Paul engaged the autopilot. His hands were shaking. He was white as a ghost.

"Are you crazy?" he yelled. "You almost killed us!"

His eyes were wild this time, probably a lot like what I'd looked like minutes earlier. I smiled to myself. For the first time in months, I felt in control.

"What is it you want to know?" He was more sullen now.

"I want to know what this contest was all about! I want to know why they're burning down the town! I want to know why all my friends are dead!"

Paul looked me straight in the eyes.

"It's all pretty simple.   The town is being burned down and dozed so no trace of it will ever be found. You or anyone else who looks for it will never find it."

"What about everyone who's buried there?"

"They'll stay there, but no evidence of them will ever be found. Tomorrow, the whole town will look just like the rest of the prairie around it. The contest never happened, and the town never existed."

That wasn't going to happen. My friends' families deserved to know what happened to them and give them a decent burial.

"Where are we?"

"That, I'm not going to tell you."

I gritted my teeth and thought about putting the plane into a dive again, but then thought better of it.

"Why did you shoot and kill all four of my friends who left and tried to find help?"

"I didn't know anything about the shootings until this morning, but, you were all warned not to leave the town. My partner had contracted a local tracker to keep everyone on the reservation, ah, in the town. I was informed that each of the contestants who tried to leave was stopped, and directed to return. Reportedly, each one attacked him, some with a knife, and he shot them in self-defense. That's what I was told."

"All four of them? That's a bunch of bullshit! I don't believe a word of that! They were all shot in the back!"

"That's what I was told. Believe what you want. It doesn't change a thing and you won't be able to prove anything one way or another. *It didn't happen.*"

"It *did* happen. They were shot in the back. We dug up the bodies and there was a hole in them the size of your fist. Who is this partner you keep referring to?"

"I'm not going to tell you that either. You didn't think I executed this contest myself, did you? To answer part of your question though, there are several of us. You will never uncover their identities—you weren't even supposed to know mine."

"What's going to stop me from going to the police?"

He shrugged as if he didn't care. "That's up to you. If you do, you won't have a book to sell. We'll make you out to be a lunatic, a screwball. You won't be able to prove a thing. You won't get your sixty thousand. You won't get a contract. Everything you went through will be for nothing. And...you may end up like the rest."

"That sounds like a threat."

He looked at me. "It is."

"Why'd you let *me* live? Why didn't you just kill me like the rest?"

"The rules."

"The rules? What rules? What the hell are you talking about?"

"There are rules, George. The winner gets to live, but only if you keep your mouth shut."

"Got it all figured out, huh?"

He was thinking faster than I was. It seemed he did have it all figured out, but then, he's had months, maybe years, to put it all together.

"There's something else, too, George. You won't like this, but you need to know now so you'll keep your big mouth shut. It's kind of a gift you gave us, our ace-in-the-hole."

"And what would that be?" I sat back with a smile on my face; confident this S.O.B. had nothing he could use against me. I almost laughed at him. He was the one who should be squirming; he helped kill nine of my friends.

"We have videotape of you, Stewart and Peter killing Harry. You electrocuted him."

I hesitated for a moment; I couldn't believe he knew. "I don't know what you're talking about." I looked out the side window.

"Deny it all you want, but we have it recorded. I'm sure the police would love to see it."

I looked Paul square in the eyes. I wanted to know if the man was lying. He didn't blink. What the hell was he talking about? How could he have a tape?

"How do you know that? What tape? You couldn't have a tape, it was at night!"

Paul looked over at me and smiled. "George, do you know you just admitted to murder? You say it never happened, but it happened at night?"

I didn't respond. I knew I'd fucked up.

"There is such a thing as night vision cameras, George. It's very clear what you three did."

"I didn't have anything to do with it. Stewart told us he was letting him go. We were exiling him." I was lying, of course. I knew Stewart intended to execute Harry, I just didn't know how until it happened. "Well, he deserved it."

"And why is that? If you really felt he deserved it, you would've done it during the day. You were there; you're just as guilty as the others."

"He raped and killed Nicki. We caught him raping Ada."

"He might have raped Ada, I don't know anything about that, but Harry didn't rape or kill Nicki. Is that why you executed him? That's what you believed?"

"What do you mean *that's what I believed*?"

"Harry didn't kill Nicki. The tracker we hired to watch and guard all of you killed her. He told us all about it. He practically bragged about it. He said she was really hot and he wanted a piece of her, but she started to scream. He put a pillow over her head and she suffocated. When we found out about it, which was this morning, he was taken care of."

"No, that can't be true. She was strangled. She didn't suffocate."

"Sorry, George, but it's true. Harry didn't kill her. Our tracker may have hedged a little to us about how he killed her, but he definitely killed her. Why would he admit to us he did it otherwise? How would he even know about it? Tell me, did you find a needle in her arm?"

"Yeah, why?"

"He said he stuck it in there to make it look like an overdose. How would I know that if he didn't tell us?"

"How the hell should I know? Maybe you had a camera in her room. You don't seem to have any scruples, what would preclude you from that?"

"I assure you, George, even we have our limits. There were no cameras in the bedrooms. The three of you executed an innocent man."

This couldn't be. I was thunderstruck. My mind swirled. The thought never even occurred to me that Harry might have been innocent. He had repeatedly denied any responsibility for Nicki's rape and death, but we didn't listen to him. We had no reason to. We were absolutely positive he was guilty.

Ada killed herself because of Harry; he *was* guilty of rape. The way I saw it, he was responsible for her death. The only problem was, she committed suicide after we killed Harry.

"How do I know you're being straight with me? How do I know Harry didn't really kill Nicki?"

"Our guy said he locked Nicki's door when he left and put her key in Harry's bottom drawer while everyone was asleep. He wanted you guys to find it if you ever searched for it. He thought you'd blame it on whoever's room he put it in, in case you figured out she was killed instead of dying from a drug overdose. Just so happened it was Harry's room. Could have just as easily been yours."

"He thought of all that? I doubt it."

"He must have. That's what he told us. Did you find the key?"

"Yes." I said quietly.

"Where?"

"In Harry's bottom drawer."

"So, you can go to the police and notify them about everything that happened, but make sure you inform them about the three of you executing Harry, an *innocent* man. I'm sure they'll give you a free pass on that because you *thought* he was guilty. Maybe we'll all meet each other in the big house."

Shit! What a predicament! I wasn't the one that killed Harry, even though I agreed to it. I needed the sixty thousand dollars, and I certainly didn't want to spend the rest of my life in a jail cell because of an honest mistake. I'd survived the two-month ordeal; I deserved the money. I'd written a great story and now I wanted to see it published. I wanted the royalties, the profits, and the notoriety.

It suddenly hit me, what would have happened if the key was put in my drawer? Would it have been found? Would they have executed me?

"Why did you do the whole contest thing? How did you expect it to end?"

Paul was ready with an answer. "We came up with the idea because we had so many assholes, like yourself, who always thought you had great manuscripts or books and were always calling, yelling and cussing at us. We chose ten authors we actually believed could write a decent novel, if given the right circumstances and the time to do it. We decided to have the contest and pick the best manuscript to invest in at the end. We didn't think so many would die. I mean, we thought there might be one or two accidents, with snakes and other natural occurrences. We even figured one of you might kill someone in the group, but you guys really surprised us. I mean, nine of the ten dead in six weeks? Who could have guessed? What a great story!"

"You're really fucked up. There're nine people dead and all you can talk about is what a great story it makes."

"I didn't kill them; I don't feel bad at all. And you only killed one." He smiled; I knew that inside he was laughing at me. *That asshole!*

"You may not have pulled the trigger, but you loaded the gun and cocked it. You're definitely responsible for their deaths. Some would have survived with adequate medical attention, which you didn't provide. You locked us away in intolerable conditions and then I watched my friends die one by one."

"Maybe. You can believe what you want."

"You know how everyone died?"

"Of course I do. Four were shot, one suicide, one snakebite, one murdered, one from loss of blood, and one *you* executed."

"How'd you find out?"

"That's easy. Some are on videotape. The four who tried to escape each gave our tracker information before they attacked him and were shot. That's what I was told anyway. Whether it's true or not, like I said, we'll never know."

"Why's that?"

"If I answered that, I might incriminate myself. Let's just say it's possible the tracker who was hired to watch over you and keep you in town isn't around to give us any more answers."

"What were you going to do if there were more survivors? You couldn't have kept them as prisoners this long and expected the losers of the contest to keep quiet. Were you going to keep us there until only one was left?"

"We had plans. That's all I'm going to say. It's like a dream," he said, spreading his arms, "it never happened."

"What about the little poems on the graves? Whose idea was that? That really took a sick fuck to write those."

He laughed. "I read those this morning. Again, that was the guy we hired. He said it was his little joke; he considered himself a poet. He thought it was fuckin' funny and made a big deal out of it, as he actually wanted anyone leaving to head south. For some reason or other, he said it would have been easier for the dog to track you."

The dog. I remembered Peter's notes to me had mentioned he heard a dog barking.

"Yep. He had a tracking dog. That's what made it so easy to find those who left the town. I told you everything was very simple."

"Yeah, real fucking simple. And the electric fence, we were out in the middle of nowhere, did you really need it? Wasn't that a little overkill?"

"The fence wasn't there to keep you in. We knew you could get out anytime you wanted. It was put up a long time ago to keep people out of the town. Treasure hunters were destroying the place."

"Could have fooled me. The place looked pretty well destroyed as it was."

"I wanted to preserve the hotel. There aren't too many of that type left. It was historical, a real high-class brothel in its day. Too bad we had to burn it down."

"Yeah, too fucking bad."

"Look, we'd planned on bringing a little adversity to your group to make the story more interesting. We wanted to bring together, in a difficult environment, ten people from all parts of the country and from all different backgrounds and see what would happen under extreme conditions. We thought it would make a great story—kind of like having a group of people who didn't know each other stuck on a deserted island. Only we didn't have a deserted island."

"What kind of adversity?"

"We were going to steal some of the food, limit your water supply somehow, maybe dump some of the gas from the generator. We thought food rations would be an issue for everyone from the start, but so many died so quickly, it never was. The tornado took care of the water and the electricity. We didn't have to do a thing."

"Weren't you lucky."

"In a way, we were. Look, you have nothing to be ashamed of. You did what you thought you had to do at the time. Now you have a great story. You thought you had to protect yourselves from a rapist and a murderer. I would have done the same thing. I doubt there are too many who wouldn't have. There was no place to hold Harry. Even though he was innocent of murdering Nicki, he *was* responsible for Ada's death. If he hadn't raped her, she would still be alive today."

"You would've probably just figured out another way to kill her off."

"Maybe, maybe not."

I looked at him and shook my head. "Good, you can be my lawyer at the trial."

I unstrapped myself from the co-pilot's seat and slowly plodded back to the main cabin. I sat down, unscrewed the cap on the Scotch and took several long swallows.

How could we have been so wrong? We took an innocent person's life. Harry was an asshole, there was no doubt about that, and he needed to pay for the rape, but electrocution? I wished I could forget about it, but now the scene of him writhing in pain under the fence played over and over in my mind.

I needed to forget everything for just a while. My head still hurt from last night's binge and I was reeling from all the information I'd just received. I couldn't process it. Exhausted, I lay back in the seat and opened the bottle of scotch. After a few more nips, I passed out.

***

The plane landed with a jolt and awoke me from my alcohol-induced snooze. We were at the small Chicago airfield. I looked out the window, welcoming civilization once again. I agonized over the friends I'd met here two months ago who were no longer alive. Would I feel the same about them if they were here today? Maybe, maybe not.

The plane taxied to the terminal and Paul shut down the engines.

"You want to come in or stay here?" he asked. "We've got a little time while they refuel the plane."

"If you're buying. I want some real food—a cheeseburger and a milkshake. And I want to wash up a little. I'll probably stink everyone out of the place."

"You are ripe." Paul laughed. "Come on, I'm buying."

He acted like my best friend.

We exited the plane and went into the terminal building. Luckily, there weren't many other passengers or customers around. I put in my order at the restaurant and went into the men's room to wash up. I reveled in the small things, like hot running water and a working toilet. I promised myself to never take these things for granted again.

I consumed the burger in about five bites and downed the milkshake in thirty seconds flat. I ordered another round and laughed when the cook asked me what mountain I'd just come off of. Paul came and sat down with me as I ate the second order.

"Order any more and I'm deducting it from your check," Paul said with a chuckle.

"Pleeeze," I pleaded, "just one more shake." I really didn't want any more and I didn't exactly feel right acting like he was a friend, but I thought I should go along with his little game until I could figure everything out. I wanted to get the money *and* make them pay. Pay big. But how I was going to do it eluded me for now.

"I have the contract here, George. I need you to sign it so we can proceed with our arrangement and I can give you your checks. It's a standard contract we give all our first time authors. We didn't change a thing in it, but I have a little something extra for you."

I held the several-page contract in my dirty hands. It was a dream come true, but for all the wrong reasons. I waited for the next part. What was the little something extra, another bagged lunch of peanut butter and jelly with a bottle of water? A ten-dollar gift certificate to a fast-food restaurant?

"I have two thousand dollars in cash here for you. It'll hold you over for a few days until you get settled again and get around to cashing your checks. You can purchase what you need and get a motel room for however long you need it. Look over the contract and if you have any questions, ask."

I nodded and started reading the contract, clutching it in one hand while holding the remainder of the cheeseburger in the other. Paul left to refuel the plane.

As soon as I scanned the contract, I believed it to be exactly what Paul had told me—it seemed like a standard contract. I was kind of surprised; I expected to find all kinds of ambiguous language like the waiver we had signed on the plane.

***

"Good, I see you signed it," Paul said as he rejoined me. Then in a quieter voice, "I take it you decided not to call the police?"

I still didn't know what I was going to do. I needed time to think about it and maybe some legal counseling. I was going to have to wrestle with my conscience, but I sure as hell wasn't going to tell Paul that, and, I wanted the money. I deserved it. Besides, I had all the I.D.'s if I ever wanted to go to the police, and that's one thing Paul didn't know.

"No. I don't want to spend years in court and possibly spend the rest of my life in jail. Hell, I don't even know where the crimes were committed. Who would I go to? Where? But, tell me, if one of us had made a copy of the letters we received from you, wouldn't that prove there was a contest and you were involved in it?"

"Oh, would it? Try to find the agent listed in the letter sometime, a Mr. Henry Wright, wasn't it? The letters had completely false names and addresses, including the name of the business and the person named as the agent. We rented a post office box for a few months—that was all. So anyone trying to trace the letter would obviously hit dead ends wherever they looked."

"Why did you pick us for this contest? Why didn't you pick some form of low-life's, like lawyers or used car salesmen?" I mean, how did you find so many gullible people so eager to enter a contest like this?

"Just look at yourself, George. Have a good look in a mirror. Most writers are loners. You all think you have a great book that will sell a million copies if you could get a break. Most are broke, living on the edge and can't even get an agent to look at their work. Dangle a carrot in front of them..."

"You had it all figured out."

"I hope so. Here are your checks and the cash I promised you," said Paul pulling an envelope from inside his shirt. He gave me the envelope then pulled out his wallet and counted out twenty, one hundred dollar bills. I looked in the envelope and found twelve cashier's checks from different banks for five thousand each; a total of sixty thousand dollars.

"Why all the checks from the different banks? And... I thought you were only giving twenty thousand up front."

"Well, we didn't think you would trust a company check, so I gave you the twelve checks from the banks. You went through so much, we decided to go ahead and give you the whole sixty. If you don't want it..."

"No, no, no. But why five thousand each?" I wasn't just curious; I still didn't trust the son-of-bitch. It didn't make any sense, but I wasn't about to turn it down.

"Ten thousand or more and the banks have to report it to the IRS. I didn't want to deal with it, and besides, this way, it's tax exempt to you. There's no record."

I didn't really believe the bastard, but sixty thousand was sixty thousand. Don't look a gift horse....

"Just in case you're wondering what the other families will do when the other contestants don't come home—we sent them a letter from Mexico saying the contestants were on a yacht, which traveled to South America while they wrote their manuscripts. A storm suddenly came up and the yacht sank and all on board were lost. A copy of the general release and liability waiver that each of you signed was included with the letter. As of today, we haven't received any inquiries from any of the families or any lawsuits."

"Sounds like you covered all the bases. How would they contact you if they did have questions?"

He smiled. "Nice try. Finish the book. Give me what you have up to now and I'll have the editing started."

"How long will it take to get it in print?"

"About a year—maybe longer. We have a lot of work to do first and it has to go through several edits, cover designs, etcetera. Let's get going; the plane's fueled and ready."

"There's gonna be a special place in hell for people like you."

"Probably...but I'll save a place for you."

We took off from Chicago and headed for New York. Not a word was said between us the whole distance. When we arrived at the Westfield airport in New York where my trip started, Paul again taxied to the terminal, but this time everything was closed up. It was two in the morning and dark—not a star in the sky. Not a light was on in the building, but a spotlight lit up the entrance. I borrowed some change from him and used a pay phone to call a taxi. Paul gave me his business card with his email address and business information. I noticed the address was the same post office number I had sent my application to.

"I thought you said this box number was a fake, and closed."

"It is. Just call or email me."

I gave him a CD containing most of my manuscript. I kept the stack of notepaper I'd continued my work on and the flash drive I'd copied the other manuscripts onto. He didn't know about that.

"I'll call you when I transcribe this and finish," I said holding my notes. "I'll email you the rest."

"See if you can get it finished within the week," encouraged Paul. "We're going to be on a tight schedule."

I knew I had heard that before. It seemed to be Paul's life.

Right now all I cared about was getting a hot shower, some clean clothes, and sleep in a comfortable, genuine bed.

As I waited for the cab to arrive, I watched Paul taxi the plane out and take off. I never did find out where the plane was stored at, but then I really didn't care. I cursed myself later, though, for not getting the tail number off the plane.

When my ride arrived, I threw my bags in the back seat and climbed in after them. The driver gave me a dirty look.

As we drove away, I could picture the first time I met Nicki, her ring-laden hand outstretched to greet me, and encountering the others that fateful day. It was surreal. And Harry, what was I going to do about Harry? God, how could we have been so wrong? I didn't even take his identification. Maybe Paul was right. Maybe there would be a special place in hell for me.

The cab took me to a motel in the small town. No one was attending the desk and I had to ring the bell for two or three minutes before someone arrived to check me in. The attendant had obviously been sleeping. I paid cash for the room. Once inside, I dropped my bags and went directly to the bathroom. I filled the bathtub with hot water, stripped and enjoyed my first hot water in a month.

***

I woke up hungry at five in the morning, still soaking in the tub. The water had turned cold. I took a hot shower, dried off and went to look for some wearable clothes. Again, I'd have to settle for the cleanest dirty clothes I had until tomorrow when I could wash everything and maybe buy some new ones. Even my cleanest were rank. I didn't want to go shopping smelling like a petting zoo, so I filled the sink with hot water and threw a set of clothes in. I scrubbed them the best I could with what was left of the small bottle of complimentary hair shampoo, wrung them out and hung them over the shower curtain rod to dry.

As I searched through my luggage for some clothes to actually wear, I noticed something was wrong, terribly wrong. Things were missing. I had placed the I.D.'s I'd collected in the top inside pocket. They were not there. Even Peter's will and Jessie's letter. Frantically, I dumped everything on the floor from both suitcases. Nothing. They were gone.

"That son-of-a-bitch!" I yelled, throwing the suitcase across the room.

CHAPTER 30
Jackpot!

Paul taxied the plane to the parking area for private planes at Kennedy International Airport in New York City. Howard was waiting for him as he entered the terminal.

"Well, James, how did it go?"

"I'm beat. Let me get a coffee and I'll enlighten you about everything while we get refueled."

"Well, at least tell me who the winner was."

James smiled. "You won't believe me."

"Shit, not again."

"George."

"George?" Howard yelled. "How could George win? That fat prick? He couldn't have!"

"It was George. You owe me," he said, patting Howard on the back.

James bought coffee and sat down at a table.

"I can't believe it," Howard said as he sank down in the chair across from James. "It can't be."

"Believe it. I have the tapes in the plane. I'm sure some of our clients will want to review them."

James sucked down his coffee, ordered another and after a short rest, both headed out to the plane. Once they were safely inside the cockpit with the outside door closed, James told Howard everything that had transpired on the flight, including the part where the plane was put into a dive.

"That son-of-a-bitch. What do we do now?" he asked.

We do nothing. He has no idea who we are, where we are...nothing."

"Did you have to tell him anything about the real contest?"

James smiled. "Of course not, but we also have an ace up our sleeve just in case he does find out something."

"What's that?"

"Just before our tracker...uh...expired, he told me how he killed several of them, and one of the contestants in particular. Seems our chaser got horned up, raped and accidentally killed Nicki."

"He killed Nicki?"

"He sure did."

"What do we tell our clients? What about the ones who bet on Nicki? Do we tell them, give them their money back?"

"Hell, no!" James said. "They'll never find out. We'd never know if the asshole hadn't told us."

"This isn't good. If our clients ever find out our employee killed one of the contestants, and we didn't tell them, they'll want our heads."

"Calm down. Reynaldo made it look like Harry did it. They all bought it and three of the guys, Peter, Stewart, *and George* ended up executing him. They electrocuted him and we have it on tape! Can you believe it? I let George know of his mistake; he was kind of upset to say the least. Since he was one of the guys who executed Harry, I don't think he'll be going to the cops."

"Shit! I owe you another two hundred G's?"

"Yep. I told you it would be someone totally unexpected who would win this time. How much did we end up taking in?"

"Total bets about fifty-two million. Our take, five point two mill since there was only one winner this time. Seems most of the odds were heavily on Harry. Poor guy. Maybe we should give George a bonus for taking him out of the game."

"I did," James said, "two thousand cash. I figured it was the least I could do. He made us a small fortune." They laughed.

James began going through his preflight checklist as the fuel tanker pulled away. "I have the tapes. The dozer was starting to take down the town as I circled over."

Howard belted himself into the copilot's seat. "I'll miss that old town."

James looked at Howard and smirked. "Yeah, right. You haven't been there in decades before this contest."

"Okay, Okay," laughed Howard. "It was historic though. I hated to destroy it. Our clients are asking about our next contest. What do you want me to tell them?"

James started to taxi the plane while he chatted with ground control. "It's not set yet. I still have to get a firm lease on the island. Email them we'll be in contact when everything is ready. This going to be a fun one; lawyers always think they're so smart and have the upper hand."

CHAPTER 31
Double Cross

Around six o'clock I went out to get some breakfast. My clothes weren't dry yet, so I had to wear some smelly ones. I was too embarrassed to actually go into a restaurant, so I opted for a fast-food joint down the street that had a drive-thru. I went to the outside window and ordered. When the lady gave me my order, she gave me a loud *thank-you*. I don't know if it was for the order or she got a whiff of my clothes and was thanking me for not coming inside.

Later, after using the motel's dryer to dry my wet clothes, I found a second-hand store down the street where I purchased a couple pairs of decent used jeans and a few shirts. I was even able to fit into jeans a couple sizes smaller than I used to. I went back to the motel feeling like a million bucks.

Finding the business card Paul had given me, I placed a call from the motel to him. I don't know why, but I was actually stunned when the message at the other end said the number had been disconnected. I dialed it again with the same results. I called the information operator, who gave me the same information. I couldn't figure out why the line was disconnected.

I then realized I had no other means of contact with Paul other than the post office box on the business card, and the email address. Paul had already told me the box was closed. Now what kind of scam was taking place? Didn't Paul want the last chapters of the manuscript?

A wave of fear shot through me. Were the checks for sixty big ones fake also? They were drawn on major banks; it wouldn't take long for me to find out.

After nine, when the banks opened, I anxiously called a taxi and went to one of the branches in Westfield. I asked to see a manager and told her I wanted to open an account, but I first wanted to see if the check from their bank was authentic. The manager took the check and went to her computer. As she approached me, I was clenching my jaw, ready for the bad news. She told me everything was in order and she could indeed cash or deposit the check.

I decided to open an account and deposit the one check, as I still had a majority of the two grand in cash Paul had given me. I was going to deposit one check a week at different branches until the sixty grand was all in the bank. That way it wouldn't attract any unneeded attention. I wanted to put my life back in order, and the sooner, the better—but I wasn't going back to the tenement dump I had lived in. Never again!

With money from the contest, I rented a condo in the suburbs of Buffalo. I really wanted to move to Florida, but until I could put everything together and decide exactly where I wanted to move, I decided to stay here for a while. I purchased a used car, rented a truck, retrieved my belongings from storage, and paid my sister back the money she had fronted me. I knew, with any luck, I could get another job teaching, if only temporarily. From now on I'd write in my spare time.

One good thing that came out of the misadventure; I'd lost almost thirty pounds.

A month later, I tried sending an overnight letter containing a CD with the final part of the manuscript to the address on Paul's business card. Yeah, he had said it was closed, but I wanted to find out if that was a lie also.

No surprise, it came back to me several days later, and in bright red letters, *BOX CLOSED, NO FORWARDING ADDRESS* stamped on it. I tried the email address, but of course, it was invalid too. It seemed Paul had been very thorough in keeping his identity secret. I started to wonder if his name was even Paul.

EPILOGUE

When George couldn't find Paul, he knew he had been screwed several different ways. He also knew his book wasn't going to be published, and he believed he had a real winner, especially since it was a true story. Since he would implicate himself in a murder, he couldn't sell it as a true story. He sent out queries to over twenty agents and publishers he had contacted before, but he never received a single response.

Of course, George added a few chapters from Peter's notes to fill in the gaps of what happened to him and Stewart in the desert. He seemed especially close to them. He also had the other manuscripts that gave him the opinions and views of some of the other writers.

He told me nightmares still haunted him. Seems Peter and Stewart were making their messages clear. Each night George was back in the ghost town standing alongside them, looking at his own freshly dug grave. They each had a shovel in their hands and they were pointing, telling George to get into the hole they had dug.

His conscience couldn't take it any more; it bothered him greatly and he wanted the truth to be known.

Two months after returning to New York, George went to the local police and told detectives the whole story. He reluctantly admitted to the murder of Harry, gave the police a copy of his story and told them everything in it had actually happened, it was a true accounting of his two months captivity. He claimed the book was to be released as fiction, as he didn't want to incriminate himself.

George waited to be arrested. The police thoroughly investigated his claims, but could not substantiate anything—George couldn't tell them where the alleged crimes took place.

He did give the police the names of the contestants and where most were from. Again, the department investigated a few, found some information on each, even a few friends, but no family could be found who knew anything about the alleged contest. They said George could have taken the names from the phone book, or maybe he knew of a list of writers.

Some of the names of those he gave could not be found or verified, along with anything or anyone from The New Writer's Agency. Maybe the pilot was right; maybe they were a bunch of loners.

The authorities finally dismissed George as a crackpot, believing he was just trying to make wild, fantastic claims that would sell more books.

He went to the State Police and the FBI, but after they checked with the local police, they also told him to go away.

I guess he couldn't take it any more. The nightmares and his conscience drove him to the verge of insanity.

The police found George in his bathtub with his wrists slit, almost dead. His sister in California had frantically called and alerted the police. She told them George had called her, told her about the contest and how no one believed him. He told her he loved her, then said goodbye and hung up.

That was two years ago.

George currently resides in a private psychiatric hospital, where he is still under constant sedation. He asked me to finish the book; see if I could get it published. The profits from your purchase of this book will help to continue the excellent help he is receiving, and, maybe repay a few of my expenses.

I've kept the original names George used in the book, and not the names he claims are the real ones.

One last thing...you may ask why I remained on this case for so long without a solid lead, clue, or income. Months after George had his nervous breakdown and was admitted to a mental hospital, his sister flew out to pack up his condo, put his belongings into storage, and take care of his financial obligations. She was a very nice lady and she asked me to help inventory and box his belongings. I agreed to assist her.

While packing some of his clothes, I came across a green plastic trash bag in a closet. As I opened the bag, a smell hit me that almost knocked me over. The clothes inside were filthy and in a pillowcase. Curious, I pulled a few of them out. A key fell out of a pair of pants. A skeleton key with a tag attached. The room number on the tag? Number eight.

Was the contest real? Was George telling the truth? If he was, why did they let him live and pay him? Did the ghost town he said was burned and leveled really exist? Did all those writers really die, or was it a figment of George's imagination combined with the psychotropic drugs he was receiving from the hospital?

You be the judge.

Rico Sanducci,
Private Investigator

Timothy M. BRAUN

Author of
WHEN THE ANGELS CRY
The Story of Arielle
An exciting, thought provoking, in-spirational novel!
Readers agree, this story will change your life!
Have you ever received a miracle?

If you liked "*The Shack*" by Wm. Paul Young or the "*Joshua*" series by Joseph F. Girzone, then you'll love *WHEN THE ANGELS CRY—The Story of Arielle*.

"WHEN THE ANGELS CRY—The Story of Arielle" is an intriguing novel with a variety of phenomenal turns." Diane Niebling, Nebraska

Recommended reading by the Colonia del Rey Book Club.

Read *When The Angels Cry—The Story of Arielle* and discover the miracles in your life. Go to www.whentheangelscry.com to read sample chapters of this exiting book!

MIRACLE OR COINCIDENCE?

Have you ever been the recipient of a miracle? Most of us probably have, whether we know it or not. Think back. How many critical situations can you recall affecting yourself or your family in which a crisis was averted? Divine intervention or twist of fate?

THE INFANT

After losing her own child to S.I.D.S. and in a deep depression, Rebecca finds Arielle on her doorstep as an infant, but possessing something so mysterious Rebecca finds it hard to comprehend. She starts to question her own sanity. As Arielle grows, Rebecca observes her daughter in conversations with an invisible presence.

MESSAGES FROM THE ANGELS

While helping a friend, Arielle is injured and placed in extreme danger. She struggles with her own resolve.

Throughout her childhood, she is barraged with questions from religious leaders who have difficulty accepting Rebecca's observations, and Arielle's angelic messages to them. The leaders are told they must change their lives, attitudes, and behaviors; start believing in and teaching about a loving, compassionate God.

After a dispute with a teacher at her school that escalates to litigation, Arielle is faced with a judge who has no tolerance for religious matters.

Who is this child? Will they ever believe her? Will they do what they are asked?

WATCH FOR:

WHEN THE ANGELS CRY
In The Line of Fire

(The Second in a Series)

As a small boy growing up, Jacob tells adults about conversations he has with angels, but no one believes him. He enters school and encounters a special teacher.

As an adult, he becomes a police officer. With his supernatural ties, he tackles situations in a world of corruption, drugs, death and mayhem that no one would want to encounter. An angel with human emotions, he must circumvent the natural desires of humanity and make decisions that would test the mettle of anyone, yet maintain his special relationship with the Almighty.

TIMOTHY M. BRAUN was born in Indianapolis, Indiana in 1952. He served for over seven years in the Army Security Agency as a crypto-analyst, spending most of that time in Japan and Korea. He retired from a Massachusetts police department as a Detective Sergeant after which he owned and wrote for the Gold Camp Journal in Cripple Creek, Colorado. *The Contest* is his second novel. He is also the author of *When The Angels Cry—The Story of Arielle*. Mr. Braun is married and splits his time between his homes in Cripple Creek, Colorado and Corpus Christi, Texas. When he is not writing, he volunteers his time to non-profit organizations.